"*The Land of Debris* is much more than your typical journey into self-discovery. What separates it from its twitching, self-absorbed kin on the shelves is a true poignancy, an insight into what we love and what we hate, what we forget and what we want to be forgotten. Plus, if you read this book, you will live like a rock star and ride on the back of a dinosaur."

Joe Reid

"...a wild ride down the oft' pot-hole filled highway of enlightenment..."

Kendall Bohannon

"The Clinton-Gore Administration and the Federal Government encourage the development and use of alternative technologies, particularly efforts such as Clearwater Publishing Company's which have the potential to create business and employment opportunities while enhancing national, regional and local economies. I encourage and appreciate your efforts and I hope that you will enjoy continued success in this worthwhile endeavor."

Fran McPoland,
Federal Environmental Executive

"I am glad to see that companies such as Clearwater Publishing are putting forth the effort to produce more environmentally friendly products. We are excited about your work."

Kathleen A McGinty, Chair,
Executive Office of the President,
Council on Environmental Quality

The Land of Debris
and the Home of Alfredo

by Kenn Amdahl

Clearwater Publishing Company

Broomfield, Colorado

The Land of Debris and the Home of Alfredo
by Kenn Amdahl

Copyright ©1997 by Clearwater Publishing Company

ISBN 0-9627815-8-4

Printed in the United States of America

Cover paintings by Susan Contreras of Santa Fe, New Mexico and used by permission.

Cover design by Janel Martensen and Kenn Amdahl.

July You're a Woman written by John Stewart, published by Chapel Publishing and used by permission.

Edited by Suzanne Venino.

Printed on "Trailblazer Paper"™ made in the United States by Vision Paper of Albuquerque, New Mexico. This paper is made from the kenaf plant grown in Mississippi and is completely tree-free, acid-free, and chlorine-free.

Clearwater Publishing Company
P.O. Box 778
Broomfield, Colorado 80038-0778

(303) 436-1982

e mail: Wordguise@aol.com

The equatorial deserts of Hell are probably hotter than western Oklahoma in August. The good news for Oklahoma sinners is that Hell is also likely to be more interesting and easier to escape.

I trudged down an endless black snake of pavement so softened by the relentless sun that my sneakers depressed it with each step. Tumbleweeds lay motionless in the ditch, all hope of a breeze abandoned, while I alternately cursed the vast featureless prairie and talked to my blisters. I was a bug beneath God's magnifying glass, slowly frying. When the heat seeping through my sneakers became unbearable, I walked on the shoulder where the round gravel twisted my ankles and jabbed at my raw feet. After my shoes cooled, I stepped back onto the pavement and shook sweat from my hair.

For no particular reason the words to an old John Stewart song kept repeating in my mind: *"July you're a woman, more than anyone I've ever known."* I pictured the songwriter driving down this very stretch of deserted road toward some anonymous gig, bored and alone, humming to himself and writing the song. *"I can't hold it on the road when you're sittin' right beside me..."*

Why name the woman July? Was the woman in his mind really named Julie but the sound didn't play as well for him? Or did he have a Playboy magazine on the car seat and Miss July kept distracting him? I decided I would never know the answer.

1

A brief gust of hot wind stirred dirt then died. In the distance a white bird soared and swooped. It rode the wind then glided the calm, twisting in a crazy pattern. As it flew in my general direction I realized it wasn't a bird at all but a scrap of paper. I stopped, fascinated, as the fitful wind carried it closer and closer and finally deposited it at my feet. Impossible odds. With a thousand acres of vacant prairie to choose from, Oklahoma chose to direct this paper to me. I picked it up and stared at a tattered centerfold. Miss February.

"Pure coincidence," I muttered, not completely convinced. "There's a logical explanation."

"Right," I argued sarcastically with myself. "Completely logical. You ask a question and then, perhaps for the first time in your life you simply shut up and wait and the answer falls from the sky. Maybe somebody's trying to tell you something."

I folded the paper and stuck it in my shirt pocket, embarrassed that I would even consider some mystical answer but not confident enough to throw it away.

"Just don't want to litter," I explained to myself as I began walking again.

The brown dirt was punctuated sparingly with short, thorny bushes, some close to the highway. Each time I passed one, it rustled wildly for a few seconds, then fell silent. After this happened several times, startling me each time, I began to consider it remarkable. Finally, as much from exhaustion and boredom as curiosity, I decided to investigate. I left the road and walked toward the nearest bush, twenty feet off the road, grateful to be walking on soft dirt.

The bush seemed completely inanimate and quiet. But I would not be fooled. What self-respecting mystery would reveal itself to a casual tourist? I lay down and stared at it, wishing it was tall enough to create shade, and made myself as still and silent as the ragged weed itself.

I may have spent a lifetime staring at that bush, holding my breath, sweat dripping from my forehead. Perhaps it was less than a minute.

And then it rustled, loud as a potato chip sack. I waited another lifetime. Suddenly, as if conjured by a heat-crazed desert genie, a lizard smaller than my hand darted out to stare at the steaming mountain that had materialized in its front yard. We communed silently for several minutes, curious man and unblinking reptile, until I understood. As usual, there was more logic here than magic. The thornbush snagged dry leaves and candy wrappers from the wind, each one as sensitive to movement as a snare drum. It also repelled large predators, like hawks and little boys. The barbed tangle formed a safe little monastary for the poor of brain and the thin of skin. To survive, lizards hid within the noisy debris at the base of the bush. But to eat, they had to venture into the brutal arena of the open prairie. At the first hint of danger, the first thud of an approaching footstep, they scuttled back to their porcupine of a home. Interesting.

A sound on the highway startled me. I looked up in time to see a state patrol car pass by, sleek, official, and shiny as a shark. The driver had not seen me.

I could have jumped to my feet and run to the highway, yelling and waving my arms. The driver might have noticed me in his rearview mirror and given me a ride.

I did not move. The lizard did not move. The bush remained silent. Finally, when the sound of the car faded away completely, I started to get up, frightening my reptilian friend into a panic of insect-quick activity as he disappeared into the safety of thorns, ancient fast-food wrappers, and faded scraps of newspaper. The patrol car was gone. But another vehicle appeared in the distance and I froze. There was something ominous and familiar about the speck on the horizon, and an instant later I was sure. The white van of my nightmares was approaching.

"It's not possible," I whispered. "It's not possible."

In seconds it would be near enough for its occupants to see me, but there was nowhere to hide and no time to run. Terror bulldozed the exhaustion from my body. My mind raced wildly and I could not breathe. I had to do something.

I sat behind the bush and furiously scooped handfuls of dirt onto my feet and legs until they were a long and dusty burial mound. Lying back on one elbow, I covered my stomach and chest. I could hear the engine now, but there was no time to look up. I dusted my hair and face, threw what I could onto the arm nearest the approaching evil, flattened myself against the earth, and held my breath. I am not here, I said to myself. I am part of the prairie, only dirt and spiders and tumbleweeds. I do not exist. There is nothing to see in this patch of emptiness.

The sound of the terrible vehicle came closer and closer, like the deliberate footsteps of an executioner at dawn.

They're going to see me, I thought. I should leap and run while I still have a chance. A scream writhed its way up from deep within me but I struggled to catch it at my throat and only a choking sound escaped. No. I must remain perfectly still, invisible as a desert lizard.

The van passed without slowing, but still I did not move. Its whine faded to silence as I slowly exhaled. Too close, I thought.

I sat up to the fanfare of dry leaves and scraps of paper and brushed myself off. The dirt and sweat had formed mud on my face and my hair was a wet clay sculpture. It doesn't matter, I thought. Nothing matters. I stood and clapped clouds of dust from my jeans, then cautiously resumed my journey.

But now I walked a hundred feet off the road, where the dirt was soft and not nearly as hot as the pavement. There was no point in staying exactly on the road when the prairie was headed in the same direction. No need to keep torturing myself with a rigid straight line when mere distance made me less conspicuous. After an hour or so with no signs of traffic, I stopped turning every ten seconds to watch the road. The van was a dream and could not hurt me. I could relax.

I bowed my head, watching for rattlesnakes as my feet plowed through dust and shimmering heat waves.

The flatness of the prairie changed to gently rolling hills and valleys, still unburdened by green vegetation. As I crested one of these low hills I was surprised to see a plot below that was different from the hundred that preceded it. A half-dozen dead trees stood like white skeletons in two straight rows, as out of place as I felt, and they drew me toward them. Someone had lived down there years before and planted trees, probably before I was born. Scattered chunks of charred wood and rusted cans hinted at the story. When the house had burned and the survivors moved away, there was no one left to water the trees, to repair the well, to fill the stock pond. All had dried and died and been consumed by scavengers, drifting dirt, and crusty weeds. Now only thick wooden ghosts marked the spot where some family had celebrated Christmas and birthdays, made love and grown old.

Set in a slight depression, it was completely hidden from the road, and I needed to rest. I sat and leaned against a smooth trunk, white as old bones, and tried to imagine exactly where the house had been and the inevitable vegetable garden. Perhaps there had been a chicken coop, and two pots near the front door with brightly defiant flowers.

I dozed off for a moment but was rudely awakened when a grasshopper the size of my thumb landed on my cheek, its feet gripping my skin like tiny lobster claws. I slapped it away and the sting of my own hand made me cry out in surprise. I was getting sunburned. My tongue felt thick in my mouth. Sleeping out here was suicide.

I struggled to my feet and my blisters reminded me that I was still a long way from any peaceful place to sleep. "Blisters won't kill you," I muttered, wincing with each step. Without looking back, I climbed the hill and continued to march through the barren landscape. My mind was very tired.

It was also very empty. Something was missing, but I couldn't put my finger on what it was exactly. I tried to retrace my journey, but somehow that was more effort than I could muster. The prairie seemed to be spinning slowly and unevenly beneath my feet, like a carnival ride that wasn't working right. My tongue was a wooden stick rattling around my teeth, and I could not blink the dust from my eyes. Something big and important is missing, I repeated. At last I realized what it was.

It was my memories. No matter how hard I tried, I could not recall where I had been. I stopped walking and stood alone in the vast heat and concentrated. All my memories had vanished like a scent in the wind. I didn't even know my own name.

Somewhere in the heat and the dust and the sweat and the boredom, I had set down part of my mind, perhaps to rest, and had forgotten to take it with me when I started walking again.

Panic crashed like a tidal wave against me and threatened to drown me. I held my breath, flailing around for something familiar to clutch — but there was nothing. My life had disappeared without a trace, a footprint on yesterday's beach. Nothing existed but the cold blackness of a deep, dark ocean. I was dead.

I started to run, but my legs refused to cooperate. After fifty feet, I collapsed face-first onto the hot ground, panting like a dog, inhaling dirt with each breath, coughing and sneezing.

Then as suddenly as it had struck, the panic dissipated, flowing off me like green water sliding from a mossy boulder. Sunlight glinted on a tranquil tide pool within me. I rolled onto my back and stared at the perfect blue sky and imagined I was staring into lovely deep water. You're just tired and dehydrated, I said to myself. Everything will be all right if you can get to some water, find some shade, and rest. My choice was simple: I could keep moving slowly and calmly, or I could panic and die. My memories could wait. All obligations were now deferred. However black my sins, they had been forgiven and forgotten. At the least, my penance had been postponed. If people loved me, they would understand. If I was hated, my enemy's malice could not touch me. You're thirty years old and in good shape, I said to myself. It was all I knew, but it was all I needed right now. I could not afford to waste energy on anything else.

I realized with some surprise that I didn't miss my memories. How could I miss what I couldn't recall? I felt loss, but no real psychological distress. My mental condition was neither good nor bad.

I reached for my wallet, but it wasn't there. My jeans' pockets were empty except for two quarters. I had no wallet, no cash, no car, no extra clothes, no home, and no one to call for help.

I started to laugh out loud. This was absurd. My body did not have surplus energy to burn by laughing, but I couldn't stop. I howled like a wolf from an old fairy tale, and rolled in the dirt until my sides ached. I had absolutely nothing.

No. That wasn't quite right. I sat up, suddenly sober, and squinted at the shimmering horizon as a single memory flickered and flared within me. Not a person or place — I concentrated very hard. There — a number. A telephone number. I repeated it several times. There could be no doubt. I knew a telephone number, and it would surely lead me back to my life.

If only there was a telephone in the middle of the Oklahoma desert.

Be logical, I told myself, look for clues. And keep walking. I did not want to go crazy, and calm disciplined thought would keep me sane.

The first clue, of course, was my own amnesia. Surely something had caused it. With both hands I examined my head for bumps or sore spots. With a mixture of relief and exasperation I concluded there were none. I had not fallen or been struck. Interesting, I thought. I don't remember the events of my life, but I do remember that a blow to the head can cause amnesia.

Perhaps drugs, I thought. I searched my pockets carefully. Besides the quarters, they were clean. Not even lint. There were no needle marks or bruises on the inside of my elbows.

I stopped in my tracks. My own instincts were my best clues. I had known to check for a blow to the head, known to look for signs of drugs, and I knew I was dehydrated. There could be only one explanation and calm logic had led me to it.

Clearly I was a doctor.

I walked with more confidence and continued my methodical examination of the evidence. How quickly I had begun to search for symptoms! Surely I was no ordinary doctor. I must be one of those really good doctors — a surgeon. That explained it. I must be a surgeon. I held out my hands. Rock steady. Not a quiver. All doubt left

left me. I was a surgeon. Probably an excellent one at that. A rich, world-famous surgeon. People would be looking for me. This amnesia would be a very temporary inconvenience.

When I looked up, I got more good news. In the distance I saw a gas station. Civilization! Water! A telephone! I was going to survive. I ignored my thirst, my exhaustion, and my blisters and walked quickly to the gas station. It was small and plain but it looked like the Taj Mahal to me. I walked directly to the pay phone in the parking lot. My troubles were over.

I knew I was in trouble again when the Pepsi machine winked at me. My hand stopped just before the phone sucked the quarter in and I blinked several times. This was not the knowing wink of two friends who share a secret across a room. This was a sly, sensuous wink. That Pepsi machine was Cleopatra, slithering on her Persian rug. "Come hither, my sweet, shy gladiator," it whispered to me.

I shook my head. "It's only a Pepsi machine," I said to myself. "Only a Pepsi machine." I ignored it and pushed a quarter into the telephone. A mechanical voice answered and my quarter jangled into the coin return.

Not in service! How can it be? Panic and nausea settled in my stomach. Again and again I pushed the quarter into the machine only to reach the same garbled, static-filled message. The words were distant and hard to understand, like a familiar but incomprehensible foreign language. It sounded something like this:

"The number you have reached, 'The Land of Debris and the Home of Alfredo' is not in service at this time. If you feel you have reached this number in error..."

I hung up angrily. The leathery gas station attendant peered at me from behind the window. A tiny electric fan ruffled old candy bar wrappers on his desk. A shotgun lay across the desktop, only inches from his hand. He turned back to his little black-and-white TV. Only two quarters, the Pepsi machine took forty-five cents, and I was very thirsty.

I went into the gas station.

"Your pay phone's not working."

"Not my pay phone," the man said. "Take it up with the phone company."

"But I need to get home."

"Where is home?"

"I'm not sure. That is, I can't remember. I think something happened to me..."

"Well, what do I look like? Your spiritual guide?"

No, I thought. He did not. But it occurred to me that it might be a good thing to have. A spiritual guide. Or any kind of guide.

"Well, how about a drink of water then?"

"Pepsi machine outside. You ain't a convict escaped from the state pen down the road are you? Maybe the highway patrol can help you get home. Maybe I ought to give them a call for you."

Convict? No, I was a surgeon. I had probably been camping... I stared at the barren landscape. But why would a world-famous surgeon go camping in Hell when he could be sipping tropical drinks surrounded by adoring young women in skimpy bikinis? The logical part of my brain shrugged and did not answer.

"Thanks anyway," I said. "I guess I'll just try the pay phone one more time."

The old man nodded but did not smile. His hand stayed near the shotgun.

I went back outside and stared at the Pepsi machine, its bright colors faded and covered with red-clay dust. The shimmering air made it look like it was moving just a little, a carnival robot waiting to be turned on one last time before it melted from the heat and dissolved into the pavement. I hadn't realized how thirsty I was until I that machine grinned the word "Pepsi" at me. I hadn't thought of anything except the phone number. The phone number that was no longer in service, the last radio link to a distant home planet, the last scraggly bush you can grasp as you feel yourself sliding over the edge of the cliff. Through all the heat and distraction I had forced myself to repeat the number, over and over again, fearful I might lose it, until it was the only clear thought in my brain.

But now there was another thought. Pepsi. The seductive machine chuckled under its breath as I held the two quarters in my hand. It batted its eyelashes at me and swayed like a dancing gypsy girl. It wiggled and twitched and giggled at me.

Sometimes a person's choices don't matter. You choose the red wine instead of the white, and regardless of the rules, it doesn't ruin your filet of salmon. You invite the waitress to ride in your convertible six hours down the coast highway and back, both of you pretending to be in love, the cool night cooperating. You return refreshed and younger, with no dark consequences to your lives.

But sometimes the choices do matter. You casually lean to the left without thinking, without knowing that everyone else in the world happened to be leaning left at that same instant. The shift of your weight is the final tiny push the earth needed. "Oh shit," the earth says, as it feels itself losing its balance, wishing it had arms to flail backward, or a God to catch hold of. You lean left at just the wrong instant and become the world's banana peel.

This is what I retained from my life. I knew that sometimes choices matter, and sometimes they don't. The rest of my brain was as vacant as a church during the Super Bowl, a hollow cavern I rattled around in.

I stood in the middle of western Oklahoma, cat-box to the universe, a blacktop highway the single element of geographical interest, and a one-pump gas station sprouting like a pimple from the dust beneath my feet. The attendant leaned into the laugh track on the television, the old show more real to him than his own life. The two quarters in my hand sweated, desperately eager to be spent.

The pay phone took a Las Vegas approach. "This might be the time, you might get lucky. Try me. What do you have to lose?"

The Pepsi machine, on the other hand, was my lover. It knew I could taste it already, feel an icy can in my hot hand, and cold, sweet effervescence sliding down my dry throat. And so it stopped dancing, tossed its long hair over a lovely shoulder, and looked away, completely indifferent. "If you don't want me more than anything in the world, it's your loss. Someone else will. You'll both put in your quarters, and then I'll choose."

I didn't know much. But I knew that sometimes choices matter, and sometimes they don't.

"Hey, buddy, need a lift?"

The voice startled me. I must have looked confused. The man laughed patiently.

"You got no car and you're staring at a pay phone like it was Miss September. What, did your car break down?"

The voice came from an big black car with old-fashioned rounded bumpers. I hadn't heard it pull into the station. The driver was in his fifties, fat and balding, in a cheap, short-sleeved shirt.

"Miss February," I corrected him.

"Suit yourself," the man said pleasantly. "I got to fill up, but then you're welcome to ride along if you want. The name's John. Which way you heading?" He reached a fat hand out the window for me to shake and instinctively I shook it. It was sweating like my quarters.

"I'm heading for..." I stopped. I didn't know where I was heading, but you can't really stop a sentence like that in mid-breath while you're shaking a guy's hand. It occurred to me that I might have just escaped from the state penitentiary down the road. I thought fast.

"I'm heading for the Land of Debris and the..." I stopped again. Maybe it was a password, or some secret place. Maybe I was the only one who was supposed to know it. I might not remember what size underwear I wear, but I wasn't crazy. I knew you have to choose your words carefully. Sometimes such things matter.

"Which way are *you* headed?" I asked. The man pointed at the spot where the thin black highway narrowed to invisibility at the horizon, where deep blue sky and white thunderhead clouds rested on the flat brown pancake of Oklahoma.

"Me too," I said. Keep your mouth shut, I told myself. Don't say too much. Anything you say can and will be used against you.

"Great!" he said. "What's your name?"

A name. Of course he would ask my name. Panic surged within me once more as no names bubbled to the surface of my brain. All I could think of was the television show on the attendant's TV.

"Desi," I said, shaking his hand. "Call me Desi."

"Pleased to meet you, Desi. I could use the company. Just let me fill the tank and we'll be off. I'll even buy you a beer. Do you drink beer?"

"I could probably be persuaded."

I put my hand in my pocket and released the two quarters. There would be another Pepsi machine and another pay phone. I had escaped making a choice and I hoped it didn't matter.

John bought gas, several six-packs of beer, and a bag of ice. He wore baggy beige shorts and black socks and his legs were fat and white. But he had a car and I didn't. He had beer and ice and a destination. He probably had memories. The universe had surely sent this man to be my spiritual guide. I rubbed the two quarters together in my pocket and got into his car.

"Sorry there's no air-conditioning," he said as we pulled out onto the highway. Then he laughed. "Well, there's air-conditioning." He pointed to a group of buttons on the dashboard labeled 'air conditioning.' "But it don't work. Bad pump. Someday I'm gonna fix that. Black car in Oklahoma, day like this, could get a little close in here. Hope the humidity don't get too high." He laughed again. "That's what they say, isn't it? 'It ain't the heat, it's the humidity.' Day like this, black car, if the temperature hits one-ten like yesterday, it ain't gonna be the humidity. It's gonna be the heat. Want a beer?" He motioned to the backseat.

He had put all the beer in a big cardboard box, surrounded it with ice, and set it on the backseat. The ice was already starting to melt and the cardboard box was beginning to look dark and wet. I thought it might have been smarter to leave the ice in the plastic sack it came in and just set it on top of the beer, but I didn't say anything. I wouldn't want some stranger telling me how to conduct a surgery. I dug through the ice and got a couple of cans of beer. There was something else in the box with the beer and the ice. I pushed the ice away. It was a dead fish.

I handed John a beer and tried to act casual.

"There's a dead fish in with your beer," I said.

He beamed.

"Isn't that the biggest damn bass you ever saw?"

I didn't want to say that I couldn't remember ever seeing a bass of any size before. My memory was pure and vacant in that area. I chose my words carefully.

"I don't remember ever seeing such a big damn bass," I said honestly. "Where'd you get him?"

"Caught him myself. Yesterday. My pole's still in the back." He took a drink of his beer. "Go ahead, see for yourself."

He didn't have to prove it to me, of course, but he obviously wanted me to look. I leaned over the seat and confirmed that there was, indeed, a fishing pole and other paraphernalia on the floor of the backseat. A plastic tackle box still wore its price tag. A mass of dying earthworms writhed limp and gasping on dry dirt in a coffee can. Empty Styrofoam cups testified to the coffee he drank early yesterday morning while he subdued the big damn bass. Tangled fishing line clutched bobbers, a couple of big flashy lures had snagged the tattered black carpet.

"You caught him, all right," I said.

John smiled proudly, sat straight, and steered with one hand. Sweat formed on his fat white legs. The old black car purred over the road.

"Always wanted to catch one really big fish," he said. "I just never had the time. Worked in a sporting goods store my whole life. I've sold a thousand fishing poles and never really been fishing. My dad didn't fish, and then, when I grew up, I got busy. Just never got around to it. Get to be a certain age and it's hard to do things for the first time. It's a small town. What would my customers think if I went fishing and came back with some tiny little fish? Or with no fish at all? I had to do this by myself, where no one would know me. And I did it. Biggest damn bass I ever saw. They're going to look at me different when they see that fish. They'll ask my advice, want to know what kind of bait I used. I'll carry that monster into the store, all fat and glistening and just act casual about it. 'Oh this?' I'll say. 'It's nothing. Just a fish I caught.' Their eyes'll get big. 'Mount it?' I'll say. 'Hell no. It's just a fish. If you want it you can have it. Make somebody a good dinner.' Then I'll give it away like it was nothing and they'll be amazed. Yeah," he said with satisfaction. "That's the way it'll be."

I just nodded and drank my beer. Despite uneasiness about my own amnesia, I felt happy for my new friend whose plan had worked. Anyway, I'd get my memories back; I'd just been in the heat too long. Beer will probably help, I thought, so I finished it quickly. Rest, drink a lot of fluids, and keep your mouth shut, I told myself.

"Help yourself," John said. I got another one.

The hot wind blew in the car window, drying the sweat on my face. The land outside was featureless, forbidding, and foreign as Uranus. We each drank another beer. The cardboard box became soggy. The highway in the distance looked wet, but the mirage disappeared as we got closer. John drove in silence, a smile on his face, rehearsing the scene of carrying his fish into the store. Every now and then I touched the two quarters in my pocket and repeated the telephone number. Life was pretty good, I decided. I was moving down the road, rehydrating my poor body. I had a friend. I had made the right choices.

I dozed off. When I woke up, we were pulling off the road onto the gravel shoulder. Steam was blowing out of the hood and the smile had left John's face. I didn't know if I should be worried or not, so I didn't say anything.

When the car stopped, we both got out. John opened the hood.

"Broke a hose," he said, pointing to a hissing cloud of white air escaping from a hole in a black rubber hose.

"Yup," I said, wanting to seem knowledgeable but realizing that any information I owned regarding engines was not available to me. I assumed that if the problem had been medical, my instincts would have kicked in immediately.

"I think I've got some tape in the trunk," he said. He looked down the road, which still stretched endlessly before us, shielded his eyes with his hand, looked up at the sky, shook his head, and waddled to the back of the car.

Without the wind blowing on my face, the heat closed in upon me. It was a malicious heat, heavy as iron, that invaded my body each time I inhaled. My sweat-soaked shirt clung to my back and the ground baked my feet through my shoes and reawakened my blisters. No bird sounds disturbed the thick air, no animal sounds, no stirring leaves. Just the clanking and quiet cursing of my friend moving things around in the trunk looking for tape, and the snakelike hiss of steam escaping the engine.

By the time John located a roll of black tape, the hissing had stopped. Using a rag to prevent burning his hand, he opened the radiator cap.

"Lost a lot of water," he said. I nodded agreeably. He wrapped the black tape around the black hose, covering the rip with several layers.

"Need more water," he said, furrowing his forehead, putting his fist against his mouth unconsciously, searching his brain for the nearest location of water. I was fascinated by his concentration. This is how the great scientists must have looked while they were inventing gravity and black holes and plastic grocery bags. God probably looked like this when He was inventing women. I'll put this here and that there — no, wait. I'll put three of these here and nothing there — no, that's not right either.

"The beer!" he said at last, with the tone of satisfied revelation God surely used when the idea of symmetrical breasts sprang into His mind. "That's it!"

Several inches of cool water lapped at the beer. The cardboard box was losing its faith in physics, the backseat was noticeably damp. John reached in, past the huge fish floating sightless in the water, and pulled out two six-packs.

"This ought to do it," he said, opening a beer and pouring it into the radiator. The grateful engine gurgled and gasped as it drank beer after beer. "With one left for each of us," he said happily, handing me a can. He closed the hood, and we got back into the car. I opened my beer as we eased back onto the highway. With a near-mystical perceptiveness he answered my unspoken question.

"Needed the ice water to keep the fish cold."

I nodded. When all the information became available, there could have been no other decision.

If the car had been hot before, it was now a pizza oven. I rested my elbow on the window for an instant and received a fry mark. I took off my shoes and socks, but the floor was too hot for bare feet. I put my shoes back on, without the socks. I swallowed my warm beer without enthusiasm. I did not feel well. I was grateful for my amnesia if my memories included many experiences like this one. We drove for perhaps another hour. Through the haze of my own discomfort, I became aware that my friend was watching the dashboard with increasing concern.

"She's over-heating again," he said tersely.

Within a minute I could hear the familiar and ominous hissing sound and could smell hot, cooked beer as we pulled over again. The tape had pulled loose. Using the last of his tape, he fixed the hose once more, his face grim and set hard against the unpleasant decision he had already made. Then, trying to make his voice sound calm, he said, "Give me a hand with that cardboard box."

Lovingly, he removed the floating fish and placed it on the seat. We slid our hands under the box, now half full of warm, fishy water, and lifted.

Boxes may have souls. They may have character and cunning and personality and heart. If they do, this was a courageous and gallant box. This was a corrugated Sir Lancelot. This was a brown and soaked Saint Peter of a box, a rectangular Richard the Lionhearted. Drenched and weakened, straining for hours against sloshing water and the battering of a dead big damn bass, it had held its aching self together. But now we asked too much. We had not moved it two feet when, with an agonized whimper of exhaustion, it collapsed into shapeless lumps of soggy paper drooping from our hands. The fish water, with remarkable, perhaps preplanned efficiency, soaked my jeans, my friend's shorts, the backseat, and the ancient carpet on the floor.

I said nothing. My friend said nothing. The fish stared, one eye downward at the hot, wet seat, the other upward at the black ceiling. None of us were feeling very well. A momentary panic flickered across John's face. We had no more water. For all I could tell, there was no other water within the state of Oklahoma.

"I've got it!" he said. He maneuvered his fat body out of the backseat, reminding me for a moment of a sea lion wiggling its way backward off a rock. "Come on."

John climbed onto the front bumper and perched in an awkward position, balancing carefully, trying to hold very still. I did not understand until I came closer and realized that he was urinating into the hot radiator. The car gurgled and gasped happily.

"Your turn," he said, bouncing to the ground, fumbling with his zipper.

I looked both ways down the highway. Despite the fact that no cars interrupted the heat waves rising from it, and despite the perfect absence of landmarks, houses, or signs that humans lived within a hundred miles, I felt a little funny. John seemed to sense this.

"I'll check the rear tires," he said.

I climbed onto the bumper, positioned myself carefully, trying not to touch the hot metal with my hands. But my zipper would not budge. It held its position like an abalone. Like a cat up a telephone pole, it entrenched its claws and would not come down. I could no more move that zipper than I could move Montana.

At that moment I realized that I needed this event to happen as badly as the car needed it. In fact, this event was going to happen regardless of the outcome of my zipper struggle.

"You about done up there?"

"I can't get my damn zipper open."

"Well, take your time."

The urgency of the situation finally demanded dramatic, decisive action. I loosened my belt, unbuttoned my jeans, and with great difficulty wiggled both jeans and underwear, still wet with warm fish water, down around my knees, aimed carefully, and relaxed.

The Grand Coulee Dam sprang a leak. I was God and the radiator was Noah. I was the Nile River and that engine was every Egyptian that ever lived. Everything was going to be all right. I would not explode and the car would run again. The universe was hot, but beautiful.

"Do you need help?"

It was a woman's voice.

"We broke a hose. How far to the next town?"

I peered over the top of the hood. My friend was standing in the middle of the road talking to a heavy middle-aged woman driving a tan station wagon. Neatly lettered onto the door were the words "Lazy J Ranch" and below that a stylized brand. A lovely young woman sat in the passenger seat. They couldn't see me behind the raised hood of our car.

"It's only about five, six miles to Jim's Place. Not much there. Buy some gas, get a sandwich. Wanna lift?" The passenger, probably her daughter, was blonde and beautiful. As the girl became bored with the conversation, she looked casually in the direction of our car.

"I think we can make it that far," John said.

I hoped he would keep talking. I felt like the cardboard box in the backseat which had held itself together by strength of will for as long as possible and then simply let go. I could not stop. I was Niagara Falls, and sick to my stomach, and hot, and my jeans were hot and wet and smelled like fish, and the engine smelled like grease and gasoline and boiled beer. For some reason, fate had perched me on the front of that old black car, a sweaty pink-skinned hood ornament. There was nothing I could do about it now. Still, I hoped they would keep talking for another thirty seconds or so.

My friend kept talking about the heat, directions to towns I'd never heard of, and college football teams. He loved to talk. Once the lady in the station wagon realized we were not in danger, she started inching the car forward, impatient to be gone. She nodded out her window, looking at John and away from me.

Her daughter, on the side of the station wagon nearer to me, stared at our old black car. As they eased forward, and the hood no longer blocked her view, she was staring at me.

There was nothing I could do. No graceful and elegant way to stop peeing into the radiator, jump down and introduce myself. David Niven in a tuxedo could not have handled it stylishly. Ronald Reagan could not have shrugged it off with a grin. David Letterman would have been jokeless.

I smiled and waved.

The girl's mouth fell open.

Even gaping fishlike at me, the girl was lovely. She stared through the window of their obviously air-conditioned vehicle with wide blue eyes and perfect skin and long blonde hair. I felt conflicting emotions. Perhaps it was only my lack of memories, but I was pretty sure no woman had ever stared at me with such open wonder and astonishment. I felt a little tingle of excitement at that. I was also embarrassed, but decided this was probably normal. I was glad this was one of those chance encounters that last thirty seconds and then you never see the person again. I would not like to try to make casual conversation with that girl at a cocktail party, being careful to avoid subjects like radiators and pink hood ornaments. On the other hand, despite the relatively unflattering position her face had frozen into, she was a very pretty girl. But if first impressions are important, I suspected that any potential relationship between us was already seriously handicapped.

Her face never changed expression as they drove away. It was the same open-mouthed, wide-eyed expression the bass wore. I struggled off the bumper and pulled up my pants. John slammed the hood enthusiastically.

We drove to Jim's Corner, refilled the gas tank, and bought more tape. "Just in case," John said. He bought a burrito and microwaved it. I couldn't imagine eating anything ever again. I tried the pay phone but only got the same garbled message.

Walking back out to the car we saw something moving in the backseat. As we got closer, a huge gray cat scrambled out the far window.

"Oh no!" John said, quickening his pace.

But we were too late. The cat had eaten huge chunks out of the slowly drying big damn bass. It no longer glistened, proud and symbolic. It had become meat.

I thought John would be devastated. I would not have been surprised to see tears welling up in his eyes. I would not have been surprised if he'd pulled a gun from beneath the seat and chased after the sacrilegious cat. But something different and stranger happened.

Nothing happened. John stared with love in his eyes at the grotesque dead thing, the abomination staining his backseat, skin ripped, fluids oozing, bones protruding. He reached in and straightened it out.

"Could have been worse," he said, wiping his hands on his shorts. "Let's hit the road."

We drove through the long hot afternoon, an afternoon choreographed by Dante, with music by Stephen King. The car was a furnace. The wet carpet in the back released years of animal smells. The fish and dead earthworms were aggressively rotting. My jeans stuck to my skin. My head ached, my stomach turned and rolled like an eel on bad drugs. The endless rolling hills outside vibrated with the heat. Oklahoma was a huge fat woman with the plague and bad breath, sweating and smelly, covered with pimples and pus who lusted after me. She squirmed and moaned and tried to be seductive. She licked her heavy lips. John did not seem to notice.

"I'll carry that fish into the store, all fat and shiny," he said to himself. "Just carry it in like it was nothing. 'What, mount it? Nah, it's just a fish. Make somebody a good dinner. You can have it if you want.'" He smiled, sat back proudly and steered with one hand. "That'll be something, won't it? Yeah, that'll really be something."

Perhaps it's time to locate a new spiritual guide I decided, keeping my face carefully in the fresh wind from the window. My stomach roller-coastered and my brain banged against the inside of my swollen eyeballs. Eternity will not seem long to me. I've already done it once.

Finally I saw houses and trees ahead. The sun was setting. I had a choice to make. I was not sure if it mattered. For just an instant I glimpsed a mailbox with a familiar symbol on it. I could not place it but mere familiarity attracted me like a beacon in the twilight.

"Let me out at the first house on the right," I said. It took a lot of effort to say anything. My voice was weak. "That's where I'm going."

"Sure thing," John said cheerfully.

He pulled over.

"I'm going on into town, see if I can buy some more ice." He gestured toward the backseat. I nodded. "If I keep on driving, I'll be home by midnight. Hey, we had a couple little adventures, didn't we buddy? Sure glad I ran into you. A trip's always more fun with some company, right? Hope we meet again real soon." He reached across the seat and shook my hand. "You take care now, Desi, you hear me?"

I nodded and watched him drive off. I did not feel so good. I was not at all sure I could be happy living as a desert lizard lives, yesterday forgotten, today's sunrise a surprise, and tomorrow inconceivable. Yet here I was and that's all I had. That and a firm confidence in the power of logic.

There were some shrubs by the road. I lay down next to one and prayed for sleep. Just before I lost consciousness, I touched the quarters in my pocket and repeated the phone number twice.

It was dark when I awoke, and the wet grass pressing lines into my cheek smelled like fresh green salad laced with mint and cucumber slices. Crickets courted each other with urgent cheerfulness, while less familiar insects joined their singing. Frogs grumbled in the distance, a cool breeze rustled through the bushes. Ten thousand stars taught each other slow and stately dances in the soft black sky. I felt a lot better.

The windows of the house beyond the hedge glowed with a warm, inviting yellow light. I lied when I told John that this house was my destination. But somehow just saying it had made it my destination. It seemed like a completely random place to go, which was oddly appealing to me. What the hell, I thought. I knocked on the front door with no idea what I would say to whoever appeared. A large matronly woman opened the door. She had graying hair and wore a loose, brightly flowered dress. She looked vaguely familiar, and I tried desperately to place her. Perhaps, subconsciously, I had remembered something.

"Malcom!" she exclaimed, "Is that you?" The name Malcom rang no bell within my vacant brain, but it didn't matter. Before I could respond, she continued. "Well of course it's you! It's so good to see you again after all these years! My how you've grown up! Why, I scarcely recognized you! I'm Virginia, but of course you already know that. Come and give me a big hug!"

She pulled me into the house and engulfed me. Had I been an orange, she would have squeezed me juiceless. Her arms were steel bands within their soft fleshiness. These were arms made to wrestle half-grown cows to the ground for branding, arms for lifting barrels of pig slop, for making love to men with locomotive muscles and steer tattoos. Instinctively I tried to return her affection, to hug her back, but my own arms were pinned to my sides and unavailable. Finally, she released me and pulled me along behind her.

"Jake, it's little Malcom! He got here a day early!" She turned to me. "Well, not so little any more, I guess." She looked me over and wrinkled her nose. "Kind of a rough trip, eh?"

Don't say too much, I reminded myself. I soon learned that would not be a problem as long as Virginia was around.

Jake entered the tiny living room, a tall, thin man with calm brown eyes and a long nose. His skin was deeply tanned and lined, and I instantly thought of the scarecrow from the Wizard of Oz. It was reassuring to know I still remembered some things.

"Well look what the cat drug in," he said in a rough voice. He shook my hand. "You got any bags?"

I looked around behind me, as if a bag might magically appear.

"No, I…"

"Well, they probably got lost on the bus, or the train or something, didn't they?" Virginia interrupted. "Don't I always say you got to keep your bag under your seat when you travel? Don't I always say that, Jake? Them people just don't care. Well, it don't matter. We all gotta learn for ourselves. Jake, you get Malcom here some fresh clothes." She turned to me. "Now honey, you go take a shower and change and I'll put another plate on the table. I hope you like fried chicken."

I wanted to explain that I wasn't at all sure that I was Malcom. I wanted to tell them that I wasn't sure who I was, but there was a telephone number I had to call and I had two quarters to pay for it. I wanted to say that I had been led to this house by my spiritual guide, a man named John, who had caught the biggest damn bass in the world, a man wise enough to see beyond the oozing, rotting carcass it had become to the essential beauty of the fish itself. But somehow I did not get the opportunity to be completely honest. I was in a bathroom, with someone else's clean jeans and shirt draped across one arm, a clean towel draped across the other, and the door was closing. I was alone. There would be another opportunity to be completely honest. Surely there is always another opportunity to be completely honest. The universe had directed me to this bathroom for a reason. Who was I to resist?

I did not remember other showers, but this one felt good. Better than good. It was a hot and soapy heaven of a shower. A steaming ecstasy. A mystical, cathartic, soul-liberating symphony of cleansing, massaging droplets caressing every inch of my body like a million tiny geishas. After I dried off and stood clean and radiant in fresh, strange clothes, I felt like a new person. Malcom, perhaps. I should not overlook that possibility, although there was no good reason to believe I was Malcom and it seemed improbable. But if you eliminate all the improbabilities from your universe, what are you left with? Certainly no anteaters, no baseball games, no crawdads, or cornflakes or glaciers. Given that reality is mostly comprised of the unlikely and illogical, given that the truth is often improbable, I decided there was a pretty good chance I actually was this Malcom fellow. I was happy I had not blurted out my earlier misgivings. Still, it would probably be smart not to say too much. I was clearly not quite myself yet.

I joined my hosts in the dining room. Virginia was putting plates around a huge wooden table while Jake moved glasses around randomly, trying to look busy enough that he wouldn't be asked to do more. Three other people had joined them.

"Malcom, this is Ted. Everyone calls him Uncle Ted. Do you remember him?"

Uncle Ted was a short, thin man with glasses and long uncombed white hair. He looked very old and frail, but when he spoke, his voice was deep and resonant. He shook my hand. "Why Malcom, you haven't changed a bit since you were eight years old. Do you remember when I took you into town that time? Well, you were pretty young then of course. No, Virginia, he hasn't changed a bit. But then, no one changes, do they?" Uncle Ted's voice had a magical quality to it. When he spoke, he no longer looked small or old. The rich baritone surrounded him like a cloud or a veil, a disguise that made him seem large and somehow substantial. I would believe whatever that voice said.

"Uncle Ted's a preacher, Malcom," Virginia said. "He's always saying things like that. 'No one changes.' Really, Ted!" She turned to the next newcomer. "And this is Earnest. He's fifteen now, and quite the student. Can't get ten minutes work out of him, but he gets good grades. Say hello to Malcom, Earnest."

"My world grinds to a standstill in awe at the unspeakable pleasure your acquaintance provides me."

I liked this kid instantly. "Me too," I said. His mother frowned.

"You been readin' again, ain't you."

Earnest grunted indignantly and stared into space. He was gawky and awkward, a pimpled heron of a kid in a too-large shirt and too-short jeans. His voice cracked when he spoke, one moment a cello and the next a violin scraping cement.

"Perspicacity burgeons in direct proportion to the quantity of variegated abstraction provided."

"Don't try to sweet-talk me, boy. I can always tell when you been reading." She turned to introduce me to the final newcomer. "And this here's Lisa."

It was not possible. At the least, it was not probable. Lisa was the girl from the tan station wagon. And now I realized that Virginia, her mother, had been the driver and the symbol on the mailbox was the same stylized brand I had seen on their car. Lisa's loose blue work shirt made her eyes seem even bluer, as they widened for a moment in recognition.

"Pleased to meet you, Malcom," she giggled. I shook her hand. It was soft and warm and small.

"Me too."

We sat around the table and Uncle Ted said grace. "Thank you, Lord, for the bounty of thy harvest, and for sending our dear Malcom to us once again, unchanged after twenty years. Amen."

A chorus of quiet "Amens" quickly circled the table. Lisa sat immediately to my left. Uncle Ted was directly across from me.

The prayer was some sort of code. The words were lovely, the voice deep and soothing and hypnotic. But what it meant was, "On your marks, get set..." The word "Amen" was a starter's pistol. A cheer rose from thousands of fans in the bleachers, an announcer's voice, distorted by the public address system, shouted, "And they're off!" Arms flashed out to grab pieces of chicken and thunking, splatting spoonfuls of mashed potatoes. A bowl of broccoli was shoved aside impatiently, bread was dealt as if by a riverboat card dealer.

I stared, dumbstruck, as this frenzy came over my hosts. Suddenly I realized that I was very hungry, and that there would be no mercy for the timid at this table. I raced old Uncle Ted's hand for a crisp brown thigh and grabbed it myself.

"The Lord works in mysterious ways," he said, looking me grimly in the eye. "If you can call it work."

I don't know how he did it. Somehow I was holding a meatless thighbone in my hand, and he was stuffing the meat that had surrounded it into his mouth. He had held onto the meat and let me slide the bone right out of it.

I lunged at another piece, a back, barely beating Earnest to it. After pulling it to my plate and surrounding it with one arm, I felt like growling to keep them at bay.

Fortunately, no one was as aggressive about the broccoli and it tasted good to me.

Once everyone had eaten three or four pieces of chicken and a half pound or so of mashed potatoes, some of the urgency dissipated. Conversation resumed as people picked more graciously at the remains upon their plates.

"So, Malcom, how's your mother?" Jake asked.

"Yes, how is Lucinda?" Lisa said. She certainly was a pretty girl. I searched the cavern of my brain for information about my mother, Lucinda. I found only bats and stalactites and echoes.

"Well, how do you think she is?" Virginia said. "Weather like they've been having, her arthritis will be bothering her, right Malcom? The poor dear. And your dad still works for the department store I'll bet, isn't that right? Do you still have that cabin in the mountains? Of course you do! Lucinda would never sell the old cabin. I bet you still go up there every summer, just like always. Remember that time we went up there with them, Jake? I never have seen such sunsets as they have up in those mountains! Well, I sure am glad to hear they're fine. You have your mother's eyes. Yes sir. I bet your folks haven't changed a bit."

Uncle Ted peered at her through his wire glasses. "Nothing ever changes except change itself," he said.

Earnest thought that was funny and laughed a loud teenaged laugh. "Paradox is the refuge of last resort for the obfuscatory mind."

Virginia snapped at him. "Now don't you be talkin' like that at the dinner table!" Earnest just grinned.

Jake looked up from his plate. "By the way, Ted, how's Bernice? When you gonna make an honest woman out of her?" Jake's eyes twinkled. This was apparently an old joke between them. Old Uncle Ted looked down at his plate.

"I only do what's best for her, you know that."

"Of course I know that," Jake said. "But, you know, I'm just a farmer at heart. Not much education. Sometimes you got to explain things to me a time or two. Like your trailer. When do you suppose you'll be telling her about that?"

Ted looked a little indignant.

"I bought that trailer for her," he said. "You know that. Couldn't very well ask her to marry a man who didn't own a home, could I?"

Jake shook his head. "I don't suppose so. How will you explain that you bought it so close before your own birthday?"

"Pure coincidence, nothing more."

"And the little birthday party you had there? The one she didn't know about?"

"I wanted to surprise her. I've been waiting for the right time. Things like this are important to women. I don't want to spoil it for her by just blurting out the first thing that comes into my head. 'Hey Bernice, I bought a trailer, let's get married.' No, that wouldn't be kind. It hurt me not to have her there, still hurts me, but it was for her own good."

"I guess I can see that. You still go over to her place for dinner Wednesday nights?"

"Most Wednesdays, I guess."

"And the time just hasn't been right."

"I've been thinking I ought to pay off the loan before I tell her about it. I mean, I'm eighty-four years old. Would it be fair to ask a woman to move into a trailer that had a loan on it, when there's no way to tell when the Lord will call me home? Would it be right to saddle a woman with payments this late in her life?"

"You'd think that trailer loan would about be paid off by now."

Uncle Ted moved some mashed potatoes around on his plate and said nothing.

"How long has it been, anyway? Let's see, it was an election year, I remember that…"

"Thirteen years."

"What Ted? I didn't hear…"

"Thirteen years. I said I bought the trailer thirteen years ago."

"Now Jake," Virginia cut in. "Don't badger Uncle Ted like that. You know it's none of our business."

"I'd just think in thirteen years there might have been one good time to bring up the subject."

"Stop it, Jake, now, I mean it! It's none of our business."

"Probably every person in the county's been to his trailer except Bernice and she feeds him every Wednesday night and I don't know what all, thinks they might get married some day. Doesn't even know he owns it. Seems like an odd kind of love if you ask me."

"Well no one's askin' you, and that's the end of it. More broccoli, Malcom?"

"No thanks."

"I think Bernice is sweet," Lisa said.

32

"A wonderful woman," Uncle Ted agreed. "A bit self-absorbed perhaps, and demanding at times. I'm trying to help her understand that she must not always be pushing to get her own way. She must learn to trust in the Lord. Good things come to those who wait." He stared into the distance. "But goodness, can the woman cook."

Jake started to say something, but a stern look from Virginia stopped him like a window stops a sparrow. He closed his mouth and his words fluttered silently, unconsciously to the ground. Earnest jumped into the vacant spot of quiet.

"Convoluted eloquence relumes a tessellated mind, that's what I think," he said. "Concatenations of unrelated ideas may titillate the imagination, but they circumnavigate true sagacity. Unnecessary complexity and random sesquipedalians may buttress a weak thought, superficially, but a cantilevered soul..."

Jake interrupted him angrily. "If you can't talk about anything but women's private parts, you can leave the table son."

"But Dad..."

"No sir. Your mother doesn't have to sit here and listen to that kind of language. And us with company, too. You go to your room."

Earnest left the table looking unrepentant.

"Where's Malcom going to sleep?" Lisa asked shyly, and I became instantly more interested in the conversation. Lisa was all sweetness and heat, a brilliant flare spinning in a summer field, shooting hot sparks across the black Oklahoma sky. Somewhere within me a dalmation began wagging his eager tail and padding toward forbidden furniture. I jerked his mental leash, he yelped and sulked back to whine beneath a dark, private porch. Virginia's face brightened. "Oh, I almost forgot about that." she said. "I've got a surprise for you, Malcom.

Remember when you were little and you'd come to visit us? Remember how we used to put a cot up in the hayloft for you?"

"Well, I was probably pretty small…"

"Of course you remember! Well, we put a cot up there again, just like you liked it! Lisa, why don't you show him. I'm sure he's exhausted."

I was not exhausted. My little nap on the grass followed by the shower and a good meal had refreshed me. But I let Lisa lead me out to the barn. With no memories to push me along, with no philosophy or religion in my brain to funnel me, it seemed reasonable to let myself be led. Plus, I liked the idea of being alone with her.

"It's a nice night, isn't it Malcom."

"A heck of a swell night," I agreed. And it was. After a long day in Hell, the coolness was a banana split for my mind. After squinting at the sun, broiling beneath its cruel inquisition, ratchetting my face tighter and tighter, it was pleasant to let my eyes relax. I'd had enough of the smells of rotting fish, wet carpet, hot beer, and urine. Now I walked through an olfactory carnival of alfalfa and cut grass, roses, pinks, carnations, and strawberries. A crowd of cicadas buzzed loudly in a tree. For all their insistence, it was a soothing sound.

The moon had risen, casting long black shadows behind trees and fence posts and highlighting Lisa's soft face and fine rippling hair. When the terrain forced us together, I could feel the warmth of her skin and smell traces of her shampoo. When she looked at me and smiled, I could actually see the moon and stars reflected in her liquid eyes. The scent of her delicate perfume sent a shiver down my spine. I knew that perfume, knew its name, and I became instantly more alert. I would follow that scent anywhere. An idea buzzed around my head like a mosquito picking its spot: Perhaps Lisa was to be my new spiritual guide.

"I'm in love, you know," she said.

"Excuse me?"

"With Mike. I'm in love with Mike. He's a salesman."

Suddenly, inexplicably, I was less sure that she was to be my spiritual guide.

"Neat," I said. "Love is neat. I mean, I'm glad you're in love."

"He travels a lot, so I don't get to see him much." She paused, then said, "Oil field equipment," in answer to the question I probably should have been thinking. I just nodded.

"He's real smart. We're going to get married someday. It's all set. Well, we never really talked about it or anything. But I just know."

The barn loomed huge ahead of us, like a gigantic black ship sailing through the dark grass and trees. Lisa was thinking hard about something.

"Malcom, do you think I'm sophisticated?"

"What?"

"You know, sophisticated. Mike wants me to be more sophisticated."

I knew the word, sort of, and associated it with people who dress well. Lisa's clothes, while not fancy, looked good on her. Her blue shirt spilled over a white skirt that fell a few inches above her knees.

"You're as sophisticated as anyone I can think of," I said honestly.

"Oh, you're just saying that to be nice. No, really, what do you think?"

I caught myself looking at her shirt, at the outline of her breasts pushing against the material bouncing lightly with each step. I decided not to tell her what I was really thinking.

"I guess it depends. What does Mike mean when he says that?"

"Well, like the time I was walking through the park, a couple months ago, and it was almost dark, and I saw him sitting on the grass with Mary Lou Schneider. They were kissing, see, and I got all upset, and Mike said I was acting childish. He said grown-ups kiss each other all the time and it doesn't mean anything at all. I said I didn't think that friends kissed each other."

"What did Mary Lou say?"

"Nothing. She seemed kind of out of breath."

"Hmm."

"That's when he said that I needed to be more sophisticated. I needed to learn to trust him. That I was just young and inexperienced. He said he loved me, then he kissed me, and it all made sense. He's a wonderful man. I just want to make him happy."

I was confused.

"But if Mike loves you, why was he kissing her?"

She looked at me like I was a child who simply did not understand such grown-up matters.

"Mike explained that all to me. He says love isn't what you do. It's how you feel and what you say. He says I'm the only girl he loves, so I shouldn't worry about what he does. Because love is all that matters. See, I told you he was smart."

"So as long as he says he loves you, you shouldn't worry if he beats you up and takes all your money?"

She laughed. "Mike would never do that. You're just playing little word games with me. Sophisticated people have lots of people that drift into their lives for a little while and then drift away again. Mike is very sophisticated."

"It sounds like he's practiced it."

"Exactly. And if I don't want to be an innocent little girl all my life, I need to have more experiences too. Big ones and little ones, all kinds, until they pile up so high I can't even remember what it felt like to be a goddamn sweet little farm girl. I'm tired of being ignorant."

"That could be a big train to turn around once you get it going," I said.

"I'll never forget who I am," she said firmly and, it seemed, a bit innocently. "No matter how many experiences I have. I'll always be just the same as I am now only sophisticated."

I felt a dull stab of jealousy when she said she'd never forget who she was. I also thought she was wrong about never changing, somehow, but didn't want to argue. How could someone not change? Or maybe I hoped she was right. After all, I'd lost all my experiences, but had I changed? I didn't think so. I did't feel particularly innocent or naive. In fact, at the moment I felt uncomfortably grown up.

"You're lucky to be in love."

"I know."

We entered the perfect darkness of the barn. The air was pleasantly moist and richly organic. It smelled like wet sawdust, or strong tea. Lisa found my hand and led me to some wooden stairs.

"Careful," she said. I couldn't see a thing. Her hand was very warm. I tried to be a perfect gentleman, but couldn't anticipate her starts and stops. I kept bumping into her.

"Excuse me," I said, grateful for the darkness because I could feel my face getting red. Lisa giggled. The stairs were steep, almost like a ladder, and as I climbed them behind her my face was only inches from her back. "Oops. Excuse me again." Moonlight spilled through a big window in the loft, casting extreme shadows. A cot sat in the center of the room with a mattress, pillow, and quilt. Bales of hay were stacked neatly everywhere, filling the loft.

"Here you are," she said. "Does it look familiar?"

"Well, it's been a long time," I said. Nothing looked familiar. We sat on the cot. The moon lit up Lisa's cheekbones and the outline of her hair, but left her back and neck completely dark. Beyond her, the blackness was impenetrable and perfect. She looked like a Mexican oil painting, a gold and yellow Madonna on black velvet.

"So you see, I'm trying to be more sophisticated," she said. "I want to make Mike happy."

"Excuse me?"

"Mike says it's an attitude. He says sometimes I'm a real hillbilly. I hate it when he calls me that. I've always been kind of shy, the way I dress and all. I just care about things too much. Mike showed me pictures of really elegant ladies dressed in these skimpy little outfits. He says these women are proud of their bodies. Did you know that at the beaches in France none of the women wear any tops at all? They just walk around and they don't care if perfect strangers look at them!" There was awe in her voice. Then she shrugged. "But, of course, they didn't grow up in Oklahoma. He says it just takes practice. You can practice not caring, and if you practice enough, pretty soon you won't care about anything at all. Not what you do, or how you look, or what anybody else thinks. And then you're sophisticated. And that's the way Mike wants me to be."

"I bet he likes you just the way you are."

"I want to be better." She looked downward and hair spilled over her eyes. "Would you help me?"

"What do you mean?"

"Well, I know you're sophisticated. When I saw you yesterday, on that black car, and you just stood there, even after we drove up and were looking right at you, and it didn't even bother you. You just smiled and waved and, you know, just... kept on. Well, that minute I knew that you were very sophisticated. Just like those ladies in France."

I did not feel very worldly. Then or now. "What exactly do you want me to do?"

"Just talk. Just sit here and talk about all the things in the world. Faraway places and smart people and books and restaurants. About anything we want. Mike says that if I act like I'm not shy, pretty soon I won't be any more. Now, what do you want to talk about?"

"I'm probably not as sophisticated as you think," I said. If there's a scale somewhere that measures a person's innocence versus their experience, my life was breaking new records right now. It was spinning like a windmill.

She giggled. "Now you're teasing me." She tossed her hair over a lovely shoulder. "Boy, it's still hot in here, isn't it?" She casually unbuttoned the top two buttons on her shirt. It was a man's shirt and two buttons covered a lot of territory on her small body. "Aren't you hot too?"

"Yeah, it's a little warm all right." To be polite, I undid a couple of buttons on my shirt as well. I rested my hand on my leg and felt the quarters through the denim of my pocket, as if the coins were magic amulets that could save me from some vague evil. "I really need to use a phone. I've been trying to reach this number…" But there was no phone in the barn, and the house stood across a vast sea of clover and wild rye, upwind and against the current, beyond treacherous reefs and swirling maelstroms. Only a fool would attempt that journey at night.

"How about farm prices?" she said. "Shall we talk about them? Jake says it all comes down to when we get rain, you know? If you keep track of the rain, you'll be able to predict the price of any crop."

Lisa knew enough about the price of various crops to have her own early morning crop report show on a radio station. She talked for a long time, and every now and then I'd hear a familiar word break through my haze. A word like "corn" or "pork bellies." Mostly I just tried not to look at her breasts as they bounced gently and hypnotically in the moonlight with each gesture. She said something about planting before a full moon.

"See, this isn't so hard, is it?"

"What?"

"Mike will be real proud of me. This was a good idea. I don't feel nearly as shy anymore. I feel comfortable. That's good, isn't it? I mean, that's how I'm supposed to feel, right?"

"I guess so. Sure." I was not comfortable at all. "You know, I bet it's possible to be too sophisticated. I bet it takes some of the fun out of things."

She stared out the window. "You're just saying that because you've seen the whole world and probably done everything and you don't think I can be like that. Well, I can be just as good as anybody. I can learn not to care about anything! I'm no hillbilly!

"But that's enough about me. What have you been doing for your whole life? Do you have a girlfriend? What are your hobbies? Are you interested in sports, or politics, or religion?"

"How about sorghum this year? I bet there's a record crop." I had no idea what sorghum was, but it sounded appropriately rural. I inhaled the scent made by trillions of microscopic creatures as they transformed dead straw and sawdust into rich living soil, mixed with the faint smell of shampoo. Humidity squeezed spicy cologne from the barn's old timbers. It did feel very warm in there.

She ignored my comment. She was obviously deep in thought. The moon made her skirt seem very white, almost glowing against her tan legs. Her breasts were calling out for company. They were shrieking like banshees.

They sang the song the ocean sings to lemmings high on the cliff. They were porch lights, and I was a miller moth. I stared out the window into the night. How was I supposed to help her practice indifference when I could feel the warmth of her long legs only inches from my own?

"I really love Mike."

"I can tell that."

"I mean, I know I'm too shy and all, and I'm afraid if I don't learn to relax a little, he's going to find someone else. Does that make sense?"

"You don't seem shy to me."

She laughed, a light musical laugh that touched something inside my mind, deeper than the part of the brain that thinks. Her voice was smooth, soft candy and a rippling stream in the desert. It was an old friend on the telephone, pulling me, warning me, trying to remind me of something important. I couldn't understand the words, but I moved toward the sound.

"That's because I'm not acting shy," she said. "Remember? That's what we're doing. I'm practicing acting like I'm not shy."

"And doing a fine job."

She leaned over and kissed me softly on the neck. I closed my eyes at the wonderful warmth and moistness of her lips, absolutely familiar yet completely new. Her hair tickled and her perfume made me shudder as shadows and phantoms swirled around within me, too subtle and elusive to catch and hold.

"Thanks," she whispered.

"Thank you," I gasped, my voice very dry and thin.

"Mike can kiss anybody. Like you see on the talk shows, how everyone kisses everyone else. I mean that's the way I ought to be, isn't it?"

"I think you're sweet just the way you are."

"And like touching. I always think it's a big deal. Mike hugs everybody. If I touch your leg like this, see, just near your knee, then I shouldn't feel bad or good or anything, right? And you shouldn't either. It should be like touching a bale of hay, or like petting a dog."

"I don't know if you should pet my leg like that..."

"Why not? Am I hurting you? Am I hurting anyone? That's what Mike would say. He'd say I have to rise above my upbringing."

"I really think you ought to stop that..."

"And if you touch me, then it shouldn't mean anything either, right? Here, give me your hand. See? It's just a leg, right? It could just as easy be an oatmeal box."

Well, it was not an oatmeal box. Her leg was soft and warm and smooth and exquisitely alive. I felt myself rising above my upbringing.

"It should be a good year for watermelons. The ones in our garden are about ready to harvest. Do you like watermelons?"

Her hand rested on my leg. I repeatedly sent messages to my own hand ordering it to return to headquarters, but the lines were apparently down. It explained that it was exploring a cardboard oatmeal box. Line of duty, it said. Following orders, it said. Return to headquarters, I yelled at it. That's an order! Shut up, stupid, I'm busy, it said.

"They're so soft and juicy," she said.

"What?"

"Watermelons," she said. "Do you like them?"

"Yes, I sure do like them."

We struggled to maintain a clinical disinterest in the reality of the moment while we discussed the abstract intricacies of produce. On a theoretical level, it was a fascinating concept, a noble attempt, a worthy case study. But Lisa was inexperienced at the fine art of not caring, and I was a desert lizard. Her smooth skin and familiar perfume summoned memories more ancient than our lives. More conversation would have violated the temple where life conducts its sacraments. Our experiment in indifference disintegrated quickly.

Whatever joy sophistication provides was lost on us. We quickly became two frenzied octopi, pumped full of hormones, thrashing at each other in a desperately primitive Neptunian ritual. Much kelp was destroyed, coral beds were decimated, and the northern lights flashed across the sky. The sea became wild and frothy, the wind raged and whipped up waves that would frighten a Viking until its ancient urgency was spent.

Finally, the clouds parted and the stars beamed serenely on the glassy water. Whales called softly in the darkness while a warm breeze breathed gently, rhythmically in my ear and the smell of seaweed faded and merged into the aroma of new-cut hay. My confusion was exorcised the way sunlight and fresh air cleanse a musty attic. This is where I belonged, where I had always been. Just before I fell into exhausted sleep, the telephone number flashed through my mind. In a near-dream, I dialed it. A disjointed voice answered. It sounded something like this: "I'm sorry but the number you have reached, the Hand of the Flea and the Loan of the Phrase is not in service at this time. If you need assistance, please remain on the line…"

But I could not remain on the line. I felt completely comfortable, and yet oddly sad. In the darkness, surrounded by warmth and that familiar scent, I pushed the sadness aside.

The voice became a chorus of crickets, the connection faded, and my little boat drifted out to sea.

The Land of Debris

The smell of frying onions and potatoes filled the house as I stood in the tiny living room staring out the window at the neat lawn and the highway beyond it. The early morning peace was disturbed only by an occasional truck roaring toward some distant city. Lisa and Earnest still slept. Virginia chattered away at Jake in the kitchen, and I caught enough of their urgent conversation to piece together the big news.

Uncle Bud had died in his sleep, but his death didn't seem to bother anyone and was not the big news. No one much cared for Uncle Bud, who lived "way up in New Mexico." A kinky old buzzard, that's how Ted apparently described him. But Earnest had written him letters, long and erudite tomes in which he discussed the nature of things few people had ever heard of, and Bud had written back equally long letters using words that neither Virginia nor Jake could understand. They corresponded like that for years, old man and young boy, exchanging dense and incomprehensible letters.

Presumably that's why, when Bud died, he left his Cadillac to Earnest. The letter announcing this came early in the morning, only hours after Lisa and I had dabbled with sophistication. A messenger delivered it, giving it God's own authority. The Moses ploy.

A movement on the highway caught my attention. I turned toward it, then dropped to the floor in terror. My heart pounded furiously as a white van cruised slowly past. I had been standing like a billboard in the window.

From the floor, peering through the curtains, I watched it continue on its way. I crawled across the carpet to the telephone and dialed as quietly as I could.

"The number you have reached..."

I hung up. It didn't make any sense, but I knew I had to get out of there.

"What in the hell are you doing on the floor?" Jake's deep voice rumbled at me, as amazed at someone sitting on the carpet as he might have been if one of his pigs had started singing opera.

"I don't know," I said honestly.

"Leave him alone." Virginia shouldered past him. "Why, look you've startled him half to death. He's as white as a sheet. Now listen, Malcom, here's the deal. How'd you like to take a trip up to New Mexico? We'll pay your bus fare and everything. We got us a little scheduling problem. And New Mexico's a helluva sight cooler than Oklahoma. Just take a few days. It would be like a little vacation for you."

There was no time for breakfast, let alone long good-byes. Earnest had to go to Taos immediately to pickup his car. And an adult had to go with him to sign the papers. Everyone else had commitments. So I was appointed.

I tried to explain that I might not actually be Malcom, but no one listened. It was just as well. How would I explain myself to Virginia and Jake if the real Malcom arrived that afternoon? How would I explain it to Lisa? For that matter, no one had ever explained how I was related to anyone. Was I (that is, was Malcom) a friend of the family? Or were Lisa and Malcom (that is, were Lisa and I) cousins? Or brother and sister? Or was I really more closely related to old Uncle Ted, the preacher with the secret trailer? In one day I had managed to tangle all the relationships of my new life into a complicated cat's cradle of interlocking possibilities. A free bus ticket to Taos sounded pretty good.

The ride was uneventful. Earnest read three books of science fiction while I slept, thought about Lisa and her lovely perfume, and drank glass after glass of iced tea from the thermos Virginia forced me to take along. Outside the bus window the terrain changed from low-altitude desert to high-altitude desert, then to prairie. The dirt changed from red to gray to brown, the sparse vegetation changed to low piñon pines and sagebrush, with huge boulders scattered like meteorites among them.

You're killing time, I told myself, as miles slipped past me. You've lost your life and you don't have many clues to help you find it and yet here you are on a strange bus with a very strange teenager chasing across the country. Be logical. Devise a plan. Figure out a course of action, then be decisive. This is not a pair of socks you've misplaced. Do something!

Right, I answered myself. Like what exactly do you suggest? Maybe you just need to ask the universe who you are and then shut up long enough for it to answer. Wouldn't that be as smart as anything? Wouldn't it be as logical as anything? Ask your questions, shut up, do nothing, and wait.

It did not seem like a good plan, but it seemed reasonably easy to try. And, having no alternative in mind, I adopted it as an interim strategy. Shut up and do nothing. But don't forget the phone number.

In Taos, a small town built of adobe bricks and tourist dollars, we signed some papers (luckily, perhaps remarkably, no one asked to see my identification — a potential adventure I had overlooked). Then we picked up the Cadillac, a peach-colored Eldorado, huge and old, but in perfect condition. Earnest called home to report our success and got permission to stay several more days to practice his driving and see the sights. We had brought sleeping bags and other camping gear, prepared to orchestrate a pleasant little adventure. No other Malcom had arrived and I didn't know how I felt about that. My new family would welcome me back, that was good. I wanted to see them again, especially Lisa. But it also meant I was more likely to be Malcom and if I was Malcom, I couldn't be anybody else. I chaffed at that restriction. I felt more free before I had a name. It was one of those good news/bad news deals, like Jesus must have felt. "Well, yeah, these nails hurt like hell. On the other hand, this is probably about the worst thing that will happen to me today."

"Hello?" I shouted in my brain. "Is anyone in there?"

But my brain only echoed back, "...in there?...in there?... in there?..." I threw a stone into the blackness, but never heard it hit a wall or splash into an inky pool. Not even bats, I thought. Not even bats.

My next surprise was learning that Earnest did

not know how to drive. So I drove the peach-colored Eldorado to the outskirts of town and began to teach him. It felt a little odd, not knowing anything about myself, and yet knowing that I could drive, that I knew everything about it. In fact, I learned that I'm a pretty skillful driver. Teaching Earnest would probably be a good experience.

He was a quick student, and I relaxed. I may have relaxed too much.

"An expedient alternative to my present course might be serendipitous," he said. I had been staring out my window deciding that sophistication is highly overrated while he practiced. We were far out in the country by now. I looked over at him.

"Excuse me?"

"The alacrity with which the impending singularity in the space-time continuum approaches has momentarily diffused my capacity for lucid thought and decisive action," he said simply. "A plethora of possibilities surely exists, a panoply of choices, yet none seems salient or inexorably logical. I assume it's my own inexperience. Perhaps you'd be so gracious as to suggest…"

His knuckles were white around the steering wheel, his eyes transfixed. I looked ahead. During my daydream, Earnest had let the accelerator get away from him. We were barreling down a dirt road at ninety miles an hour and the biggest cow in New Mexico was standing a hundred feet directly ahead of us, staring with mild disbelief at the approaching peach-colored apparition.

"Hit the damn brake!" I screamed. "The one on the left! Brake, dammit!"

Immediately his expression changed. Oh yes, now I remember. The pedal to the left. He slammed his foot onto the brake pedal. Only he must have swung the steering wheel hard left at the same time, because the Eldorado started sliding sideways down the road. Then it was sliding backward. It spun completely around two or three times, dust and gravel flying everywhere, brakes and tires squealing. I covered my head with my arms, but I knew deep down that it was useless. I was dead. Earnest was dead. The cow was meatloaf.

Within seconds there was a bone-wrenching collision, I was thrown sideways against Earnest, his door flew open, and before we knew it both of us were lying on the ground. The Cadillac was stopped crossways straddling the road. We lay there for a moment before we realized that it was over, and that we were alive.

"Thanks," he said, his vocabulary apparently gone for the moment. "That was a good plan."

We got up slowly, brushing dirt off ourselves. The cow had vanished. My terror changed into anger.

"You could have slowed down," I said tersely. "You could have honked your damn horn. You could have steered away from the cow, onto this flat parking lot of a prairie. You could have asked for advice more concisely. Something like 'what should I do?' Then we might have had time. And what in the hell were you trying to do, going that fast anyway?"

"Excellent suggestions, every one, in retrospect," he said pleasantly, cleaning dust off his glasses. "But, of course, an excess of alternatives can be counter-productive to the decision making process. Had I had access to a surfeit of possibilities, the time required to process them, to distill them to their essences for comparison, might have consumed the available window of opportunity for action. No, your simple suggestion, implemented without deliberation, was certainly the optimum solution." We started walking around the car, looking for damage. "Anyway, what cow?"

"That one," I said, and pointed. The tail of the

spinning Cadillac had whacked into the unfortunate beast, leaving it cleanly, instantly, and irreversibly dead on the gravel.

"Oh," he said. We stared at the bulky creature that lay motionless before us. I ran up and down the vacant cavern of my memory looking for clues. Had this happened to me before? Did I know what to do? Was this a common problem?

A man's voice startled us both.

"This don't look good." He was big and burly, perhaps in his fifties, astride a fat gray horse. His face was deeply tanned, his hair was long, black, and scraggly, and a huge belly distended his red flannel shirt and hung like a sack of beans over his belt. A single pheasant feather protruded from the band of his well-worn black cowboy hat. He puffed on a fat cigar, but his face was otherwise motionless. The rifle he held casually across his saddle made him seem menacing. I decided this might be one of those times when choice of words mattered. I paused while Earnest, perhaps more familiar with situations like this and always eager to talk, took up the slack.

"We have had an automotive-bovine juxtaposition with adverse, in fact, terminal consequences to the organic component of that equation."

"Hit the cow with your Caddie, eh?"

"Well, in a matter of speaking…"

"Killed it, eh?"

Earnest just nodded. The man looked at us for a long time.

"Just bought it, didn't you."

Earnest and I looked at each other in amazement. The man was obviously a psychic, a New Mexican shaman so in tune with the spirit world that he saw the Truth beyond the mists and confusion the rest of us are condemned to live within. How else could he have known about the Cadillac?

51

He pointed at the car. "Temporary sticker. Where you from?"

"Oklahoma," I said. It was the simple answer. "He inherited the car. We came to pick it up."

The man nodded and inspected us silently for a few moments. Finally he nodded again, this time with more authority.

"I'm Chief Heliotrope," he said, sliding off his horse. "That was my cow. You owe me money." He slid the rifle into a holder on the saddle and walked toward us. As he walked, he pulled a long, nasty-looking knife from his belt. Earnest and I stepped backward in unison. When God finally decides to gut the Devil, he will use a blade like this one. Excaliber with a hickory handle, a scimitar for lopping off buffalo heads. A big knife. I decided quickly that a firm and fair explanation was in order. We had, after all, killed the man's cow, but that didn't mean he ought to kill us. Surely there was some sort of Indian code that respected honesty and firmness and courage. We had no money, that was the first problem. I would be a man and calmly negotiate an equitable settlement. He would understand, agree, and then we'd smoke a peace pipe or something. I could do this.

But when I opened my mouth, the voice that spoke was a ten-year-old kid's who had broken the neighbor's window with a baseball and was whining about it.

"But we didn't mean to do it," I said. "Honest."

Chief Heliotrope ignored me. He walked directly to the dead cow and began cutting on it. It took me a minute to realize that he was removing a square of skin with the animal's brand. When the outline was complete, he peeled the skin away, leaving a bloody red square of meat exposed. Then he looked in each of the cow's ears, located something and cut one ear off. He put it on the square of skin, rolled it like a newspaper and whistled.

"Custer!" he yelled. "Here boy!"

Within a heartbeat, a yellow cur appeared, a gaunt assemblage of mange and drool and toothy cunning. This was a serious dog and I could tell right away that things mattered more to him than they do to me. If he and I had a disagreement, the dog would win. His basic life premises were clear and well defined. Things like bones that still had some red meat attached were clearly nonnegotiable. So was cowhide. Custer bared his teeth briefly in my direction, a simple canine restraining order, then trotted over to his master. He seemed to know what to do. He took the rolled skin in his mouth and loped off toward the hills.

"Why'd you do that?" I asked in amazement.

"Old Indian custom," he said. "Return the cow's spirit to the earth. Very few white men have seen the ritual. You swear secrecy." He took a step toward us, wiping the bloody blade on his jeans.

"Scout's honor," I said quickly, and Earnest crossed his heart and hoped to die.

"Hmm," Chief Heliotrope grunted. "That was a six-hundred-dollar cow."

He stood there, waiting.

"Cash," he said. "No checks."

We all stared at each other. Earnest spoke timidly.

"We are, unfortunately, impecunious."

I don't know if the chief knew the word, or simply understood the tone. Perhaps he deduced its meaning from the clear fact that no money was changing hands. He did not pause or flinch.

"I'll take the car."

Suddenly there was a thought in my brain. A small but good idea cartwheeled across my mind like a naked cheerleader at the Pope's birthday party. Everything would be fine. I could solve this problem. It could not fail. I knew what to do. I felt happy and proud and confident. It was a strange sensation.

"Won't be necessary," I said. "You'll get your money."

Both the inscrutable chief and Earnest looked surprised. I savored the moment. I paused, I waited, I let seconds tick away. Finally I released them.

"Insurance!" I said gleefully. "We bought insurance when we picked up the car. Complete coverage! We don't have any money. But insurance companies have more money than Switzerland. We'll report the accident to the police, and to the insurance company, they'll send an investigator to look at the damage and then pay you for your cow!"

"Hmm," Heliotrope stared into the distance. "Don't know. How much cash you got on you right now?"

"About sixty bucks," Earnest said.

"Hmm. It's not much. But if it's all you got..."

"That doesn't matter," I said firmly. "The insurance company will pay you whatever the cow was worth." I spoke with confidence. Earnest was the closest thing I had to family and I felt protective of him. "The boy needs his cash for gas to get home. If you just direct us to the nearest telephone..."

"His rates'll go up."

"What?"

"Insurance company'll screw the kid."

The man had a point. I could picture a rate schedule with a line for teenage boys who use their cars to kill cows on deserted country roads the first time they get behind the wheel.

"On a purely actuarial basis, there is some statistical veracity…" Earnest began.

"Better idea," Heliotrope interrupted. "You can work it off. Five days work. No cops, no insurance, no money."

"You mean, if we work for you for five days, you'll just forget about the cow?"

"I accept that offer." Heliotrope stepped toward me and extended his hand. The hand without the knife. Instinctively I shook it. "Done deal," he said.

I looked at Earnest. He looked at me. Heliotrope was shaking his hand. Earnest shrugged, as if to say, 'What just happened?' I shrugged back. 'Hell if I know.'

Still, I felt proud. I had negotiated for our lives and won. It occurred to me that major league negotiating skill like that can only be developed by years of practice. There could be no doubt. I was some sort of professional negotiator. But what kind, exactly? Perhaps someone who has to deal with cultures different from his own…

It hit me like a rock to the forehead. Ambassadors. This was just like being an ambassador. That had to be it. I was an ambassador. I started to tell Earnest but caught myself. He thought I was Malcom. I could not break his heart. Sadly I decided that, for his sake, I must continue my charade a bit longer. At last I knew who I was, but could tell no one. Once again, the smart plan was to keep my mouth shut.

That's how we became Chief Heliotrope's indentured servants for five days.

He rigged a travois out of fence posts and bush branches, produced a rope, and tied the unlucky cow's legs together. Then he fastened the rope to the frame of the caddie. With the chief on his horse leading us, we slowly dragged the carcass behind the car. After traveling across most of the state of New Mexico, we reached

the chief's ranch, a perfectly barren wasteland at the end
of a barely discernible dirt road. The only improvements
were a tiny gray shack and a large, rusting metal building
he called the barn. The barn was stuffed full of machinery, tools, car parts, and junk. The land itself was scruffy
and dry. No trees, no fence, no lawn in front. If you held
a rifle waist high and aimed in any direction, the bullet
wouldn't hit a thing before it ran out of steam and drifted
to the ground. And, I realized, no one would hear the shot.
As soon as we dragged the dead cow to the vicinity of the
barn, Heliotrope took the car keys. Then he put us to work.

First he had us cut open the cow and remove its
intestines and other organs. Custer got the liver without
discussion or negotiations. With dripping red meat hanging out both sides of his mouth he growled a brief closing
statement, then trotted to a patch of hot shade next to the
house.

The inside of a cow is a marvel of wet things. There
is apparently no way to get them out without grabbing a
slippery handful and pulling hard. I was surprised that it
was still so warm in there, and surprised at the various
smells. Once we had created a cavern where the cow had
conducted its bodily business, Heliotrope had us hoist the
beast with pulleys so it was hanging head downward.
Then, using his knife and a handsaw, he cut off its head.
Blood poured out for a few moments, then slowed to a
trickle. While it was draining, he gave us knives and pli-
ers and made us skin the thing. He sat on a wooden crate,
a beer in one hand, a new cigar in his mouth, and directed
us. He seemed to know what he was doing, but was unin-
terested in participating.

It is much easier to kill a cow with a big car than it
is to transform the carcass into meat, which is very hard
work. When the last of the skin was removed, he made us
rub a mixture of salt and pepper into the surface of the

body. He filled gunny sacks full of ice from a rusting ice machine that still bore the name of some defunct New Mexico bar. We stuffed the interior of the cow with these bags, and draped them over the outside.

"Best to cool it quick," Heliotrope said. By then it was dark.

To his credit, Heliotrope brought us each a huge bowl of steaming stew. We sat outside the barn, leaned against the warm metal, and devoured it as the stars appeared. When we were done, the chief lit his cigar, belched loudly, then raised his face to the sky. Exhaling white smoke, he howled like an animal in a high falsetto voice, long and calm, until he'd expelled a lungful of smoke as if this were his nightly post-dinner ritual and it didn't occur to him that a stranger might find it odd. Just the sort of idiosyncrasy a man who has lived alone for a long time would develop. Earnest looked at me quizzically, but we said nothing. Heliotrope belonged in this place, the way sagebrush and dry heat belonged. I felt a twinge of envy.

"That was great!" I said at last. I did not recognize the flavor, but attributed that to my amnesia.

"Mm," our host agreed. "Nothing like stew made from fresh heart." He wiped his mouth with his shirt sleeve. "Tomorrow you can start your five days working for me."

"Tomorrow!" I said. "What about today? We worked hard for you all afternoon! That's not fair! We had an agreement! We had a contract!"

"No," he said quietly. "We had a treaty. You sleep out here tonight. Keep the coyotes from the meat."

"Coyotes?"

He nodded. "This will help." He produced a hand-sized transistor radio. "Tune in the Albuquerque talk radio show. They hear the voices, they usually stay back. Sleeping bags on the shelf back there."

He stood up and dissolved silently into the shadows. Earnest and I were suddenly alone on the vast vacant prairie with the stars and coyotes, the dead cow hanging like a crucifix behind us.

A coyote howled, and I shivered. It was the voice of the vast, lonely unknown. The voice of my past. The voice of death. Of my future.

As I drifted reluctantly to sleep, a strident woman was complaining about potholes on some Albuquerque street. And I was noticing how it feels to sign a treaty with a guy who's holding the keys to your Cadillac.

I repeated the phone number to myself. I didn't want to lose it.

The next day we painted Heliotrope's house. Then
we painted his metal barn. The day after that we dug a pit
for cooking the cow and roamed around the ranch gathering small boulders. There was going to be a big parade,
with a feast afterward, a big party for all of Heliotrope's
friends. I could not imagine that he had many friends. We
were going to have a lot of leftovers

The chief did not display much emotion and he
rarely talked. But I could tell he loved one soul, at least,
on the planet: his old gray horse, Michelle ("after the
Beatles' song"). She was mostly Appaloosa, over fifteen
years old, and had been a gift from his father just before
the old man died. Every morning after Heliotrope gave
us our instructions, the old horse would amble over and
nuzzle him for treats. The Indian would whisper nonsense
in her ear and caress her forehead. After this ritual fore-
play, he'd spring lightly onto her bare back and ride away
slowly with Custer scouting ahead at an easy trot. Custer,
the dog, was his friend, his partner, his co-conspirator.
Michelle was his lover. In his eyes she was still young
and proud and swift. A beautiful young woman. And,
judging from the ease with which he mounted her and his
alert posture as he rode, on her back he was no longer
unkempt and overweight and aging. He was a young and
untamed brave from another time.

The day before the parade, we began having visitors. First a young man drove up with a flatbed truck full
of firewood. He had dark skin and eyes and black hair

like Heliotrope, but wore jogging shoes and a black rock
'n roll T-shirt. The two of them leaned against the house
drinking beer while Earnest and I unloaded the truck. The
firewood consisted of broken fence poles, weathered sections of telephone poles and cracked pallets.

"A few more days of ultraviolet stimulation to our
subcutaneous melanin and we'll pass for one of them,"
Earnest whispered. "Perhaps then we can effect an escape."

It was true. We were getting pretty badly sunburned. More Indians drifted onto the ranch, some in
pickup trucks with sacks of potatoes that needed to be
unloaded, others with bushel baskets of unhusked corn.
Many pulled horse trailers. Michelle soon had a lot of
equine company, horses of all sizes and shapes, some wary
of each other, others sniffing and nuzzling each other like
old friends.

Under Heliotrope's watchful gaze Earnest and I
got things ready for the feast. We stacked firewood in the
pit, balanced a large metal grate on several rusted rail-
road rails, and piled stones on top of the grate. We lit the
fire and cooked the boulders all afternoon. Whenever the
fire died down, we added more wood. By sundown the
rocks were hot to their granite hearts and the fire was
allowed to dwindle. Using asbestos welder's gloves, a
half-dozen quiet men helped us remove all the rock and
the grate. The pit was lined with the baked rocks. Other
men butchered the cow carcass, cutting it into a dozen
large pieces. The sections were wrapped in aluminum foil,
laid into the pit, and covered with more rocks. Unhusked
ears of corn and whole potatoes were thrown in, then more
hot rocks. Finally the whole thing was covered with a
foot of dirt. Wherever smoke and steam escaped, more
dirt was added. I could not believe that hot rocks would
bake a whole cow in a hole in the ground. And I'd never

heard of traditional Indians using aluminum foil. I asked Heliotrope about it. He shrugged.

"I saw it on TV," he said. "This is how they do it in Peru. Anyway, it tastes good, not much hassle. Easy way to cook, if someone else digs the hole."

He had me there. Heliotrope's total effort toward the project consisted of drinking beer and smoking cigars.

As darkness settled over New Mexico, the visitors left. Earnest and I spent one more night in sleeping bags on the dirt, guarding the smoking ground and watching the horses. The horses raised a haze of dust, pungent smoke filled and dried our noses. A coyote howled, not too far away in the darkness. I did not picture a doglike creature making that eerie sound. I pictured a woman, with long black hair and pale skin, who wandered these hills endlessly, insane from loneliness and filled with an overpowering sense of desolation and despair. A woman whose tongue had been cut out years earlier in some barbaric ritual. Now, unable to form words, she could only moan her deranged agony in rising yelps and falling howls that echoed in the darkness and sent a shiver up my back. I repeated the phone number a dozen times before I went to sleep.

Early the next morning, pickup trucks began arriving, and more horse trailers and dilapidated cars. Along with these were flashy sports cars and practical modern vans and station wagons. By dawn a hundred or more men stood in clusters, smoking cigarettes, drinking coffee from Styrofoam cups, and chewing tobacco. Small yapping dog packs raced through the scrubby weeds. All the men were Indians, although many distinct groups were represented. The conversations were modern. What football team got the Heisman Trophy winner in the draft. Those fools in Washington. Those crazy fools in the

Middle East. Can you add a turbo-booster to a Dodge 318. Some very old men with long white hair stood like fragile dolls and looked bored. Young men clowned with each other and looked a little embarrassed to be here. Some came to please a father, or an uncle, or a wife. This had nothing to do with them. They had good jobs and houses in town and insurance policies. Their ancestors had been fools and victims. They wanted no association with their past. Yet here they were.

The young Indian's lives were populated by two varieties of ghosts. Ancient warriors haunted them in campfire smoke and stories told by old men. Stories of lives the young ones could never lead made them nervous and embarrassed. Those times were gone forever.

Other ghosts visited them in the form of wealthy country singers who twanged on their pickup truck radios. Their tales were of beautiful women and life on the road. The songs they sang were of hard times and jukeboxes, but their voices had the softer edge of Mercedes and swimming pools in Nashville. You could never quite believe them. These were ghosts of the present, as distant as their ancestors.

Many preferred the ghosts on MTV, as shadowy and unreal as any legendary chief. However unlikely, those lives were possible. The flickering crowd of city youth dancing in the videos — that was their tribe. Those were their brothers. Someday they would join them.

But for the next day or so, they would visit the old ghosts. They would parade as warriors have always done and join the festival. They would celebrate the kill or the victory; survivors would gather with their families, proud of their success, grateful for breath, humbled by the dark shadow of death lurking beyond the firelight. With song and food and laughter and old stories they would keep The Cold One beyond their circle a little longer with rites as enduring as the oldest stone altars of those who hunted before names had been invented.

By midmorning the crowd of men started mingling with the crowd of horses. Some of the men still wore flannel shirts and faded jeans. But a lot of them had changed into the traditional garb of their various heritages. Many of the young men simply removed their shirts and wore a headband, their costume dark skin and well-defined muscles. As they mounted their horses, a subtle transformation occurred. Mechanics and grocery store clerks and bankers and social security recipients faded away. The distinctions of jobs and status, possessions and education disappeared. Embarrassment faded. All the narrow words that defined their everyday lives blurred to insignificance as they were replaced by the overwhelming common bond of the moment: They were Apache. They were Navajo. They were Hopi. Ancient enemies bound together by a world that had spun past them. A certain calm arrogance came over them, obvious in their unblinking eyes and set jaws. Call me a Native American when we're in court trying to get money for our school children. Use my tribal title when you're negotiating for my oil rights. But now, with my powerful horse beneath me, surrounded by sky and prairie, I am an Apache. Not merely because of chromosomes and my dark hair and eyes and the shape of my nose, but because I have done things you have not done and will never understand. You are domesticated, fearful of the world beyond your self-made cages, but I have slept beneath the stars without tent or lantern or anything with the word Coleman on it. I have eaten wild meat the day I killed it. As a boy, I danced around a campfire, shouting and singing words that made no sense, and it was only partly a game. I have held my anger within me without a flicker of it showing on my face as you could never do. I have become a tenant on land that my grandfather owned, yet I work it with pride. And I have prayed to the moon without feeling childish, and known in my deepest heart that my prayers were heard.

I wondered if I had such a heritage.

"I have two extra horses. You will ride with us," Chief Heliotrope announced.

"Gee, thanks and all," I said. "But we'd better stay and watch the meat cook."

"The women will do that," he said. "You will ride."

I don't know if this was supposed to be an honor, or the final humiliating climax of our punishment. Either way, I felt outnumbered.

"I've never ridden a horse before," I was quite sure that was true. Heliotrope just nodded. "Sit up there."

Horses are big animals. Standing as tall as I could, I could not see over the top of this brute. It's leg muscles were bigger than my chest. It kept shuffling its tremendous feet and moving its head around like it wanted to eat me. But I got up there, somehow, and straddled it. I had no idea what made it start or stop. I assumed that you turned the beast like you turn a bicycle, by pulling one of the little leather straps attached to its head and leaning, but I wasn't sure. Luckily, the horse didn't care what I did or said. When the other horses started walking down the road, it went with them.

It took a long time for our procession to reach Taos. One of the younger Indians rode up beside Earnest and me.

"Who are you guys?" he asked.

"This is Earnest and I'm... I'm Malcom."

"I'm Franklin. Nice to meet you. You been helping old Heliotrope."

"Well, we had to. We made a deal. We killed one of his cows."

Franklin smiled knowingly and nodded.

"Heliotrope never owned a cow in his life," he said. He shook his head and laughed quietly. "Well, enjoy the parade," he said with a little salute. "See you tonight at the feast." Then he rode forward to talk to one of his friends.

Earnest and I rode on in silence. I felt very foolish. I felt angry. I began to wish that terrible things would happen to Heliotrope.

But not what really did happen. I would hate to think that my angry thoughts had anything to do with it.

The streets were lined with tourists as we rode through the little town. Every shop seemed to sell Indian art and pottery and Kachina dolls. The pale people standing on the sidewalks watched us with a trace of fear and awe in their eyes, and perhaps envy. They all saw what I had seen earlier, a residual wildness in these riders, old and young alike. Thunderstorms and lightning flashed behind cold eyes, disdain twisted mouths downward. The riders' comfortable cocky posture on their horses made the tourists jealous because the raw confidence carried a taunt: once you surrender the wildness in you, when you bow to the rules and customs of committees, you lose something that cannot be recaptured. You discover a cave within yourself.

I rode along, a brightly patterned blanket over my shoulders despite the heat, not part of the parade, really, but also not part of the watching crowd. I was in a separate set of bleachers somewhere, and both the horsemen and the people on the sidewalks were on the playing field before me.

The parade ended in a small green park. Everyone dismounted, horses were tied to trees and fences, and most of the men drifted back toward the central business plaza to get something to eat and drink and to flirt with the pretty girls. Earnest and I stayed with Michelle and Custer in the park.

I lay on my stomach on the cool shady grass. My muscles were sore, my legs rubbed raw, and my hands ached from clutching the reins. That horse needs a new suspension, I thought. Families from New Jersey and Denver and Chicago walked past, taking a closer look at the horses. The adults tried to look casual. The children were obviously excited.

"What's your horse's name?"

I looked up. It was a little girl with huge brown eyes and blonde pigtails in a light blue dress. She was probably seven years old and heartbreakingly sweet.

"Her name's Michelle, but she's not my horse. She belongs to an Indian chief."

"My name's Jenny. I'm going to have a horse someday too. A pretty one, like Michelle."

"What will you name yours?"

She thought very hard for a minute. "I think I'll name her Princess Jasmine."

"That's a pretty name."

She nodded. I could see it in her eyes. It had all been decided. The horse's name, what it would look like, and the little bow she would tie into its mane. I felt a huge urge to pick her up and hold her, but of course I did not. It wouldn't be appropriate, and would probably get me thrown in jail. But it made me feel good that she trusted me enough to talk as if I were an old family friend.

"Jenny, you better come over here by mom and daddy now. Don't talk to people you don't know." Her mother's voice was pleasant but firm.

"Bye," she said.

"Bye."

She skipped away merrily. Custer made a low throaty noise beside me.

"What's the matter, boy?" I said. He had something in his mouth he wanted to give me. I was wary, but looked closer. It was a dollar bill.

I took it. Earnest sat on the grass beside me. "A capitalistic canine!" he said, his voice cracking. He peered at me through his thick glasses and pushed a little mop of hair off his forehead.

"What Pavlovian programming do you suppose Heliotrope has employed on that pup?" The alliteration was his attempt at humor.

"Beats me," I said as the dog scampered away again. A few minutes later he returned with another dollar bill in his teeth. I took it, he ran back into the crowd. I wondered if he had been trained to retrieve windfall money, the bills that are lost and trampled in the normal course of any gathering, or if he had been trained to pick pockets. Whatever his method, he was very good at it. He brought me a steady stream of bills, despite my efforts to explain ethics to him, and I soon had twelve slightly damp dollars in my pocket.

Earnest and I were trying to figure out what to do with Custer and wondering whether we'd be considered accomplices, when we heard a buzzing in the distance, like a chain saw. The sound got louder. A teenaged boy on a small motorcycle raced toward us across the grass. The visor on his black helmet covered his face and made him look like some sort of insect, a creature from another world. He weaved and circled and made the dirt bike jump across grass moguls.

"That looks fun," I said. Then the boy gunned the bike and headed straight for us. We sat up. The bike accelerated with an angry snarl that increased in pitch as it gained speed and got louder and louder as it approached. Time compressed.

The kid was going so fast I didn't think he'd be able to swerve away. The noise became deafening, a terrible bumble-bee sound. The horses were terrified, moving, neighing, trying to pull back from their tethers. Earnest and I scooted backward on the grass. At the last possible instant the rider swooped away, strafing us with grass and dirt divots. Behind us the horses squealed and stamped and pulled to get away from the horror. I heard a snap behind me.

The motorcycle rider never looked back. We watched him disappear into the trees beyond the park. Then we turned to the horses.

Michelle had broken her tether and moved backward. Her eyes were wide, her feet were still moving rapidly up and down. There was something on the ground behind her, a bundle of cloth. It was light blue.

Earnest leaped to his feet and caught Michelle's halter. Avoiding her pounding feet, he soothed her with his voice, using words that neither she nor any human present understood.

A woman's voice called out, first in concern and then in terror. "Jenny, where are you? Jenny!"

I wanted to move. I knew that I must get to my feet and enter the scene, but I could not. I was in the bleachers and this was happening out on the field of play. I was lying on a bed, half asleep, and this was happening on the television. I could not move. My body had become completely hollow and a cold wind whistled within me, an icy devil lashing wildly at the inside of my skin. It slithered up my throat and into my brain, then whipped back down to form a huge aching ball where my stomach once had been. I doubled over with pain, holding my belly to keep it from exploding.

The mother ran to kneel beside the little girl who lay motionless on the ground and cradled her in her arms, shrieking hysterically. Other people, drawn by her cries ran toward us. "Call an ambulance!" a man shouted. "Somebody call an ambulance!"

But it was too late for ambulances and I couldn't move. I wanted to pray for a miracle, but I did not know how. My brain was empty and my body filled with broken glass swirling madly in a deep, cold vacuum. The only prayer I knew was the telephone number I had memorized, and I repeated it over and over.

There was no miracle. I don't know if there ever are miracles. Jenny was dead. A life had somehow escaped through a rip in the universe. The mother kneeled on the ground cradling her daughter's limp body. A crowd of people gathered in a ring around them as if their bodies could seal the awful leak. No one spoke. Sirens began wailing softly in the distance, their whining arpeggios a slow crescendo. Police cars and vans with flashing lights raced impotently to the park. Urgent men in green uniforms pushed their way through the crowd. Crowd control men ran to the scene and shouted orders to the other equally helpless people. Finally, the dead girl and her wailing mother were put in an ambulance. It drove away without flashing lights or siren. The police began asking questions, taking names, writing things on little pads of paper. People talked quietly. Children asked loudly what happened and were shushed by their parents.

My throat felt like a tennis ball had lodged in my vocal cords. I stared at the spot on the grass where Jenny had talked to me, and she seemed as real and alive as anyone in the world. I whistled for Princess Jasmine, and a meadowlark answered. This sort of thing happens all the time, I reasoned. I didn't even know her, not really. But it didn't matter. I could not swallow, or speak, and my eyes kept filling with tears. I pushed the feeling down, trying to stuff it into some suitcase that was already too full, using all my weight to hold it in place while I struggled with the zipper until it was safely contained.

The police had left and the crowd dissipated by the time Heliotrope returned. I explained what had happened as simply as I could. He listened without any sign of emotion. He stared into the distance for a long time. Then, without a word, he mounted Michelle, his proud young lover, his beautiful woman, his wife of fifteen years. Earnest and I struggled onto our own horses with much less grace and followed them home.

Young men with shovels and asbestos gloves opened the pit and took out the rocks and dirt. The rocks were still too hot to touch, twenty-four hours after they were buried. Steaming food was set on several tables. The pit was filled once more with wood, and a bonfire lit. Wives and mothers, daughters and sons had joined the gathering. A keg of beer sat at one end of a table. Music blared from a PA system. Horses milled beyond the barn.

The warm night air was full of the smell of roast beef and wood-smoke and beer. The bonfire leaped and crackled. The music was cheerfully modern and urged the young people to dance. But no one danced. Everyone was quiet, subdued by the terrible accident. People in small groups talked quietly together. Heliotrope stood off to one side. People came up to him, talked for a moment, then drifted away. Every few minutes he disappeared in the direction of the horses.

About ten o'clock a sheriff's car pulled up and a young deputy got out. Several other cars stopped a hundred yards or so down the dirt road. No one seemed surprised. A child had died in an accident involving an animal. The horse would have to be impounded. The girl's parents would need some show of justice, a price paid, a feeling of retribution. If they demanded it, Michelle would probably have to be destroyed.

I slipped away and ran toward the horses to find Heliotrope. When I found him, he had his rifle in one hand and was riding bareback. Franklin stood watching him.

"He's not going to try to fight his way past that officer, is he?" I asked.

Franklin spoke softly. "No."

"What's he going to do?"

He didn't answer for a moment. When he finally spoke, his voice was so quiet I had to strain to hear.

"He'll ride for a long time, probably get somewhere in those hills." He pointed into the darkness. "Some place that's special to him, that he thinks holds magic. He won't let them make his horse a prisoner. He won't let her die among strangers. He'll find a place where her body won't be disturbed..."

"You mean he's going to kill Michelle?"

He nodded, then continued.

"There's a new law. Any death involving an animal, they got to kill the offender. It was meant for pit bulls. One dog wound up killing twice, and folks got crazy. But they didn't word it carefully enough, and now the folks that oppose the law have been making a big stink. Any death at all, they scream, 'letter of the law.' They figure if we kill a few pretty horses, or cats that run into traffic and distract someone, the law will get pulled."

"And Heliotrope?"

"He'll stay with his horse all night, mourning, probably chanting. In the morning he'll cover her with stones so the coyotes don't get her. Then he'll start walking home. It will take him several days to get back." He paused. "By the time he does, he will be much older."

Obviously this was a situation that called for the negotiating skills of an ambassador. I would reason with the sheriff, negotiate a compromise of some sort. I walked quickly toward him.

As if they had planned it, the Indians slowly assembled around the officer and his car. He stood in the center of a circle of emotionless faces. Dozens of dark, unreadable eyes stared calmly at him. There was no malice, no threat. But many of the men stood with legs apart, arms folded across their chests. They would not fight, but neither would they move. Franklin had told me that his two favorite Indians were Chief Joseph and Mahatma Ghandi. I'm not sure why I thought of that now.

The young man from the sheriff's office was equally inscrutable and completely unafraid. His hair and eyes were as dark as theirs, his skin as brown. Despite his neat, close-cropped hair and gray uniform, he did not look out of place. He was tall and lanky, his movements slow and athletic. He looked up at the stars, inhaled the crisp night air and leaned back against his car. Without ever looking at the crowd around him, he pulled a pack of cigarettes from his shirt pocket, shook one deliberately into his hand, and tapped it against the hood. He lit a wooden match by chipping at the tip with his thumb as he raised it, so it looked like fire simply sprang from his fingertips to light the cigarette. He blew white smoke toward the sky. Still without looking at anyone, he said, apparently to the stars, "I need to talk to Heliotrope."

By now I had worked myself to the front row.

"I'm a friend of Heliotrope," I said.

He nodded calmly, took another slow drag, and spoke again to the stars. "Don't believe we've met."

"My name's Malcom," I said, my voice confident and richly diplomatic.

For the first time he looked directly at me. "Are you an attorney?"

The question startled me. It was an intriguing possibility and would explain a lot. I did seem to possess the logical mind, the negotiating skills, and the common sense of an attorney. Plus, I seemed inclined to help people, whether I stood to gain anything or not. But right now it didn't matter. I ignored the question and tried to sound friendly.

"I'd like to help Heliotrope. This whole thing is a big misunderstanding."

The young deputy stared at me.

"A misunderstanding," he repeated softly. He flicked ashes to the dirt. His voice was very gentle. "A child is dead. Maybe you'd like to explain this misunderstanding to her parents."

Behind him, beyond the crowd, a shadowy figure on horseback glided silently through the evening. An old man with a potbelly on a gray Appaloosa. In the deceptive moonlight, it could have been a young brave on his war horse. As long as the officer was looking at me, he would never see them. Not an eye glanced in that direction. No horse whinnied, no twig snapped, no dog barked. I forced my eyes to stay on the young deputy and realized I was holding my breath.

"What did you want to say?" he asked me. The ghostly horse and rider disappeared beyond my peripheral vision. I searched the black sky for words, kicked up a tiny puff of dirt with the tip of my shoe, and exhaled slowly.

But there was nothing to say.

He turned away to speak to one of the old men and I worked my way back through the crowd, my face hot, my eyes welling with salty tears. Beyond the crowd, Franklin stood alone as if waiting for me. Neither of us said anything for a long time.

"It was a good thing you did out there," he said softly, his voice husky. "Distracting the sheriff. Took guts, risking an obstruction rap. Honorable. Because there was nothing in it for you. Not many white guys are honorable like that."

Then he remembered something. "Here, he said to give these to you."

He handed me the keys to the Cadillac.

The next morning I drove the Cadillac to the outskirts of town so Earnest wouldn't have to contend with
city traffic, although it didn't seem to bother him. He was
a natural driver, as long as no cows were in his way. As
we turned onto the highway that led south to Oklahoma, I
glanced in the rearview mirror and nearly put the car into
the ditch myself. A block behind us a white van had missed
the green light and was stopped.

"Are you all right?" Earnest said as beads of sweat
grew from my forehead.

"Sure," I lied. "Just a little stomach problem I get
from time to time." My stomach was, in fact, as tight as a
golf ball. I punched the accelerator and the huge engine
responded like a thoroughbred. "Listen, do you think you
can get this thing home alone?"

We accelerated like a peach-colored jet until we
were flying down the road at eighty-five miles an hour.
"Just burning off a little carbon," I said as he glanced
nervously at the speedometer. "What do you think? Are
you ready to solo?"

"I believe I am cognizant of all applicable proce-
dures and regulations," he said. "On a purely theoretical
level, I'm aware of no significant impediment to bringing such a task to a successful conclusion. Yet I cannot
help but feel a certain vicarious unease at your own
malady."

I forced myself to laugh. "Don't worry about me," I said, trying to sound completely casual. "I'll just hang around here for a day or two until my medicine arrives."

"At least let's go back downtown…"

"No!" I said, and my voice sounded sharper than I wanted. I smiled again, glancing in the mirror. No van. "Sorry, just a little pain. What I meant was, the walk will do me good." My blisters snickered at the comment. "Besides, some business has come up I can probably handle better from here. If I get wrapped up in it, I might not be able to get back to Oklahoma for a while. Tell everyone not to worry."

"Indeed I shall. And might I, in turn, make a small request?"

"Of course."

"The events of the last few days, while amusing anecdotally, might cause some domestic repercussions that seem entirely unnecessary…"

"I understand. There's no reason anyone has to know about the cow. Forgetting things is what I seem to do best. It never happened."

"Thanks."

An abandoned gas station appeared ahead of us. Perfect.

"One last thing," I said. "I don't like long goodbyes. I'm going to pull off the road up there and I want you to slide over here and take off immediately. Do you understand?"

"Probably not completely."

I nodded. "Get used to the feeling. That's life. You give everyone a big hug for me, you hear?" He agreed. I screeched to a stop in front of the gas station and jumped out.

"Hurry, hurry!" I said as he slid over to the driver's side with a bewildered look on his face. The white van had not yet come into view. He fastened his seat belt and extended a hand through the window. I shook it quickly.

"Listen, Earnest, when you start looking for a career, you might consider writing high school text books. You'd be a natural. Now get out of here."

"Thanks," he said, then pulled away. I ran behind the ruins of the filling station and waited. In a few minutes, the van drove past, in no particular hurry, like a stalking predator that knows its prey can't outrun it. My heart beat fast until the van was gone. Then I walked back to the highway and stood beneath the huge red star of the abandoned Texaco station, once the last outpost of fuel, coffee, and civilization before the complete desolation of uninhabited New Mexico. Now it was beyond the last outpost. It was part of the desolation.

I tried to focus on my amnesia, but it eluded me like a faint star. The harder I tried to look at it, the less distinct it seemed. I would have to look a different direction, but that idea appealed to me anyway. I had twelve bucks in my pocket, thanks to Custer. The New Mexican summer morning was cool but the sun was bright, and suddenly I was optimistic. I only needed a plan.

I was trying to devise such a plan when a pink speck appeared on the highway far away, approached, and revealed itself to be a long pink limousine. It slowed and stopped beside me. The windows were dark and I couldn't tell if there was anybody in it or not. It could have been a ghost limousine as far as I could tell, a phantom, the New Mexican version of the Flying Dutchman. A back window lowered itself a couple inches, but I still couldn't see in. Bits of a hurried, urgent conversation escaped but I could only catch quick whispered phrases and pieces of words.

"He's the right height...dead ringer...doesn't look too bright...impossible to connect us..."

Three men got out of the limo and walked over to me. They were in their twenties, very thin, with shoulder length hair. They wore jeans and expensive-looking sports coats with the sleeves pushed up to their elbows and T-shirts underneath. They looked me over closely and nodded approvingly. The tallest one spoke.

"My name is Jim Gold," he said, shaking my hand. "But everyone calls me Goldie. This is Frank, this is Morton." I shook their hands.

"Call me Mort."

"OK." They didn't ask my name.

"This is your lucky day," Goldie said.

I already felt that. Although I couldn't get little Jenny out of my mind, I had made progress in my quest. Earnest had retired from the cow-slaughtering business and had not killed us in the process. The sun was bright and...

"You wanna make a thousand bucks?"

Somehow I suspected there was more to the question, really, than whether or not I wanted to make a thousand bucks. I wondered, briefly, how many people would answer that question negatively. Still, my instincts said that these guys knew something about the Land of Debris. That made me nervous, but it also intrigued me.

"Sure."

"Let us buy you breakfast and we'll talk."

I got into the backseat of the limo and they took me to a McDonald's restaurant in town. Over a sausage McMuffin with egg, hash browns, and coffee, they explained their proposition.

"We're in charge of security for Billy Billy."

"No, wait, Goldie," interrupted Mort. "He's changed it, remember? Now it's Billy Billy Billy. Says no one will forget it. Right?"

"Oh yeah, that's right. Anyway, you've heard of Billy Billy Billy."

"Does it matter?" I listened to my memory, but there was no Billy...etc. There was only the sound of water dripping from stalactites.

"Of course you've heard of him. Everyone has. Biggest rock sensation since Elvis Presley. Well, we're in charge of security for his big concert in Mexico City. And we have a plan. We're going to hire you as a ringer."

"Elvis Presley?"

"We don't have time for jokes. We need a ringer. You know, an impostor. A look-alike. A decoy. Someone for the crowds to follow so we can slip him out a backdoor and onto his plane.

"The concert's in five days. A thousand bucks for five days work, plus a vacation in Mexico and a backstage pass to the biggest concert of the century. What do you say?"

I munched on my sausage McMuffin with egg. I thought about the twelve bucks in my pocket. My schedule seemed pretty open for the next five days. I compared their offer with Heliotrope's deal. I wondered why they wanted me, rather than someone else. I tried to think of any possible reason not to do this easy thing. Of course it would delay my quest for my identity. On the other hand, perhaps the universe was trying to direct me. Maybe I should just shut up and see what happened. I must have been quiet for too long.

"OK, two thousand bucks, but that's as high as we can go."

I was stunned. What was going on here? I needed time to understand this. I tried to stall.

"I need to make a phone call."

They looked at each other in shocked silence. Then Goldie nodded. The others shrugged in agreement.

"OK, you win. Five thousand. But that's the whole budget. And no, you can't call your agent first. No agents.

He said we could split the difference if we could get somebody cheaper. But we need an answer right now. We have to leave in an hour. Twenty-five hundred up front. The rest when your plane lands in Portland, Oregon, five days from now. You're too damn tough. But you look just like him. Deal?"

He pulled a roll of hundred dollar bills out of his pocket, counted out twenty-five of them, and waited for my answer.

I swallowed my last bit of coffee. Sometime decisions matter, and sometimes they don't. And sometimes you have decisions to make but no real choice.

"Call me Billy Billy Billy," I said, and put the bills in my pocket. Half an hour ago I was broke, without memories or transportation or a place to sleep. Now I was rich, with a good job, and more names than anyone was entitled to. And I was on my way to Mexico City. Maybe I had found the Land of Debris.

It occurred to me that some places might not accept hundred dollar bills. I also knew that I might need a lot of quarters for telephone calls. "Just a second," I said and went up to the counter. I gave the girl a hundred dollar bill and asked if she could change it. She was a tiny Oriental girl with shoulder-length black hair. Her name tag said 'Sue.' She said she'd have to ask the manager. Before she turned away, she smiled at me and it was as if someone turned on a bright light. The sun broke suddenly and explosively through dark clouds. A sparkler hissed and caught fire, showering the area with a million brilliant little flares.

As she went to find the manager, Goldie whispered, "Want to take her out?" I nodded. "Ask her to come with us," he whispered.

In a moment she returned. It was OK. She made change. "Come to Mexico with me." I said. She looked

80

startled, then smiled again. That smile. I felt like I was standing outside a pitch-black house when someone threw open the door, blinding me with the light that flooded out.

My face was hot, as if I'd never asked a girl out before. Altogether possible, I realized.

"I have to work," she said. The sense of rejection was very familiar. She looked over at the manager. Goldie was standing next to him. The manager was putting money into his pocket. He smiled and motioned for her to go.

"No strings?" she said.

"No strings. Just for company."

She shrugged "What's your name?"

"You can call me Bill."

I don't know why she wasn't nervous about me. I might have been a ruthless, deranged killer who would leave her body beside an abandoned road somewhere, mutilated beyond identification. Maybe I don't have that kind of face. Anyway, that's how it happened that Goldie, Frank, Mort, Sue, and I were thrust together by the huge tectonic forces in charge of such things. A dazed maybe-Malcom-pseudo Billy Billy Billy, a Japanese girl with a plutonium smile in a McDonald's uniform, and three flashy hipsters in a pink limo the size of Detroit cruising together down one fine glowing path in the space-time continuum that leads from Taos. We drove south to Santa Fe and boarded a jet-black Learjet bound for Mexico. Billy Billy Billy always flies in a jet black Learjet, they explained. It's one of his many trademarks.

The prospect of sudden wealth excited me. It opened worlds of possibilities. More than that, I was excited at the idea of doing something useful, not merely drifting from scene to scene, deuteragonist in my own life, an actor on stage with no part to play.

An actor! Of course, why hadn't it occurred to me before? What had I been doing since Oklahoma except acting? First one part, then the next, each one utterly real while I performed it. Who but a professional actor could slide from role to role so effortlessly, so instinctively?

And now I had been given a big, important part to play, by people who were willing to pay well for my experience. My new friends had recognized me immediately. My talent must radiate outward like an airport spotlight, inescapably obvious to anyone who looked. There really was no other explanation.

"This is how it will work," Goldie said, a few thousand feet above the mountains of New Mexico, which looked like a badly rumpled bed below us. "You've got four days to become Billy Billy Billy. We'll work all day and most of the nights. You must perfect his mannerisms, the way he walks, all that stuff."

"I thought you were just going to whisk me into a waiting limo."

"Well, of course that's the way we hope it works. But you're getting paid a lot of money. If anybody sees you up close, or you have to talk to anyone, we want them to believe you."

"What about me?" Sue asked.

"You can be his current girl friend. No one will think it's odd for Billy Billy Billy to have a pretty girl on his arm. They'd probably think it odd if he didn't. We'll get you some hot clothes in Mexico."

We did not land in Mexico City, which surprised me. Instead, we landed somewhere in the desert and took a van to the nearest town. The old adobe hotel was pleasant but not extravagant, a relic from some time when the town had been a popular resort. It had a pool and a bar and restaurant, but paint was peeling from the interior walls and the tile floor of the lobby showed dust. We occupied several of its best suites on the top floor.

Immediately they began training me.

"The Man has a little limp," Goldie said. "All his fans recognize it. He sort of drags his left foot like this."

"Like this?"

"No, that's too much. Here, we have videotapes."

I practiced limping, I practiced a facial tic, I practiced a nervous cough. This Billy Billy Billy was a walking compendium of neurotic symptoms. They gave me very expensive clothes: long flowing pink shirts with embroidered designs in black and red, and tight white pants, and wrap-around sunglasses, and a snakeskin headband.

"But no one will see me in this hotel room," I protested. Goldie shook his head.

"Don't matter. He wears this stuff all the time. You got to put on the outfit and get comfortable with it, the way he's comfortable. You got to believe you're him. If you believe, then everyone will believe."

I put on the clothes and practiced being this very famous man, this rich and successful singer. I tried to imagine what he must feel like, this man I'd never heard of with the absurd name. I wore his clothes and his style and his facial tic and his limp and his nervous cough for three days. I watched endless video tape. I went to sleep surrounded by his music and woke to eat his favorite breakfast and drank diet cola, because that's what he drank. Mort complimented me on my ability to forget my own identity and assume this new one. I thanked him politely.

Of course, I tried the phone number, but got only strange clicking sounds on the other end. Sadly, I hung up.

On the fourth day, Goldie wanted me to practice in front of people. I limped down to the pool, dressed in my tight white pants, my embroidered pink shirt, my sunglasses, my snakeskin headband. Sue had been swimming and sunning for three days and looked perfectly relaxed. She climbed out of the pool.

"My God, Bill," she said in awe. "You've done it. You're him."

"Thanks," I said, coughing nervously. I took a sip of diet cola while people near the pool whispered to each other and pointed. A couple of giggling teenaged girls wanted my autograph. I'd practiced it, and they were ecstatic. I wrote them each a personal note. I was as excited as if this was the very first time I'd ever been asked for an autograph. I caught myself. Of course, it probably was the very first time.

I spent the morning in town, looking in little shops, drinking diet colas in dusty cafes, watching a playground full of children playing soccer. Everywhere I went people thought I was the famous singer. There was admiration and awe in their eyes, and something more. There was love. People wanted to be close to me. They wanted to touch me. They tried to give me things. Shopkeepers wanted to give me hats and coffee mugs. Children made drawings on Big Chief paper and waitresses slipped me their telephone numbers.

"This is not bad," I thought. Sue played right along, dressed in rock-video clothes, flashing a few megatons of smile every now and then, letting tourists take her picture. It was better than working at McDonalds in Taos. At least for four days.

Late that afternoon I was trying to make the television work in my hotel suite when someone knocked on the door.

"Yes?" I said, opening it.

"My name is Abdulla. May I speak with you?"

The man was small and swarthy, with short black hair and the intensity of a tiny rodent. His black suit fit perfectly, his shoes gleamed, and he wore several large diamond rings. His dark eyes moved quickly from side to side as if scouting for danger. He bowed stiffly from the waist.

"I guess so," I said and opened the door wider.

"Come on girls," he said, and two young women that had apparently been standing to one side of him beyond my vision followed him into the room.

"This is Donna," he said, introducing me to a tall buxom black girl in a very short skirt. "And this is Crystal." Crystal was as tall as Donna, equally bosomy, and dressed just as provocatively. But her skin was white as paper, her hair the lightest shade of blonde, and her eyes pale watery blue. The two girls wore dreamy, confident smiles as they shook my hand and looked at me as if they knew something about me that I didn't know. It was entirely possible, I thought. He motioned for them to sit on the couch. They did so gracefully, crossed their legs in unison, and waited for further instructions.

"Your manager is a crook," Abdulla said, sitting in a chair, motioning for me to do the same.

"Goldie?"

"Yes. He takes advantage of you. Look at this dump!" He waved his hand.

"This isn't so bad," I said. I had been watching television and was amazed to recognize shows and actors. I even remembered many of the stories. It almost felt like being home. At least a part of home.

"The greatest singer the world has ever known is staying in a fourth rate hotel in a fourth-rate city in a fourth rate country. You could buy this town. I bet your TV doesn't even work."

"I think it's just the fine tuning…"

He gestured impatiently.

"You have power," he said. "Real power. People

believe in you. They will do what you say. You could own the world. Yet you sit here adjusting a television set."

"They were going to have a Gilligan's Island festival on Channel 4..."

He stopped me with another gesture.

"Do you like these girls?"

"Well, sure. They seem like nice people." They smiled at me.

"I mean do you want them. Right here, right now? A little gift from me to you. For all the pleasure your music gives the world, aren't you entitled to a little yourself?"

"Gosh, I don't know..."

"You can own these girls. And any others you want. I can give them to you. Does your manager do that for you?"

"Well, he encouraged me to ask Sue out..."

He snapped his fingers and the two women surrounded me. Their closeness was distracting.

"How about drugs?"

"What?"

"Does he get drugs for you? And I don't mean a little nose candy now and then. I mean hard-ball, mainline, train-wreck stuff. Exotic stuff. Wild stuff. Whatever mood you want to feel, whatever planet you want to visit. I'll do that for you."

"Isn't that kind of dangerous? I mean, don't people die from drugs?"

He laughed. "You're Billy Billy Billy. You're never going to die. Come here." I followed him to the window, a girl on each elbow. "Look at this city, at the people, the cars, the buildings," he said. "And beyond that at the land, the oceans, the other cities, all of them full of people waiting to do whatever you ask them. Because of who you are. Because they love you. You can have everything you can imagine. And all you have to do is drop your old manager and hire me."

Abdulla's voice was smooth and soothing and persuasive. And there was some truth in what he said. I'd seen it earlier in the day. Girls who would not have eaten a taco with me a week ago now wanted to bear my children. Restaurant owners who would not have hired me to wash dishes now wanted to feed me their lobsters and steaks for free. All because they believed I was Billy Billy Billy. It occurred to me that I could get a lot more out of this act than five thousand dollars. I was curious.

"What about spending money?"

"You sign with me today, I'll give you as much spending money as your pockets can hold. How about fifty thou?" He reached into the pocket of his suit coat. That's when I felt a little chill. This kind of power was scary. It didn't really matter who I was. People believed they knew me, and because of their belief, I could have fifty thousand dollars in my hand for the asking. I could have the glamorous salt and pepper sisters for nodding my head. I could ride in limousines and Learjets and eat elegant meals and get stoned out of my aurora borealis. Anything I wanted...

You don't get that kind of life without paying some kind of price. And scary power probably costs a scary price. I shook my head.

"No offense, man," I said. "But Goldie got me this far. I'm gonna pass."

Abdulla started to protest, but I held up my hand. "Later, man," I said. Eyes flashing angrily, he turned and stormed out of the room, Donna and Crystal flowing behind him. I felt like I had just escaped something.

The next day, before dawn, we flew to Mexico City. By the time I looked out the window, the plane was

The Land of Debris

already inside a hangar. Sue was no longer with us. She'd met a guy and decided to stay. While still on the plane, I changed clothes and was out of costume for the first time in several days, wearing jeans and sneakers and a T-shirt. Goldie didn't want two Billy Billy Billy's to be seen. I would earn my pay that night at the concert. A van took me to a much nicer hotel than the last one and Goldie told me to relax for a few hours incognito. Suddenly alone and invisible, I decided to take a walk.

Mexico City is huge. Parts of it glisten and gleam like new silverware. But as I walked farther, the city deteriorated. Ragged urchins begged for pennies. Unhealthy women made sad propositions. Twenty minutes with them for the price of a lunch. Five minutes for the price of a cup of coffee. Old men leaned in doorways, tired and without even hope enough left in them for begging. Groups of young, tough looking boys watched like wolves as I walked past.

I came to a vast park that was covered with makeshift dwellings, dilapidated tents and cardboard houses and car hoods propped into lean-to's. Small, smoky fires dotted the area and a wood-smoke haze blanketed everything. Hundreds of people were living in that park, thousands perhaps, and there was fear and weariness in every pair of eyes. Gaunt men and women huddled with scarecrow children. The smell was terrible. I couldn't understand the language, but I understood, on some level. These people were refugees. There had been a flood somewhere, or perhaps an earthquake or a war. The lives they had known were gone, their histories, their homes. They had come to find new lives, new jobs and homes, but the city could not absorb them. There wasn't even enough food to eat, and no government program large enough to accommodate them. The scene was vaguely familiar to me. Some low sonorous bell rang softly in the distant echoing chamber of my mind. I wondered, could this be it? The Land of Debris? I didn't know. But I wanted to help. There ought to be something I could do. I had about fifty bucks in my pocket. It was nothing. The twenty-five hundred back at the hotel was almost equally insignificant compared to these masses of starving people.

But the real Billy Billy Billy, he had millions. If I could talk to him, I bet he'd help. Why not? I started walking back toward the hotel, feeling excited for the first time in my new life. I had something to do and a reason to be alive.

I passed a fast food restaurant, a fish-sandwich place named Fishy Wishy. There was a commotion in the alley beside it. A group of refugee children came racing out of the alley with an angry man in hot pursuit. The man was dressed in the Fishy Wishy uniform. He was an American. He stopped at the sidewalk, cursing at the disappearing children, shaking his fist.

"Damn kids!" he muttered. It was nice to hear an American voice.

"What's the problem?" I asked.

"It's those tent-city kids," he said, still watching them run. "They get in the dumpster and steal the damn garbage. They always make a helluva mess while they're at it. I try to cut them some slack, most of the time, but not goddamn today. The big boss, I mean the number one main guy of the whole damn company's going to be here in an hour. Supposed to be a surprise visit, you know, he's always doing stuff like that. I got a friend at headquarters tipped me off. You know what it means, he finds a bunch of trash behind the store? It means my goddamn job, that's what. Damn kids! Why today?"

He was shaking his head. I had an idea.

"How many sandwiches can you guys make in a day?" I asked.

"I don't know. A few thousand. This ain't the hottest corner in the universe for selling fish sandwiches. Damn kids!" He went back into the store, muttering the whole time. I heard him yell at an employee to go out back and clean up the mess. I trotted back to the hotel, eager to implement my plan. I had no idea where it had come from but it was brilliant. I did not need my memories, or experience, or money, or political office. I did not need a lot of time, or well-connected friends, or the organization of a church. I needed no permits, no licenses, no paperwork. I didn't need the Mexican government, or any other government. I didn't need consultants, or committees, or shareholders, or tax-exempt status. I didn't even need Billy Billy Billy. I just needed the outfit.

The chauffeur was surprised when his boss got into the limo, but he didn't ask questions. I gave him the address and he drove to Fishy Wishy's. If I could fool the chauffeur, I could fool anyone. We pulled up to the curb behind another limo and I got out. Eyes widened as I limped and twitched and coughed into the restaurant.

It was easy to see who the owner was, the Big Boss, the man who started one fish sandwich store twenty-five years ago and built it into an empire bigger than Paraguay. He was the heavy, balding man in the short-sleeved shirt surrounded by all the nervous workers. The man checking the grease traps, getting down on his hands and knees to see if the crew had cleaned the floor under the grills. Employees whispered, or held their breath, as they watched him. They followed him like disciples and wrote down his words. Their jobs might depend on how well they had cleaned the grill or the floor drain. And with their jobs, their homes and families and dreams.

I walked into the room and stood motionless, saying nothing. No one in the store had ever been in the presence of a man of Mr. Fishy Wishy's stature, a world-famous businessman, the boss of their boss's boss, a man who held their lives in his shirt pocket. But gradually the attention shifted from that very important and rich man to the god who had just limped in. One by one, people's eyes turned from the owner of the company to stare in amazement at the most famous man in the world. The crowd moved away from Mr. Fishy Wishy a little, but he was busy with his inspection and didn't notice. Suddenly he realized how quiet the room had become and looked around. His eyes also widened in shocked recognition. I sat at one of the small plastic tables without a word and motioned to the chair across from me. The crowd moved back, as if we were two gunslingers at noon. He cocked his head, judging me, sizing me up, wondering if he could out-draw me in a contest that mattered. He was experienced enough that he gave no clue what he decided. He did not seem particularly impressed.

But then, I was Billy Billy Billy. I feared no one. As long as I wore the outfit, I was invincible. I gestured again toward the chair across from me.

He walked over and sat down. I got right to the point.

"Here's the deal," I said. "You're going to feed the refugees in that tent city. For free."

"Why would I do that? There must be two thousand of them! I'm a businessman, not a..." I held up my hand and he stopped. The crowd gasped that someone dared interrupt their boss. I was not nervous or confused or shy. This seemed obvious to me. And, smart and rich and experienced as he was, Mr. Fishy Wishy did not want to irritate Wyatt Earp without good reason. He bit his tongue and listened.

"And you're going to keep feeding them until they get their lives straightened out."

He held in his anger. He didn't understand. I could sense his trigger finger twitching nervously.

"And I'm going to eat lunch right here."

He stared at me for a long time, searching my face for the nature of my insanity. Was this a trick-shot, or a bluff? Had I pulled a silver bullet from my belt and scratched his name on it, or had I been munching loco weed in the desert?

Then a light came on within him. He did some quick, practiced mental calculations. I could almost hear the machinery within him clicking and whirling. Then he smiled. "Deal," he said, reaching across the table to shake my hand. "Give me a half hour?"

"Deal," I said. He got up quickly, barking out commands and his employees sprang to animated life like puppets in a hurricane. I sat at the table twitching and coughing while he made half a dozen phone calls. Within minutes, trucks were pulling up in front of the restaurant and disgorging television crews. When exactly thirty minutes had passed, I rose from the table, limped to the counter and ordered a sandwich, some fries, and a diet cola. Six or seven television cameras filmed the event, three from major U.S. networks. The most famous man in the world was eating a fish sandwich at Fishy-Wishy's, perhaps as a show of solidarity with the owner who had just promised to feed an entire tent city full of starving refugees. I took my meal to the table and ate it with obvious enjoyment, twitching and coughing while film crews preserved the moment for future generations. No one had ever seen Billy Billy Billy eat. He had never endorsed a product. Nor had he expressed a political opinion or helped another human. Until now, he had been pure. This was news.

The owner could hardly maintain a properly serious face as they interviewed him. He kept catching himself grinning. He had just completed a major coup. An endorsement from a celebrity of this stature had to be worth ten, maybe fifteen million dollars. The airtime to play commercials during the six o'clock news would cost more than buying the state of North Dakota. Yet the network news would show this event all over the United States and the rest of the world for free. And all it was costing him was a few thousand of these goddamn fish sandwiches. He was a genius.

After lunch, I had the chauffeur drive past the tent city. Sure enough, bright Fishy Wishy step-vans were unloading meal after meal. Television crews beamed the scene to all parts of the globe. Humanity at its best, people helping people, the warm and fuzzy side of capitalism. Starving people are not news. Charity is news. Billy Billy Billy eating Fishy Wishy's is news, and news is good business. Free publicity goes right through the advertising budget undigested to perch serene and Buddha-like on the sacred Bottom Line. I hoped I had made the right choice. I hoped I had not screwed things up somehow for the real Billy Billy Billy. I hoped he would not be irritated, perhaps refuse to fly me out of the country. Stranded in Mexico City, I could be in a bit of a pickle myself.

I shook my head. This was a choice that mattered. And, when all the information became available, no other decision had been possible. I told the driver to go back to the hotel.

Halfway back, we got stuck in a traffic jam. My driver got out to see what the problem was. He came back a few minutes later, disgusted.

"A man's trying to jump off the bridge ahead. Nobody wants to drive past him because they're afraid they'll miss seeing it. He leaned back in the seat, pushed his hat down over his eyes as if to take a nap. "Shouldn't be much longer. He looks about ready."

I got out of the limo and walked through the lines of parked and honking cars. The man was frightened and drunk, sitting balanced on the railing of a steel span bridge, a half-empty bottle of tequila in one hand and an ugly river far below. The man did not need to speak. His cheeks were wet with tears, his eyes vacant and hopeless. This was no joke, no prank. He was oblivious to the cars, to the people, because in his mind he was already dead. The actual leaning forward, releasing his hold, the slipping through the air was not important. Anticlimactic. It would happen this instant or two minutes from now, it didn't matter. He was already dead.

He looked absently in my direction as I approached. Despite his daze, he did a mild double-take. The famous American singer Señor Billy Billy Billy was walking toward him. He cocked his head to one side and stared at me in confusion and amazement.

"Do you speak English?" I asked.

"Si," he said. "Some leettle engleesh."

"Good." I said, and tried to think of something else to say. We stood there looking at each other. I could not solve this man's problems. I probably couldn't pronounce his name. Shoot, I didn't even remember my own name. Yet I had put myself here, a few words in the last paragraph of a man's life, as if I had something to offer him. And I wanted to help him. To give him some comfort, something. To make him feel less alone.

But I could thing of nothing to say.

"Can I have a drink?" I asked. He handed me the bottle, I put it to my lips and drank. It burned my mouth and throat. My lungs were on fire. I gasped. Despite himself, the man smiled at my grotesque expression. That seemed like progress. Still having nothing to say, I took another drink. I began to cough and handed the bottle back to him. "Thank you," I said.

"De nada," he said. "You're welcome."

The cars lined up behind me had stopped honking. I shook my head while everyone waited. My mind was blank. Something had happened to this man, maybe a lot of things, that made his own life appear worthless, perhaps even part of the problem. And he saw no future in which it would change. The man was completely out of hope, that was the immediate problem. But I knew he was wrong. Maybe that was me up on that bridge, before I lost my memories. Maybe that was still me up there, if I ever got them back. Now I knew that it's possible to start completely over, that there's always hope, but I didn't know what to say.

"Things might get better," I said at last. "They might. It's worth a shot. Things might get better."

He stared at me for a long time. I was not sure he understood. Then he nodded and climbed back off the railing to stand beside me. He shook my hand and together we walked off the bridge. If a man like Billy Billy Billy said that things might get better, then certainly they might.

I climbed back into the limo and woke my driver. "Let's go home," I said. This power thing fascinated and frightened me. I wondered what that man would have done if I hadn't been wearing the guise of an important person. I wondered if I'd still have that power. Or if he would have jumped.

Somehow the driver managed to pick his way through the traffic, but we got stuck one more time, in front of a soccer stadium. People had followed us, there was a crushing crowd on every side of the vehicle and no way to move. Everyone wanted to see the famous star, to touch his car, to posses some bit of him. I felt like they would pickup the limo and smash it with their loving hands. I could feel it rock from side to side. I started to understand why it was worth five thousand dollars to be a decoy.

"I knew this was a mistake," the driver said. Suddenly a policeman was beside the car. The driver cracked his window.

"We will help," the policeman said with a big grin. "Follow us theez way please." Somehow the authority of the man's uniform had an influence on the crowd. Or perhaps it was the casual way he swung a .38 special over his head. The people moved back a foot or two and the policeman led us through a gate. We drove into the stadium and out onto the middle of the field. It had been transformed for a day into a baseball stadium and a game was in progress. The stands were packed with fans. The game stopped.

"Senor Billee, Billee, Billee," he said through the window. "This is my plan. I half called more officers who shall be soon here. We will open a pathway for this car off yours so you can leaf. Eef you would please be so kind as to say some words to your many fans, then my friends will half time to arriffe."

There was a big grin on his face. He had thought of this all by himself. If I would just make a little speech to forty or fifty thousand people in the middle of the sixth inning, everything would be fine. I was trapped. He handed me a wireless microphone and I stepped out of the limo.

Immediately the crowd began to roar in gleeful recognition. I limped over to the pitcher's mound and waved. The sound of all those people was like jet engines with all their noise focused precisely on me, and I shivered. Abdulla had been right. This was like holding the trigger to a hydrogen bomb in my fingers. I was nervous that whatever I said to these people who loved me, or loved who they thought I was, might matter. Be brief, I thought. Hello, nice to be here, and then get the hell out.

"Mexico is not my home," I began. The speakers shrieked with feedback, and the announcer translated over the PA system. "But you have made it feel like my home." The announcer translated, the crowd roared, I felt the surge of excitement and power. Don't screw up, I thought.

Then my mind went completely blank. Not a word leaped from my vocabulary. Fifty thousand adoring fans were perfectly silent waiting for my next bit of wisdom, a leaf or twig from the tree they loved that they could memorize and carry home with them. But my mind was eastern Kansas under a foot of snow: pure and white and featureless. The powerful feeling quickly deteriorated to panic. I had to say something, but I really didn't have anything to say. The crowd became restless. I coughed. I twitched. The announcer cleared his throat over the PA system. Just say anything, I thought. Perhaps it will gain significance in translation.

"I won't be in town long," I said, "So I'm glad I got to catch a baseball game."

The announcer translated, the crowd roared. I wanted to say something about the tent city. How easy it had been to help, how good it made me feel. I wanted to mention the man on the bridge, whose life had become better simply because someone bothered to tell him that it might. I'd seen poor people and rich people. Shoot, within the last week I'd been both desperately poor and infinitely rich. And I'd trade both lifetimes and all Billy Billy Billy's money and fame for a few pieces of old comfortable furniture for the empty cavern of my brain. There was no way to say any of that. Better stick to baseball.

"I've learned things from you," I said. "I've learned that you shouldn't feel bad if you've got bad seats. At least you're at the game. And you shouldn't feel too proud if you have good seats. You'll get just as wet if it rains." I wasn't even thinking by now, just saying random thoughts, hoping that any confusion would be attributed to the translation. "It's easy to cheer for your own team, but the opposing players are all somebody's fathers and brothers and sons too. And the best thing is doing something for somebody else when there's nothing in it for you. Thank you. See you tonight at the concert."

The crowd roared and screamed in ecstasy, as if I had shared with them a vision of Heaven. Helluva translator, I thought as I got into the limo and we sped away.

Back at the hotel, I told the driver not to talk about our little adventures. He shrugged.

"You're The Man," he said. I did not feel like The Man.

Walking into the hotel, a feeling of melancholy and exhaustion swept over me. The idea of sitting in my empty room for a couple hours depressed me, so I wandered over to the hotel bar, a dark little hideaway of brass railings, thick carpet, and muted music. Bright green ferns contrasted against the dark wood. I was already tired of being the famous singer and ready to be just another human. That might not be easy in Billy's costume.

The bar was nearly empty, which suited me fine. If I was going to feel lonely no matter what I did, I'd rather not have a bunch of people around. I walked up to the bar.

"Diet cola?" the bartender asked. He was very cool in the presence of an apparent celebrity.

"Nah," I said. "Give me a Margarita." He looked surprised but made the drink. I surveyed the room. A woman was sitting alone at a table in a dark corner, candlelight glowing on her face. She was a pretty woman, maybe mid-thirties, with frizzy brown hair and a prominent nose. I could picture her with a guitar. Perhaps she was a famous folk singer. Or maybe she simply resembled a famous person the way I resembled Billy Billy Billy. Or perhaps by outrageous coincidence I had stumbled onto someone I actually knew, a friend, a soul mate, a former bowling partner. She might be a link to my past. Part of me wanted to walk over and see if she recognized me. On the other hand, I was tired and wanted to be alone.

I could be alone anytime. I carried my drink to her table.

"Aren't you..." I began. She looked up as if startled and opened her eyes very wide. In the dim light I couldn't tell if they were green or blue.

"No, I'm not," she said, with the finality of a door slamming shut. It didn't matter who I thought she was. She was not going to be that person. She looked back at her drink, as if by looking away from me I would cease to exist. And, remarkably, it almost worked. Standing in the artificial twilight of an empty bar being ignored by the only other human within reach, wearing outrageous clothes, I felt like a fishing bobber whose line has broken.

So I sat down.

"Don't you know who I am?" I asked. She raised an eyebrow in irritation and pointedly looked at my snakeskin headband, my sunglasses which had automatically lightened in the dim light, and my flowing pink shirt.

"No," she said simply. "Do you?"

She had me there. This woman could be cruel.

"Have you ever heard of Billy Billy Billy?"

"Are their last names Gruff?"

"No, the rock star. They always play his videos on TV."

"I don't watch TV." She took a long pull on a brown cigarette and blew the smoke straight up toward the ceiling. Looking bored and impatient she pushed her hair back from her forehead. Obviously, this was a common and annoying routine for her: a man tries to join her for no good reason, she has to get rid of him efficiently but politely. "Look, I'm sure you're a nice man and all,

but I really just want to be alone. Don't you have groupies or something to handle this sort of thing?"

"Well, sure. I mean, there's groupies, of course. I
wasn't trying to...I thought you were a folk singer. You
looked familiar. That's all."

She sighed.

"Everyone thinks they know me. Nobody does.
No. I'm not who you think I am."

Obviously this was my clue to get up and politely
remove myself from her life. There was no point in re-
maining within her cold aura when I was seeking a quiet
corner of warmth. What a strange fire, I thought, that burns
so bright yet radiates coldness. I wondered how many
eager moths had swarmed around it only to be surprised
at their frostbite.

But I had nothing to lose and the cold light fascinated me as it radiated from the woman. So I just sat there
for a minute, sipping my drink, saying nothing. We had
something in common. People thought we were someone
else. She looked at me again. I thought she was going to
make some more specific comment about my immediate
departure. I suspected it would be practiced and pointed
and unanswerable. Then she smiled a little shyly and her
face transformed. Now she was a little girl. "I just happen
to be a writer," she said. "Science fiction. And I just sold
my first book."

I don't care how much she said she wanted to be
alone. She did not. The chill remained, but now I could
ignore it. In fact, I didn't even notice it.

"Congratulations!" I said, raising my margarita.
She raised her glass of wine, we clinked them together
and drank to her first book. I took off the headband, and
the dark glasses. She told me about the book and why
she'd written it and how the writing of it had changed the
way she saw herself. I was glad she wanted to talk about

that, because I had only calcite formations and echoes to discuss. My life, as I remembered it, would make for a short conversation.

"It will probably change more than your self-image," I said, picturing the changes that celebrity had brought me.

"It already has," she said, looking into space. "But it's different than I expected." She paused, thinking. I waited. "I'm forty years old. I thought I knew who I was, and knew the people around me. I was wrong. My boyfriend got weird when I sold the book, kind of jealous. Now I'm not sure I even know who he is. You know what I mean? People want things from me. They treat me differently. I didn't want that. I didn't expect it. You know what I mean?"

I couldn't answer that. But I felt comfortable sitting there listening. I sat and listened for a long time. It was pleasant to be free of my role for a while.

"It's hard to lose your past," I said. "But it happens more than you'd think." I considered sharing my problem with her, but decided against it. No one had been very interested in my life.

"The price you pay to be a butterfly," she said a little sadly. I liked the phrase. I preferred the idea of metamorphosis to the idea of loss.

"So why does he have to be like that?" The anger in her voice was punctuated by a sharp pain in my foot. She was digging her high heeled shoe into it. "My boyfriend. Why does he?"

"I don't know," I answered, trying to pull my foot away without causing a scene but it was effectively nailed to the floor. "Maybe you just need to talk..."

"He won't talk about it!" She wiped the corner of her eye as her heel dug sharply into my other foot. "Men never talk about relationships."

I winced and slid my chair backward, trying to think of something comforting to say to this obviously troubled woman, but the pain made it difficult to concentrate. It seemed petty to ask her to be careful where she stomped those stilettos and I was certain she was completely unaware she was doing it. Still, my own eyes began to water, not merely from sympathy.

"Is it me?" she asked in a rhetorical way. "Can it be something I've done?"

"Ouch!" I said as she inadvertently kicked my shin with a hard-pointed toe. She had probably just been crossing her legs beneath the table.

"No, I can't imagine it's anything you've done," I said through clenched teeth. She kicked me again.

"Well, what then?"

"Ouch! He's probably — ouch! — just jealous, like you said." That seemed to calm her. I swiveled in my chair to be out of range. "Anyway, don't they say we only hurt the ones we love?"

"Not him. He hurts me because I'm handy. It has nothing to do with love. I hate him for that."

Sounds like a perfect match, I thought.

"I bet you're a good writer," I said. She didn't say anything, but smiled sweetly and drank her wine. There wasn't anything else to say.

I finished my drink, returned to my room, and went to sleep. I did not resist unconsciousness. I let it flow over me, welcomed it, and part of me hoped I would never wake again. Turtles have the right idea. They're only awake when they need to be. Briefly I wondered why people flashed through my life like falling stars only to vanish just as quickly.

It was dark when Goldie woke me.

"Showtime," he said. I nodded groggily. I was supposed to pretend to be someone, I knew that. I searched my soggy brain. Water dripped onto a glassy black pool, then dripped again. The sound echoed against cold stone walls, then faded, like a tiny bell struck gently by a careful Himalayan monk.

When I saw the flowing pink shirt and the rest of the outfit, I remembered. I put on the clothes and the facial tic and the limp and the nervous cough. Billy Billy Billy stared at me from the mirror. Showtime, I repeated to myself. One more time.

I was whisked into a waiting limo and driven to a huge stadium, perhaps the soccer stadium I had visited earlier. In a garage area beneath the stands we parked next to an identical white limousine. I could hear the pounding music and the screaming fans and could feel the excitement. The music stopped abruptly, the crowd roared and stamped its thousands of feet. Then I saw myself, in my flowing pink shirt and my snakeskin headband and my tight pants and sunglasses. I was running toward myself. When I got close, I got into the adjoining limo and looked in my direction. It was spooky. I rolled down my window. Then my reflection rolled down his. We stared at each other. He saluted in my direction, we pulled away, and I left myself sitting in the other limo in the dark garage. Security guards kept the people back as well as they could, but we still fought through an ocean of arms and legs, the car creeping like a bug through molasses. It took nearly an hour to get to the airport. The entire time we were surrounded by a mass of bodies and had to drive slowly.

"By the way," the driver said over his shoulder. "The Man heard about that stunt you pulled at the tent city."

I tensed.

"Yeah, he was real pissed at first. Then he got a call from his record company. People are lined up all across America to buy his CD's. It's like a frenzy. People figure every CD they buy is helping world hunger or something." He laughed. "You're a marketing genius, I'll give you that. Of course, Goldie is taking all the credit. There's your plane."

A sleek black Learjet sat on the runway, light streaming from its windows.

"Who's that?" I asked. Two men in dark suits guarded the doorway.

"Customs officers." he said. "Special deal. The crowds make it hard to inspect the planes for contraband. So they inspect it in the States and these guys stay with it every minute of the trip until its back home. Otherwise somebody could make a mint running dope."

"Who'd ever suspect Billy Billy Billy of smuggling dope?"

The driver smiled over his shoulder. "They don't. That's why they're willing to do it. Anyway, as long as those customs guys are watching the plane, it would be impossible wouldn't it?"

"It sure would," I said. But we had a more immediate problem. We would never be able to get close to the plane. Moses could not have parted the mass of humanity that separated us from it. I asked the driver about that problem.

"It's all part of the plan," he said. "It's why you're here." He flashed his headlights, the customs men waved, and we drove away from the plane.

"We're driving away from the plane," I said. He just grinned in the rearview mirror. Most of the crowd stayed by the airplane, assuming that sooner or later, we'd circle back. Without the mob, we were able to increase our speed. Suddenly, ahead of us in the middle of the vast vacant airfield, lights came on in a second black Learjet. The crowd saw it at the same time and a shout of surprise and rage erupted from their several thousand throats. They all started running after us, an angry amoeba of loving fans who felt tricked. They had trusted me. They had bought my records. They had hummed my songs in the shower. They would show no mercy if they caught me.

"Can't we go a little faster?" I asked as calmly as I could.

"We don't want them to lose hope of catching you," he said cheerfully. "That's the whole idea. Right about now The Man will be pulling up to that first Learjet. Without lights on the plane or on his car, who's going to see him? Anyway, as long as they're chasing you they won't look back. In about five minutes he'll be on his way back to the States. By the way, how fast are you?"

I looked back at the mob pursuing me. There were some pretty fast runners in that group. And some heavy droolers. You don't really need to speak Spanish to understand Mexican curses. In this case, they meant, if we catch you, we'll kill you. It occurred to me that I didn't really know how fast I was. Was I a track star? Or did I have a trick knee? Would I take four fast steps and collapse onto the runway to negotiate with my on-rushing fans? This might be one of those situations where previous choices converge on a guy like talons. I decided that the job had not been adequately described to me in advance.

"Well, if they start gaining on you, give up the limp and go for it," the driver said. "It's probably not worth dying for."

"Probably not," I agreed.

"Great, here you go," he said, pulling to a stop. "On your mark, get set..." But I was already out the door and running. Out of deference to my employment agreement, I maintained the limp for about ten seconds. Then I recognized some of the phrases that were being shouted by my pursuers, and my feet were inspired to transcend their role. I gathered that the general plan revolved around primitive surgery, without benefit of anesthesia, designed to reduce my need for a family planning counselor. As they gained ground on me, my limp became rapidly less pronounced, my desire to father children increased. I became a cheetah headed downhill, sure that God had commanded me to populate the earth. I pulled away from their hands as they ripped the shirt off my back and leaped up the stairs. The door closed behind me and the plane began to move.

"Not bad," a man's voice said. "Last guy wasn't so fast. The name's Jack." A blond linebacker of a man held his hand out. I shook his hand. He crushed mine. I was taller than him by several inches. But he obviously lifted water buffalo every morning. And I was quite sure that I did not. He wore a white T-shirt that bulged everywhere it could bulge and a red baseball cap. Disorganized yellow hair stuck out from it around his ears. I chose not to mention this. His face was freckled. He seemed pleasant enough, but I decided on the spot to agree with whatever political or religious persuasion he espoused. Yes, I thought. I've always admired the Hindu faith. Voodoo? Of course I'd like to be a voodoo priest. Catholic? Sure, I guess, why not? Even Catholic.

"What do you mean, the last guy?"

"That crazy Goldie!" said Jack, shaking his head. "I keep telling him it will work better if the ringer knows the whole game ahead of time! But he's got to do everything his own way. I think he likes the drama. Every big concert, we have to do something like this. It's just too dangerous to risk The Man. Do you have any idea what it would cost the organization if he even sprained an ankle?" He shivered, not wanting to try to picture a number so large. "A lot, that's how much. Anyway, sorry we're cramped. You can sit there. These babies really move. You'll be home in no time."

All the seats had been removed from the plane and the space filled with cardboard boxes, jammed floor to ceiling. Only the front few feet were clear. A wall separated us from the cockpit. There were two beanbag chairs on the floor. Jack sat in one, I sat in the other. Then all the lights went out.

"This is my own special touch," Jack's voice said in the darkness. I could feel the plane moving. Ahead of us I could see the other black Learjet taxiing down the runway, lights blazing. We followed it like a dark shadow. It increased speed, we increased speed. It lifted into the air, we lifted into the air.

"See, we'll fly dark all the way home, just above and behind Blackjet One. If the radar picks us up at all, they'll think we're an echo."

That made sense, although I could not imagine why we'd want someone to think we were an echo. It took no time at all to reach Los Angeles, where we landed right behind Blackjet One. I assumed we were Blackjet Two. Blackjet One's lights led us because we were completely dark. A light fog blanketed the field and I hoped our pilot would turn on his headlights, or whatever you call them on an airplane, but he did not. I hoped he knew what he was doing. I had no idea that being a celebrity involved such remarkable security measures.

We taxied through the black fog for several minutes following the lights ahead of us. When Blackjack One stopped, we stopped a hundred yards behind it.

"Got to let the Feds off," Jack said. "Then we'll refuel and be off to Oregon." We sat in silence, waiting, while Jack listened to the other plane's pilot through headphones. After a few minutes he said, "All clear! Our turn. Like candy from a baby." Then the lights went out on

Blackjet One, our lights came on, and we were moving again.

"I don't get it," I said.

"The Man is going to stay in town for a couple days. Put on some jeans and sneakers, you know, a disguise. You gave him the idea, actually. You two could be twins, but nobody notices you at all. He thinks it's because you don't wear the outfit or travel with bodyguards or ride in limos. You look and act like a regular guy so it never occurs to anyone you might be a celebrity. I haven't seen him this happy in years. He's going to try it. Go to Disneyland, hit the beach, take in a movie at a suburban shopping center. Maybe go bowling. The Man loves to bowl, but of course he can't very well go to a public bowling alley. If the whole world believes he's somewhere in Oregon, he thinks maybe he can put on a T-shirt and have a real vacation. Frozen pizza, cheap beer in cans, and bowling with fat women on a Thursday night. He dreams about it. It's all he can talk about. He's finally gotten up his nerve to go for it. Grab for the brass ring. Rent some bowling shoes."

I felt proud to have a part in fulfilling someone's dream. I waved conspicuously at the small crowd of fans that surrounded the plane as we refueled.

Then we took off again. Once in the air, Jack handed me an envelope. "Here's the rest of your paycheck," he said. "You did a good job. Best ringer we've ever used. Might have to call on you again sometime." There were twenty-five one hundred dollar bills in there.

"Think I'll take a little nap," he said and popped a handful of pills into his mouth. "Helps me relax," he said, holding up the little bottle. "Help yourself to some refreshment." He gestured in a general way to the back of the plane. "Plenty to go around, and you sure earned it. You trip much?"

I laughed. "You bet," I laughed. It seemed like all I did was travel.

He looked at me skeptically then shrugged. "Well, my own little pharmacy is in that cabinet. Feel free."

"Thanks," I said. "What are you hauling?"

Jack lay down. "Flour," he said. "Many hungry children in the Pacific Northwest." Then he closed his eyes.

I felt both relief and sadness that this adventure was ending. But I had learned not to question the workings of the universe.

The plane hit some turbulence, which made me nervous. Jack probably had the right idea. I ought to just go to sleep, but I was too keyed up.

"You suppose I could borrow one of those sleeping pills?" I asked, but Jack was already snoring. I moved closer and saw three or four medicine bottles beside him. That made sense. He probably spent a lot of time on these airplanes touring all over the world on flights of varying lengths and would need different strength sleeping pills for different trips. None of the bottles were labeled. I took a few pills from each one, went back to my beanbag, swallowed the smallest pill, and waited. Nothing. I took another. Still nothing. Perhaps some of these pills were for headache or congested sinuses. It's not good to mix medications, but these others weren't affecting me at all and I really needed to sleep. I took a couple of each.

Still I was wide awake. Darn, I thought. Maybe if I had a blanket, got myself nested and cozy, then I'd relax. There were cabinets above me; perhaps one held blankets.

The first one did not hold blankets. It held wine and wine glasses and a corkscrew and little cocktail napkins. I felt like I was being guided as I took out a bottle. This was fate. I selected a glass while the Muse held my hand. I found a corkscrew and opened the bottle, confident this was part of the galactic order of things. And I knew, with my first sip, that this was better wine than I was accustomed to. This wine was alive. It was magical. It sang and danced within my mouth and cooed and laughed as it slid down my throat. This wine loved me.

The second glass loved me even more. It leaped passionately into my mouth. This wine was a woman who had not had sex in ten years. I tried to fight it off but there was no denying it. This wine wanted me very badly.

The turbulence no longer disturbed me. It was fun. But I was having trouble keeping my balance. I decided to take one of the boxes down and use it as a table beside the beanbag. This could be an elegant little celebration. Metamorphosis, not loss. I set the wine carefully, lovingly on the floor beside my glass. Then I got a box.

But the box was too heavy and it slipped from my grasp.

"Oops," I said, then laughed at my own clever remark. The box had broken open. White bags fell from it onto the floor. Worse, one of the bags broke open, spilling flour onto the carpet. "Oops," I said again.

I flopped down onto the beanbag. I felt bad for the children. I had ruined one of the bags. "They probably won't miss one bag," I said to myself. I put the good bags back into the box and set my glass just so on my little table, with the wine bottle beside it. I adjusted their position until the makeshift table looked very elegant indeed. "Now, what do I do with you?" I asked the broken flour sack. I picked it up and flour spilled all over my hands, onto my lap, and onto the floor. "I guess I'll just have to vacuum you up." Unfortunately, I didn't know where the vacuum cleaner was, so I set the remains of the sack back down and returned to my little celebration.

"I believe a toast would be in order," I said to Jack, who snored and grunted across from me. I refilled my glass. "To toast!" I lifted it in his general direction and took a drink. "And to the flour we make it from."

I began to wonder what kind of flour we might be carrying. Whole wheat? I smelled some of it on my hand, as if that might awaken a vast arsenal of flour knowledge within me. I heard no response within my brain. I smelled it again. Seminola? I had no idea where that word even came from, but it seemed like progress. Anyway, what was the question again? Oh, yeah. Flour. I smelled it again. Bleached? Unbleached? Sifted? Wild flour? Cut flour? Flour power?

I shook my head. The information was unavailable to me. I blew the white powder from my hand and laughed at the funny cloud it made. I wondered if anyone had ever done that before. I was making fog, I realized, right here in this airplane. The air was thick and white. I never knew how easy it would be. I ought to write it down, I thought, so I don't forget.

It was a shame I had spilled and wasted some of the flour, but it could not have amounted to more than a couple of handsful. Still, things were a bit of a mess. I got up and hid the broken sack beneath its many brothers and brushed the residue out of my clothes and off the table. Dust filled the air, but then settled inconspicuously around the plane. I hoped my new friends would not be upset.

At that moment I realized that the airplane was in the grasp of a huge flying iguana, a creature from a very black lagoon, a nightmare on steroids. Terror gripped me. I tried to remember what to do in this situation. The evil presence of the reptilian hijacker, huge and loathsome, squeezed the poor aircraft like helpless prey, filling every cubic inch with its disgusting self. I needed help.

"Jerk!" I said loudly, trying to wake him. Wait a minute, was that his name? "Juke!" I tried again. It didn't matter. He was dead to the world. I was in this one alone, just me against the iguana. My enemy knew it had me where it wanted me. It materialized inside the tiny compartment. Despite myself, I gasped. It was the most gruesome apparition I could have imagined. It had cold banker's eyes and a used car salesman's gaping grin. The cold indifference of a prostitute oozed from every pore. It's teeth were from a divorce attorney's contract and its claws were from a collection agency. I was an easy trophy for its wall, a Bambi to display among many heavy antlered heads. It would use me cruelly, as a junior-high school gym teacher would, before dashing me senseless. It was the prom queen and I was the guy who understood algebra. It was the Internal Revenue Service and I had lost my receipts. I was helpless.

The monster possessed the airplane like a devil with a purple raging hatred boiled up from the depths of Hell. A shimmering fog surrounded me, sparkling with billions of tiny colored lights, and I could see nothing for a moment. Just as quickly, the fog dissipated and I faced the beast once more. I forced myself to stand my ground as it approached, sure I was about to die. It began to move toward me, one horrible scaled foot after the other.

But I would not die without a fight. I leaped at the beast, aiming my clutching hands for its crusty neck, but it avoided me and I crashed into the wall. I aimed a karate kick at its swollen green belly, but it vanished before my eyes and reappeared behind me. I learned, as I fell to the floor, that I do not know karate.

"Magic, eh?" I shouted. "Well, if it's magic you want, then magic you shall have!" I'd show this slimy air-iguana a thing or two. Without thinking, I drew my sword from its jeweled scabbard and we began to duel. My sword could not pierce its ancient skin.

Finally my proud weapon fell to the carpet and was transformed into a pencil. I was getting desperate. I reached into my wizard's bag, the special secret one with big stars on it, and pulled out a furry green hex with huge ears and red eyes and flung it at my opponent. The iguana shrieked. The hex shrieked. I shrieked. The hex got the iguana by the neck and started chewing.

"Take that!" I yelled. "This is the Cranberry Tree and the Home-Study Shave!"

But he was not finished yet. From the corner of my eye I saw something red and shiny moving toward me. I whirled to confront this new challenge.

The floor was covered with half-full catsup bottles. Instinctively I understood these were his minions, his legions. It was all the catsup bottles that people use in restaurants, the half full bottles that disappear and are replaced by full ones. There were millions of them. Of course! They had to go somewhere! They were marching in a slow waddling cadence toward me. Luckily, they moved lethargically. I drew a line on the carpet with my foot. "You can't cross that line!" I said. They were evil, but not very bright. It would hold them for a while.

The iguana pulled the hex from its neck and smashed it against the wall. The hex lay in a heap whimpering. I reached into my bag. It was nearly empty. With a growing feeling of helplessness I pulled out two small curses and flung them at him. He laughed. There was an epithet in there, and some fine print and a handful of scornful remarks. He brushed them all aside easily and began lurching toward me again. The look in his eyes and on his scaly prehistoric face said it all. It was the first memory I could be sure of. I had seen that look in the eyes of an opponent, when I'd lobbed a ping-pong ball high and soft into his forehand smash, when his knight attacked my chess king and queen simultaneously, when I've said, I

113

don't care what it costs, I need it repaired by tomorrow. That look of complete victory. Now that he'd had his fun, he could kill me and destroy the airplane.

It became important to me that I die with a certain amount of dignity. I owed at least that much to the children of Portland. I stood straight and tall and stared that nightmare square in its oozing red eyes. It squinted and glared at me but I refused to look away. The monster stopped its approach.

I was confused. Why didn't the beast just finish me off? It seemed mean to toy with me this way, even by reptilian standards. Still I did not look away and I realized that its expression had changed in some subtle way. It still steamed with hatred, but now there was something else in those eyes as well. I stupidly took a step toward the creature without thinking about what I was doing, just to get a better view. The eyes widened and I understood.

Some part of that creature feared me.

Astonishment chased away a tiny fraction of my terror. Why in the world would this apparition fear me, of all people? If I were a priest, perhaps, or an exorcist, but...

An exorcist! That's it. It knows. It senses who I am the way a deer senses a hunter. I must be a professional exorcist! It probably thought I was vulnerable without memory of my incantations. It wanted to destroy me while it could.

"Too late, old friend," I said, stepping toward it again. I had finally realized who I was, and that beast was no match for me. I was the Chicago Bulls, and the beast was the girl's team from Angola. I wouldn't even work up a sweat. It hesitated and raised one reptilian eyebrow in obvious confusion, as if thinking, "Interesting. The man covered in white flour wants to attack."

My only problem was that I couldn't think of a single incantation, no magic words, no spells, and certainly nothing like a prayer. I desperately tried to remember a phrase, any phrase, in the hopes that a lifetime of conducting exorcisms would have left deep tracks within me that my wheels could follow even in the dark. I decided to trust those instincts.

"One incantation is as good as another," I said. "It's all in the delivery. I'm only going to warn you once."

The nightmare before me did not move.

"All right then, I warned you." I raised one arm slowly and pointed at those cruel eyes like Moses pointed at the Red Sea. "Mary had a little lamb," I pronounced in my deepest, most threatening voice. "Its fleece was white as snow!" I took a step forward, the beast stepped backward, crouching a bit and raising its claws to protect its head from my attack. "And everywhere that Mary went..." My mind went blank. "Da-duh, da-duh, da-duh!"

Visibly shaken, the creature slithered backward, but I showed no mercy. It was, after all, a devil. I had just begun.

"Louie-Lou-eye—hey, baby, we gotta go!"

I spoke loudly as magic words sprang into my mind of their own volition.

"If I'm elected, I will lower taxes and balance the budget!"

The creature turned away. Then, like a ghost, it simply went through the wall of the airplane. I scrambled to a window. It was out there all right, flying right along side of us. Somehow it had grown larger. Its huge body straddled the fuselage and it grasped each wing with crusted claws. It reached its long neck down and back and grinned horribly at me through the window. It only took a moment to figure out its plan. It was hanging on to the wings. It would not let them flap. How can something

115

fly without flapping its wings? It would force us to the ground and we would die in a fiery flour-dust explosion. My magic words had not been powerful enough. The children of Portland would starve.

Not if I can help it, I thought. Grimly I forced myself to stand in the center of the plane. I stretched my arms out, shoulder high, and began to move them up and down. I could feel the connection to the wings, feel the shiny metal slowly move as my arms moved, despite the reptile's massive strength. We struggled for a long time, me using every ounce of strength to keep the plane's wings flapping, the iguana resisting every movement. "The Land of Debris and the Home of Alfredo," I said, over and over again. "The Land of Debris..."

I must have closed my eyes for a moment, because when I opened them I was standing on wet pavement. Rain was dripping from my hair and the plane had vanished. The sign in front of me said, "Astoria, Oregon."

"...and the Home of Alfredo," I said one last time, flapped twice more, just to be sure, and then lowered my aching arms.

Everything was wet. A trout-colored cloud hovered in the trees and spittered and spattered cool mist on my face. Emerald grass, lush and dripping, encroached on the glistening black pavement. Douglas firs, like gigantic Christmas trees, stretched upward, their trunks a dark shade of wet cinnamon punctuated by huge clumps of moss, their upper branches muted to invisibility by the fog. The air was heavy with the smell of rotting sawdust and rhododendrons and the fishy salt and iodine smell of the ocean nearby. I was walking on the yellow-striped center line of a two-lane road that curved into the trees.

I moved to the side of the road and walked past the "Astoria, Oregon" sign.

"Hello?" I said to myself, then listened. A breeze whispered through a sprawling underground grotto within me, making a low and breathy sound, like the biggest pipe-organ pipe, barely played, fading to silence.

I felt a little funny. Maybe that fish sandwich yesterday hadn't been such a good idea. You just can't tell how pure the food is in other countries. I kept getting these odd little thought fragments, stronger than daydreams, very vivid, but unconnected to my current activity. Something about a lizard…but the image faded.

I felt disconnected from my body. I floated on a wine-colored sea that surged just beyond the surface of everything. I touched the solid asphalt to feel it on my fingers, cold and rough. Yes, it was real, but beyond it, or below it, or in a different dimension of the same space, I sensed an ocean as tangible as the road. I could not focus on any one subject for long because my mind was cotton candy, wisps and swirls and strands, without substance. I needed a cup of coffee.

My mind drifted to Heliotrope and the subject of love. He had loved that horse the way priests love God, but I wondered if he had ever loved a human that way. Maybe he had loved a woman and she had died, or left him, and Michelle had become a symbol of her. The horse became his church and cross and he worshipped and did penance at the altar of love, disguised as an old Appaloosa. And finally, because of love, he had to destroy the thing he loved.

Is there a cosmic rule that you only get one real love in your life? A lot of infatuations, attractions, affections, and friendships. But only one love so big it fills up everything, eternal and magnificent the ways thunderheads are magnificent, or the Rocky Mountains. When things change around you, and you change, and the beloved changes, and the thing itself dissipates with the hard sun of years, something is still there: the silhouette of the love, the shadow and scent, so that reality is marked forever. When that Big Love changes, it leaves a hollow spot inside you the size of Jupiter. Maybe you fill it with something, like a horse or religion, so you don't implode from the awful pressure of all that is not love.

If there is such a rule, I wondered if I had had my Big Love yet. If it showed up, I decided I would pick it up with both hands and move it gently, and never leave it outside unprotected.

I shook my head. Bad fish, I decided.

I wore jeans and jogging shoes, a red-plaid wool shirt and a bright yellow hooded raincoat. All were brand new. I had nearly five thousand dollars in my pocket. I walked into town.

Oregon is not an acrylic painting with bright colors and sharp edges. It's a watercolor of greens and grays, punctuated by bright red and white azaleas and rhododendron and trees hung with pastel fruit. Blackberries prowl each open area, choking out less hardy thornless vegetation. Only the road itself was a perfect black, a wide ink line regularly washed clean by slow rain and rarely subjected to brutal heat or freezing. The cool air was full of the smells of lumber: the fresh sawdust smell of new construction, the sweet wood smoke from a dozen chimneys, and the mildly bitter smell of decomposing mountains of sawdust at the lumber mills.

I was no longer Billy Billy Billy. And the other one, the real one, was in L.A. disguised as a normal person. At least for the time being, the celebrity was dead.

I took deep breaths of rotting wood and mist as I walked into town.

Astoria is an old town of small wooden buildings, most of them white with brightly painted trim, that have sprung up like sleepy mushrooms on the forested hills of the western tip of Oregon. A few are painted bright colors, completely incongruous with the setting, as if their owners wanted to strike out at the gentleness of the surroundings and paint was their only weapon. The Pacific Ocean nestles up to the town like a cat, purring and hissing while it sharpens its claws on the rocky shore. The Columbia River sweeps majestically past, huge as a lake. The sky is persistently overcast. Crackers do not snap in Astoria, they bend. When you can see a spot of blue in the sky, the weatherman says it's partly cloudy. Moss grows in the sidewalk cracks. The big industries are fishing, lumber, and cheese.

What am I doing here, I wondered. Can you make a wrong turn when you don't know where you're going? Whales sometimes crawl up on the beach to die. Is that a mistake, the madcap universe in a goofy mood closing its eyes and being silly with the darts it throws, or is it part of some Grand Schematic? Does God ever giggle and say "Oops?" Or does He solemnly intone that man's childish understanding is simply too limited. Men are salamanders in My terrarium, trying to fathom the events beyond the glass. They are flying insects that develop an aesthetic curiosity about the lovely pattern of silk a spider dangles in the tulips. They are wildflowers that sprout blissfully optimistic in a field that will soon be plowed to featureless mud. Like deer are drawn to the highway and salmon to the net, pretty young girls are drawn to the city and young men are drawn to battle.

And I was drawn to Astoria. I walked past shops and offices and cafes.

Music drifted into the street from behind a door, a man singing a low and soothing country-western song. Merle Haggard. The name leaped into my mind like a tarantula pouncing on a grasshopper. I knew someone's name! A real name, a real person, in the shadows of my brain. And I recognized the song! In fact, I knew the words. I could not stop myself. I stood outside the Webfoot Bar, singing along. A young woman walked toward me on the sidewalk, her little boy beside her in a sailor's hat. I must have looked dangerous standing alone in the mist, singing along with Merle, because she took her son's hand and crossed the street to avoid me. I didn't care. The song did not summon any memories of my own life, yet recognizing it was exciting and miraculous as the birth of a baby.

The pay phone in its little booth summoned me. Still humming the song, I stood and leafed through the phone book, a huge idiotic grin on my face. Nothing under Land of Debris.

A white van stopped at a sign two blocks away and I quickly turned away, feeling suddenly exposed and vulnerable on the street. With my back toward the van I moved quickly toward the music.

The song ended as I opened the door to the.Webfoot Bar. I stood inside for a moment, waiting for my eyes to adjust to the darkness.

The Webfoot seemed familiar, the way the song had seemed familiar. Maybe I was onto something here. I rubbed the two quarters together in my pocket, walked over to the bar and sat on a stool.

All the lighting had been provided by beer distributors. Every ray of red and blue phosphorescence that illuminated the place shown through the name and slogan of a different brand of beer. Bottles of good liquor lined the back bar, while a couple bottles of everyday stuff was convenient to the bartender's workstation. A TV mounted near the ceiling played some soap opera, but the sound was turned off. Two pool tables graced the far corner of the room. The room smelled like cigarettes and beer and Old Spice cologne. In the corner, a young thin man played an ancient pinball machine that clattered and buzzed and flashed at him as he twisted his body back and forth to influence the capricious silver ball.

"What'll you have?" The bartender was a sixty-year-old woman in jeans and a sweater. She had cold indifferent eyes and a no-nonsense manner. Instantly, we both knew she could beat me in a game of pool. Or a knife fight. She had seen everything in the world, heard every lie that could be told in a bar, knew more swearwords than I knew words, and could probably rebuild the engine in her pickup truck. I glanced at the man sitting next to me and ordered the brand of beer he was drinking. The bartender nodded and turned away.

I watched her deliver bottles of beer to the men at the bar. Most were dressed in wool shirts and dark stocking caps. Each of them had a little stack of money in front of them. She'd give them a beer, they'd slide her a dollar, she'd insult them, and they'd insult her back. They were obviously all friends. When she got to me, she slapped the bottle down.

"That'll be two bucks."

"That's an expensive beer," I said.

"You ordered it."

"I guess I'll drink it then," I said. "But then I better go. This place is too fancy for me." I handed her a one hundred dollar bill.

She didn't say a word. But when she brought back my change, she gave me another beer.

"Happy hour," she said.

I stacked the change on the bar and sipped my beer.

The man sitting next to me was middle-aged, with long silver-streaked brown hair and an athletic build that had sagged with gravity and time. His back was wide as a door. There were deep lines in his face. He hunkered over his beer, protecting it, focusing on it. If his world was small enough, as small as one beer surrounded by his elbows, he could cope with it. Every now and then he looked up quickly, as if startled, and his eyes widened. Then he said a few words to himself, very quietly, and returned to his meditations. He wore a black leather jacket with a motorcycle insignia. He turned his head toward me slowly, cautiously, as if it were a periscope scanning enemy waters.

"She's OK," he said softly. The words required a lot of effort. "She's just been on her job too long. She's a fisherman at heart."

I almost corrected him. Don't you mean a fisherwoman? I glanced at his huge arms and shoulders and taped a note to my mental refrigerator: Do not ever be a smart-ass with a drunk lumberjack in a Harley jacket. Do not discuss politics, religion, or Californians with him. Simply smile, nod, and buy him a beer. I motioned for the bartender to bring him another.

"And what are you?" I asked pleasantly.

Once again his head swiveled slowly in my direction, his eyes wide open, alert and menacing. Had I invaded some private territory? Broken some bar law? Was I about to die?

"Excuse me?" he said.

"Just being friendly," I explained quickly. "I just asked what you are."

He stared at me for a moment. Then his face relaxed again, and he turned back to his beer. "I'm a cliché," he said softly.

"What?"

"I'm a story everyone's heard a thousand times." Words did not flow from him. He squeezed them out. "Had a lot of big dreams, fell in love young, then went off to fight a war no one understood." I had asked what his job was. He wanted to tell me his life story.

"That must have been hard." The bartender brought his beer, I slid a dollar across the bar and she took it without comment. She glanced at my new friend, a little nervously I thought.

He shrugged and drank his beer.

"Came back without the dreams, my girl had moved on. Nobody's fault. A cliché. Haven't had a good night's sleep in twenty years. Get a little disability, work odd jobs. Can't keep nothin' steady. Same old thing. A million guys got the same story. Best not to talk about it much."

123

We drank in silence for several minutes. He wiped his mouth with the back of his hand.

"You know what's funny?" he asked.

I shook my head.

"Geese."

Yes, I thought. Geese are kind of funny.

"I killed folks, or helped kill them. Lots of 'em. Even kept track of how many for a while. And I watched good friends die. Some were pretty bad. And I got shot up, and hid in mud and lived on worms and beetles for a while. But what I remember most is the geese."

I could think of no appropriate comment, so I just drank my beer.

"With all the surveillance shit we had, the night vision glasses and the satellites and the guards — all that shit — it was the geese we listened to. Kept some on the periphery all the time. You just can't sneak up on geese. Anybody tried to approach, them geese started honking like Chicago on a Friday night."

"That's a neat idea."

He nodded.

"Yeah. Except now, every time I hear geese, I'm back there again, and my buddies are getting blown to hell and I've got some thirteen-year-old kid in my sights. Tried to live in Minnesota for a while, and then Nebraska. No go, man. Too many damn geese."

"Aren't there geese in Astoria?"

He stared at me for a minute, deciding if I was being sarcastic. A cold look came into his eyes and I wondered if he was armed. Finally he decided I was merely stupid. His face softened and he looked away.

"Not many, not along the coast. Too cool for grain, too wet for grasshoppers. They go where the food's easy. And how about you? What's your story?"

It was the first time someone had really asked me that question and expected an answer. I decided this was not a guy to bullshit. He had lived in it, and would recognize it. Besides, his story was more improbable than my own. Touch of amnesia, no big deal.

"Something happened to me, too. I just can't exactly remember what it was. My life disappeared. I'm sort of starting over."

He nodded. "So you're a cliché, too," he said simply. "But a lucky one."

"I guess so."

He reached over to shake my hand. "The name's Pete."

"I'm...I'm Merle."

We raised our glasses in a silent toast to clichés and drank them down.

"Wanna shoot some stick?" A young man with bulging muscles stood behind me and fondled a pool cue.

"I guess I could try," I said. He racked and I broke. His name was Stephen and he worked for a lumber company. I assumed his job was pulling redwoods up by their roots.

"Let me feed the juke box," I said. Stephen shrugged. I chose a Merle Haggard tune and searched through the songs for something else equally zippy and uplifting. Suddenly a name jumped out at me. There was a song by Billy Billy, before he added his third name. I couldn't resist. I punched the number and returned to the pool table.

I am apparently not a very skillful pool player. We played for a dollar; he won while most of my balls were still on the table. Merle Haggard finished singing his sad song, I put some quarters into the pool table.

A heavy rock beat came from the speakers, then a familiar voice began singing. I smiled.

There was a sound like an explosion behind me, then breaking glass. Instinctively I fell to the floor and turned to locate the source of the commotion.

A thin young man with long hair fired at the juke box again and more glass shattered. He fired once more and the music stopped. The bartender shook her head and looked disgusted. Most of the men at the bar twisted in their stools to watch, little smiles on their faces. In the split second before I looked up, Pete had leaped to the floor, spun toward the sound, and crouched to attack. His eyes were wide, his mouth open in a snarl, but he froze in place as his mind struggled to transport him to the present.

"Ah, Mack, did you have to do that?" the bartender said. Her voice was perfectly level, but somehow a baseball bat had materialized in her hand.

"I'm sorry," Mack answered, his gun still pointing at the offending equipment, prepared to finish it off if it revived. "But I warned you! I said I'd shoot that thing if anybody ever played that damn song again."

"But this guy's a stranger. He didn't know."

"I said it. I had to do it. A man's word's gotta mean something. Ever since that creep sold out, I just can't stand him."

"You're gonna have to pay for the repair."

"I know that. I'll pay. But I won't pay to have that song replaced."

"Fair enough. But I've told you twenty times not to bring a gun in here."

"Hell, it's only a twenty-two."

"You could'a put somebody's eye out with all that glass. And you're damn lucky Pete didn't break your fuckin' neck. Rules is rules. Now you just take that thing home. I don't want to see you back here for the next couple weeks. And then you can pay for the repairs."

"You know I told you." He sounded sheepishly defiant.

"I know. Now get on out of here."

"What's he got against Billy Billy?" I asked Stephen.

"He sold out."

"Did not!" A woman in her early twenties walked over and sat at a stool near the wall. "He just made a commercial. And all those people got fed."

"Mack don't see it that way. Thinks it was a big publicity stunt."

"Well, I don't."

"Made him a million dollars. Hell, you just think he's cute."

"He ain't cute. He's gorgeous. I'm in love with him."

"You and every other girl in the damn country. At least until he sold out."

"He didn't sell out!"

"Whatever. We're trying to shoot some stick here. Do you mind?"

"Can I buy you a beer?" I said. She was a lovely lady, and she was in love with my twin, Billy Billy Billy. It seemed a reasonable opportunity. She stared at me as if I were horse droppings on her new carpet.

"Get lost, creep," she said.

A couple of Stephen's friends joined us. Jim, a wiry spring-loaded Airedale of a man, worked on fishing boats when there was work. Mark looked Swedish, tall and pleasantly fat with pinkish skin. He worked for the cheese company.

They patiently taught me a local variation of the game, a game that four people could play, but one guy would win all the money. Immediately my luck improved. At a buck a game, I won several dollars and used my winnings to buy them each a beer. It seemed the friendly thing to do. In the same spirit of friendship, they suggested we raise the stakes to five dollars a game. I must have been very lucky, because they all seemed to be better players than me, yet I continued to win. Even after paying for more beer, I must have had thirty or forty dollars of winnings in my shirt pocket. But I didn't want to keep taking their money. These guys had befriended me, a stranger, cheerfully giving me their money, including me in their afternoon.

But they insisted we play one more game. I protested, but they seemed to think I was just being polite, that I was bored playing with such amateurs. Finally they left me no choice. They would be insulted if I refused to play one last game, and just to make it interesting for me, we'd each bet a hundred dollars, winner take all. To my mind that was an incredible gesture. Between them, they were going to set three hundred dollars down on that pool table just to keep our friendship going a little longer. This despite the fact that I had won every game. I was touched. I would have handed them a hundred on the spot, no questions, no game. I had plenty. Surely I was very close to the Land of Debris.

But I was pretty sure that a gift would insult them. So I put my bill on the table next to theirs and determined that I would simply play my worst. I'd miss every shot. I'd let them win, then we'd go sit down and talk for a while, I'd explain my problem, and maybe they could give me advice. This was going to be the best investment I had ever made. An investment in friendship.

They seemed happy that I agreed and determined that I should break. I chalked up, trying to look serious. They looked at each other, smiled and nodded. Right then I realized that there had been an empty feeling inside me larger than the vacant cavern of my memory banks. I had been lonely. The people I had encountered had all been pleasant and helpful, some of them valuable spiritual guides, some delightful to spend time with. But I didn't really have any friends, not like this. People who wanted to be with me even if there was a price to pay. True friends. The universe had make no mistake. Within an hour it had filled an emptiness within me I had not even realized existed. Emotion swelled in my throat as I aimed the cue ball at the tightly racked balls.

I closed my eyes, pulled back the stick, and hit the cue ball as hard as I could. I kept my eyes closed as I heard the sharp smack and clatter of the balls flying around the table. Life was good, I thought.

"Shit!"

I opened my eyes.

"The bastard sunk the eight ball!" There was amazement and disgust in my new friend's voice.

"I don't understand..." I said.

"Like hell you don't," Mark the cheese-maker said. "You conned us! Hustled us!"

The woman behind the bar looked amused. "What's the problem, boys?" she said. "Can't take a little of your own medicine?"

"Take the damn money," Jim the wiry one said, ignoring her. "And get the hell out of here."

"But what did I do?"

"Sank the damn eight ball on the break, as if you didn't know. How many times in a row can you do that? Ten? Twenty? I've heard about guys like you."

"But I didn't mean to..."

"I said take the damn money." He pushed it into my shirt pocket. "Nobody's gonna say we welshed on a goddamn bet. Now get the hell out of here. And don't think you're gonna be able to pull that stunt in this town again. Go back to California, or wherever you came from. You're not welcome here."

I tried to argue that I was not a pool hustler, although of course I couldn't be sure. Sinking a nearly impossible shot had seemed easy to me, even with my eyes closed, but I didn't feel like a pool hustler. First of all, I hadn't done well in the earlier games. Surely they remembered that. I tried to imagine what it would be like, wandering from town to town, pretending to be something I was not so the locals would bet money on our games, living by instinctive, practiced skills. An acrobat of life, flying high and dangerous and alone without a net.

I couldn't picture it. My imagination was simply not that good.

They grabbed my arms and pushed me out the door. I looked for Pete, but he was huddled over his beer, holding it with both hands, shivering like a wet dog and talking to ghosts.

Suddenly I was alone once more, standing in the cool gray drizzle. So that's friendship, I said to myself.

I walked down the street. Maybe Astoria had been a mistake, after all.

The bus that took me out of Astoria traveled through paradise. The sky was gray and overcast, but that seemed good planning on God's part. It provided a wonderful contrast for the tall green trees. We passed orchards rich with fruit and miles of raspberry fields and acres of flowers planted and blooming just for the joy of it. The ground was so full of life that it could not contain itself, erupting everywhere in a delirium of vegetation. When the road curved near the river, sleek steel-colored fish were leaping into the air. I was Alice riding a bus through Wonderland.

The guy sitting next to me did not agree. He grumbled and growled and complained, then took a swig from a bottle wrapped in newspaper. He was about my age but had already gone to seed. His clothes were disheveled, his face a sour stubble field, his eyes red and narrow and his hair uncut. He was drunk enough that he was willing to share his wisdom with me.

"Oregon stinks," he said flatly. I took careful note of his opinion, sure that he was prepared to document the evidence. "Everything's always wet. Sun never shines. Damn blackberry's take over your yard if you let 'em. Whole state smells like apples. People don't do nothin'. Stay inside and read their damn books and play their damn guitars. The place stinks." He took another swig. He reached out his hand and I could not avoid shaking it. "The name's Oliver. Frank Oliver. But everyone calls me Olive."

"I'm Merle," I responded.

"It's the friggin' hippies, that's what it is. Took over the whole damn state in the '60s and just never left. They deserve each other, that's what I say."

I ventured a question. "So why are you here?"

"Last place they'd look for me," he said and I decided not to question him further. Smiling politely and nodding, I turned back to the window, but he was not quite done explaining his life to me.

"I mean, who'd ever look for somebody in·Oregon?" he said. "They'd figure living here was punishment enough, right? Unless you're a guy who likes strawberries." He said the word with derision, as if strawberries were the culinary equivalent of slug bait or fresh sheep turds.

"It wasn't like it was a lot of money, either," he elaborated. "Not to them, anyway. Those Vegas guys get so serious about money. Hell, and they never did prove anything."

"We ought to be in Portland pretty soon," I said cheerfully. I was not at all sure I wanted to know any more about the man.

"One time! I only did it one time. One friggin' Keno card. I mean, somebody's supposed to win every now and then, aren't they? Isn't that the whole idea? Don't they plan on having to pay a winner once in a while? So why not me? All I did was change the time on one card. My girlfriend picked the numbers off the sign, slipped me the card, and I made it look like she gave it to me before the game closed. What could they expect for what they were paying me? Anyway, what's a lousy twenty grand to those guys?"

"Sometimes life isn't fair," I agreed.

"You got that, buddy," he replied, offering me his bottle. I declined. "But sometimes I miss it anyway." He got a far away look in his eyes, remembering. "Those huge neon signs. The constant clank and rattle of coins in slot machines. Hotels with four thousand rooms, every one of them identical. Plastic sculptures lit up at night like Christmas trees. A million flashing lights on every ceiling and miles of mirrored walls." He shook his head sadly. I thought he might cry. "God I miss it!" he said. "Sometimes I think it would be worth it to go back. What's life all about anyway, if you're not willing to take a risk for the things you love?"

I nodded. That sure sounded right. What's life all about, anyway, if you're not willing to take a risk for the things you love. For just a moment I wondered if I might not have a new spiritual guide on my hands. But I decided to be cautious. I would not commit so easily this time. Perhaps one rotting fish in the backseat does not make you a mystic. Perhaps removing your shirt does not always mean you're in love. I even considered this possibility: there may be people wandering the world, apparently functional, with vaster, emptier caverns within them than me. Selecting a spiritual guide is not as simple as buying a chili dog. I moved to a different seat, but five minutes later my new friend sat beside me again, as persistent and irritating as an August fly.

"So, tell me about yourself," Olive said, but I could tell he didn't really want to know. It was a ploy so I'd let him sit there. Then he could ramble on some more.

"I've forgotten most of my life," I said. He probably wasn't listening anyway.

"Ah," he said. "So you're a free man."

"I guess so."

"Nothing in the world like freedom. Hang on to it, buddy."

The bus reached Portland, an old city of flowers and grass and trees and clean streets. With eighty inches of rain per year there is no dust in Portland. The moss eats it.

In the bus station I was accosted by a middle aged man, obviously down on his luck, who wanted a dollar. He carried an old black lunch pail, the kind with the rounded top, a sturdy metal one. My friend with the bottle and the unhappy associates in Las Vegas walked beside me.

"Leave us alone," he said gruffly.

"No, wait a minute," I said. "What's in the lunch pail?" He looked at me like I had asked him to eat a hamster.

"My lunch," he said. "Braunshweiger sandwiches. The Man don't hassle you so quick if you got a lunch pail."

"I'll give you fifty bucks for the pail and your lunch."

He stared at me, wondering if this was some sort of joke, or a police sting operation, or if I was merely another loony tune fresh off the bus from San Francisco.

I pulled a fifty dollar bill out of my pocket. He quickly decided I was simply crazy and the exchange was completed. I excused myself for a moment, retreated to the men's room and planted over five thousand dollars beneath those braunshweiger sandwiches. The lovely aroma of the ground liver meat product made my mouth water, and I was sure I had made a wise business move. If I was mugged, I would gladly hand over the fifty or sixty dollars I had left in my pockets. I doubted that the most ambitious and thorough thief in Portland would steal a man's braunshweiger sandwiches.

I rejoined the guy from Las Vegas. That is, I walked out, he scurried to my side. He seemed nervous.

"We may have a little problem," he said. I wondered how "we" could have anything. Almost immediately I understood. Two rather bulky men in identical dark blue suits approached us.

"Mr. Oliver," one of them said, revealing no emotion. "I believe you owe L.V. an explanation. And some cash." His words carried a threat, but the tone of voice did not. He might have been reciting bus schedules.

"I don't know what you're talking about, Mike."

Mike smiled at the apparent misunderstanding. His face was deeply suntanned, his hair jet black and perfectly cut. But his smile was a mask without warmth. A simple revealing of teeth. A rat or an alligator might smile like that. No warmth at all. He opened his suit coat casually. He wore a large gun in a shoulder holster. A howitzer. A bazooka. A cannon. A big gun. He made no reference to it. It might have been sheer luck that we saw it. He continued smiling. To anyone passing by, business associates were arranging lunch next week. I tried to slowly back away, but the other man stood behind me. I felt his very firm hand on my shoulder and decided to stay.

"I believe you do know, Mr. Oliver. And L.V. would like to hear your side. He really would. In fact, he'd be happy to fly you to his home in Nevada to discuss it." He turned to me as if I might feel slighted. "And, of course, your friend here too."

"No, wait, that's not necessary," I babbled. "I just met this guy on the bus, I've never even been to Las Vegas. Well, not that I can remember. See, I was in Mexico City. Well, before that I was in Taos, and it's kind of a long story, but none of it has to do with Keno…"

He just smiled the way a cat might smile at the mouse between its paws, listening to its pitiful and utterly irrelevant squealing. When I said the word 'Keno,' he raised one eyebrow.

"I insist," he said. "You will be our guest. I'm sure L.V. will want to chat with you as well."

"This is America," Olive said indignantly. "You can't just kidnap us! If we don't want to go to Las Vegas, you can't make us."

"Of course not," the man in the suit responded. "But if you decline, my orders are specific." He pulled his coat back more deliberately this time. Boy, that was a big gun. "It really doesn't matter to me." A funny look came over his face, as if he'd never thought about it that way before, and it surprised him to realize it was true. He repeated himself with a little wonder and even more conviction. "It really doesn't matter to me. Either way." Then he was all business again. "It's not the money. It's the principal of the thing. You get away with it, someone else will think they can too. Don't want to start an epidemic. If you think there's a chance you can convince L.V. that you're innocent, or if you can pay back the money, or cut a deal with him, you ought to come back." He paused, then smiled his cold shark smile again. "If not, you might be better off with a quick one through the brain right here in Portland, Oregon. Right now. While you're still a little drunk. He turned quickly to me, almost apologetic, afraid I'd been left out of the conversation too long. "And you too, of course."

"I'm just looking for The Land of the Feel and the Woman We Crave," I blurted.

"That's Vegas," he said. "Shall we go?"

L.V. lived in a palace outside Las Vegas and beyond hyperbole. His house was a sprawling tentacled adobe growth behind a huge brick wall. It must have cost millions of dollars. Lush grass and flowering shrubs contrasted with the arid surroundings outside the wall. Sliding glass doors opened onto a sparkling swimming pool. The red tiles of the roof matched red brick pathways. Beautiful young women in bikinis lounged around the pool like living decorations, while muscular men in short-sleeved shirts, white slacks, and cell phones paced alertly.

Our new friends in the business suits escorted us up a path, into the house, down a hall and through a wide wooden door.

"Well, well, well, Mr. Oliver. What a delightful surprise." L.V. sat behind a massive desk uncluttered by a single scrap of paper. He was a small, bald man, a little paunchy, with a prominent nose and quick eyes. He wore a pink golf shirt. Except for the hyper-alertness that emanated from him, he looked more like an accountant than the rich and powerful man I had expected. His voice was deep, like a radio announcer's. "Do you have my money?"

"Like I told them, this is all a big mistake. I didn't take your money."

L.V. studied him for a moment, then nodded.

"Take him out in the desert and kill him."

"Yes sir."

"Wait a minute, you can't do that!" Olive tried to pull free, but could not.

L.V. grimaced. This show of emotionalism was clearly distasteful to him. Amateurish. Unbusinesslike. "Please don't insult my intelligence," he said. "You stole money from me. You ran away and spent it. Now you're lying to me. You leave me no choice."

"What about me?" I said hopefully. I had, after all, done none of those things.

"I'm sorry, I almost forgot you." He thought for a minute, then turned to the man with the big gun. "Him too. No one would associate with Mr. Oliver because of his sparkling conversation. This fellow—what was your name?"

"Merle," I said. I had been humming the country western song to myself on the drive. It seemed as good a name as any. It sounded like it would not have to last me a long time.

"Thank you. Pleased to meet you. Anyway, Merle here must be in on it too. Don't take them too far out. We want their bodies to be found." He turned to me and explained. "We like to inspire hoesty in our employees." Then he had another idea and turned back to the man in the suit. "Listen, run over the bodies a time or two, when you're done with it. People seem to remember that a little more. But for christsake, take the limo through the car wash afterwards this time." He looked at his watch. "Now if you'll excuse me, I've got to meet Wayne on the golf course." He stood up, signaling the end of the meeting.

He handled it all so smoothly, I thought. A well-run meeting. A few important points to cover, everyone pleasant and efficient, very little digression. The unpleasant decision made, a committee appointed to carry it out, then on to the next matter. Sort of like a loan officer who decides he can't make you the loan, and of course he's sorry you'll be losing the farm, but then business is business. And by the way, wouldn't you like to join the bank's Christmas club?

Still, I felt unsatisfied.

"Excuse me, sir."

"Yes, Merle?"

"Is it possible we have not explored all the alternatives?" I tried to sound as gracious and businesslike as he had. He thought for a moment.

"Well," he said thoughtfully. "There are alternatives, certainly. There's drowning, strangulation, choking, poison...let's see. Stabbing." He was checking them off on his fingers. "There's probably a lot more. But a gun is so quick and effective. Anyway, a man develops a certain style and he hates to deviate too much..."

"That's not what I mean. Of course you can't have employees stealing from you. We all understand that. But I really don't know anything about all that. I wasn't involved. Surely there's some way Mr. Oliver could pay you back that would be just as good a lesson."

He considered that idea for a moment, then shook his head.

"Nah. He had his chance. He split on me. Get 'em out of here."

"I have an idea!" Olive said. He was pale and shaking. "Let me go undercover for you. There's probably a dozen guys working for you stealing more than I ever did. And if anyone can find them, it's me. Takes one to catch one and all that. What d'ya' say?"

L.V. contemplated the proposition. You could tell he was a guy who wanted to be fair. He glanced at his watch.

"Oh, hell, all right," he said. "You got one week. Trade me one other thief from my payroll for your lives. Or give me back my money. Let's see, you took twenty grand, I could have doubled it by now. Forty grand, one week from today, or a worse thief than yourself. Fix 'em up with collars, Mike. Now, I really must run." He shook our hands as he walked quickly out of the room, I suppose from force of habit. Mike looked disappointed as he led us down the hall.

The collars that he put on us were heavy metal ankle bracelets that contained a radio transmitter.

"Find you anywhere in the world," Mike said, flashing his joyless smile. "They keep improving these things. This is the part I like." He showed us the inside of one. It had a little needle recessed into a hole. "You try to cut it off of your leg and it triggers this little syringe. You wind up giving yourself a shot of rat poison. It ain't fast or pretty, but it sure does work. A little touchy, though. You try to slide something under the syringe and pop! Injection city. Bang it into a table…" He drew his hand across his neck, then completed his task. The collars were secure on each of us. "Personally, I think you made a mistake. Could'a been all over with by now. This way you got to think about it for a week." He shrugged. "I guess it's none of my business. See you in a week."

One had to admire the ingenious device. Fitting snugly around my ankle it was even sort of attractive. The rat poison part was a distraction, of course. But then beautiful things often disguise something darker.

"This will be a snap," Mr. Oliver said as the limo dropped us off in front of the nicest hotel on the strip. "Piece of cake. Everyone's a thief in this town. And we only need one."

I cringed at the word "we" once more, but it was appropriate. I had a metal bracelet on my leg just like he did. My altruistic instincts had been awakened. I would do whatever I could to help this guy.

"And if we can't find one, we'll set one up. One way or another, we're getting out of this thing alive. And then I'll be able to stay here." He made a broad, sweeping, happy gesture that encompassed the state of Nevada. "Might even get my old job back."

I eagerly agreed.

But it was not a snap. Everyone in every casino knew who he was and what he was up to. They would not talk to him, or stand beside him, or deal cards in his presence. The clanking of coins stopped when he walked by. The clatter of roulette balls in their spinning wheels became silent. No one was going to give him any chance to accuse them of anything. Purity surrounded him like a cloud as he moved from casino to casino. He could have been the pope.

Lisa had thought me sophisticated because I peed into a radiator. Las Vegas would have redefined the word for her. It was crowded with people so rich they could pour coins into machines all day long without a blink. So sophisticated they didn't care that they wore gaudy shorts and flapping sandals and over-sized T-shirts that advertised someone else's business. People who dwelt in that stratospheric region of sophistication where it's OK to insult the waitress and send back meals for trifling errors, and then fail to tip. I was very impressed.

After a couple days we got desperate and Olive started plotting ways to come up with forty thousand dollars. He worked on ideas for removing the collar around his leg. He wondered if there wasn't some remote country where he could go without being followed. One of the fundamentalist Islamic countries, for example. Maybe they'd be able to track him there, he figured, but it wouldn't be worth their time to actually enter the country. Not for him. He wasn't worth it. It became his most intense hope. That he would be considered worthless.

I would have preferred not to be involved at all. And I wasn't really much help, having no gift for scams or tricks or plans. I could not guess how a thief might work. Olive quickly realized my helplessness. He showed me some of the basic elements of self-preservation in this environment, and then started leaving me alone in our hotel as he jitterbugged around town in search of a thief or a scam or both. Sitting alone in the pleasant room, I realized that the issue of my immanent demise was not very frightening. I had, for all practical purposes, been alive for such a short while. It wasn't much of a life to lose. The pain aspect of it was disconcerting and I was not eager to die, but, if losing all your memories is like dying, it wasn't worth fretting about. Whatever root I sprang from would surely survive to sprout yet another tangled weed of a guy. I'd be back.

One thing I had to say for L.V: he was a good host. We had a fine suite of rooms near the top of the hotel, with God's own view and great air-conditioning and a kitchen stocked with food and liquor. He was giving us a fair shot, without having to spend time on hustling food. Of course, it also made us convenient to locate. My lunch pail was in the refrigerator, my braunshweiger sandwiches untouched and graying, and below them, my cash. I knew I couldn't spend it. I'd never be able to explain its source to L.V.'s satisfaction. If I started gambling with hundred dollar bills, Mike would surely appear to ask me about it. He would consider it proof of my guilt. Death was not a terrifying prospect, but being used as an example in some extended demonstration of cruelty did not appeal to me at all.

The first time I was alone in the hotel room, I tried the phone number.

"Passion Flower Escorts," a lazy female voice answered. I hung up the phone, quite sure that was not what I was looking for. Perhaps I had simply misdialed. I started to try again, but hung up before I finished. There wasn't really much point.

It seemed a waste to spend the rest of my probably short life in that lovely room. I went outside to a grassy area with little round tables and chairs near the swimming pool and sat down. A pretty waitress asked if I wanted a drink. She wore a bizarre little outfit that consisted primarily of long legs, high heels, and cleavage. I said yes, mostly just to please her. If she had been selling dried codfish, I would have bought some.

It was hot as a glass factory in the sunshine. A few people lounged by the pool. A man in baggy blue shorts wore the vacant stare of someone who's gambled too long and been drained of their money and their brains. A few rich wives and widows sipped oddly colored drinks. They already owned more money than they could spend; gambling meant nothing to them. Las Vegas was just one more lark. Win a few thousand, lose a few thousand, go to a bawdy show and then return home and complain about the service to all the other bored country club women.

The waitress brought my drink, a multi-colored contraption with flowers and plastic palm trees. I pulled out my new wallet and smiled. The wallet held a half inch stack of hotel stationery in it, carefully cut to the size of money, with a few real bills on each side. It looked like I had an awful lot of money in there. Olive had shown me this little trick. By using this device, he explained, I would always get the best seat in the restaurant, and a lot of my drinks would be free. It would help me fit in. Las Vegas is in love with people who carry around lots of cash. You will find it the friendliest town in the world, he said. In many ways, the man was a genius.

I paid with a single one hundred dollar bill. When the waitress brought my change, I gave her a ten dollar tip. Why not, I thought. I was going to die in a couple days anyway, and five grand that smelled like braunshweiger would wind up in a dumpster. She leaned over and kissed my cheek and asked if there was anything else I needed. I couldn't think of anything. She left with a promise to take care of me. I watched her walk away.

"That's my table."

I looked up to see a beautiful young woman, mid-twenties, with long red hair holding a drink from which she had removed the vegetation.

"I'm sorry," I said and started to get up. She motioned for me to remain.

"No, stay," she said, and laughed. Her eyes were green. "That's not what I mean." She sat down. "It's just that this is my lucky table. Yesterday I sat here and then went inside and won a lot of money. You don't mind, do you?"

I stared at her. Why would I mind if she won a lot of money? Why would I mind if she had a lucky table? I must have looked confused.

"You don't mind if I sit here with you for a few minutes do you?" she explained, speaking slowly and enunciating clearly. "Just for luck?"

Oh, that. She obviously did not understand my situation. My life, as far as I could tell, consisted of being an Indian's slave, a rock star's decoy, and the victim of a huge flying iguana. I had been kicked out of Astoria, Oregon, as a pool hustler, kidnapped to Las Vegas and day after tomorrow someone would be merrily driving a Buick back and forth across my corpse, probably while whistling a Barry Manilow tune. She was concerned that I might be offended by the opportunity to sit near an angel with skin like fresh cream and a dancing vibraphone of a laugh, a goddess radiating sweetness and wholesomeness. A lovely woman who seemed a little out of place. Too nice. Too naive. Too pretty.

I shrugged. "Suit yourself."

"My name's Jane," she said, reaching across the table to shake my hand. "I'm from Iowa."

"I'm Merle," I said. "Oregon." It was the short answer.

"Oh, it's so neat up there. All the trees and the ocean and everything. Do you come to Las Vegas a lot?"

How could I answer a question like that?

"This is my first trip," I said. That felt true.

"Me too. And it's just, I mean it's all so..." She searched Nevada for a word. A word that would do justice to the million flashing lights, the mirrored walls, the enforced circus atmosphere. "It's all just so glamorous." She nodded happily. Yes, that is what it was.

And of course, to a girl on her first trip from Iowa, it probably was. A girl who kept all the buttons on her blouse neatly buttoned and whose pants were not shrink-wrapped, day-glow, or transparent. A girl who believed in lucky tables. A girl named Jane.

"I really like the blackjack tables," she was saying. "Except you know, it's hard to add up the cards so fast. I mean, I don't know how the dealers do it. They always have to wait for me. What do you do in Oregon?"

Another tough question.

"I'm sort of between things. Starting over. I was in the import business, for a while. Kind of an agent. Flour, mostly."

"Oh, so you're a businessman! How neat! I bet you just sold your business and now you're relaxing for a while trying to decide what to do next. Isn't that right? Didn't you just make a lot of money?" She laughed. "You don't have to answer that. It's none of my business. My friends say I talk too much. I like to guess things about people. Did you ever think about buying a farm?"

It was my turn to smile.

"Actually I may be buying a farm in a couple days." That was pretty good, I thought. A joke. Buying a farm. One thing I had discovered about myself was that I didn't think of funny things to say very often. I smiled.

"Well, I bet you'll like it. Farms are just wonderful. Boy, it sure is hot out here."

"You're dressed pretty warm. You ought to go put on a swimming suit." Instantly, against my wishes, my brain dressed her in a swimming suit. Stop that, I said to myself. As if rebelling against being told what to do, my brain dressed her in a bikini. She looked very nice in it. Then my brain started applying suntan oil to her back and legs and even the bikini was fading.

"Stop it!" I said out loud. "She's not like that."

"Excuse me?"

"Nothing," I said. "Just daydreaming."

"Well, you're probably right. It would feel good to go swimming. Back home we have lakes that are so private you don't even need a suit. But this isn't bad."

I told you so, my brain said defiantly. Shut up, I said.

She fanned her neck with her shirt collar. Suddenly I smelled bales of hay and fried chicken and alfalfa. Just as quickly, the scent vanished.

No, I thought, I guess it's not too bad. Sitting here is not worse than guarding a dead cow from blood-thirsty coyotes armed only with a transistor radio.

"People are pretty casual around here." Somehow I had finished my drink; the waitress noticed and brought each of us another.

"Your drink is so pretty," Jane said. "Can I taste it?"

"Sure." I slid it across the table.

"Mmm, that's good." She sipped through a straw shaped like a little plastic native girl, then leaned forward across the table. I concentrated on keeping my eyes on her face. She whispered "Don't look now, but isn't that the movie star who's in all those nightmare movies?"

I turned in my seat and scanned the tourists.

"Which one?" I said, turning back to Jane.

"I guess it's not," she said. "Here's your drink. Thanks."

We talked for a few more minutes. This second drink seemed stronger to me. I found myself feeling increasingly relaxed and less concerned with my prospects. I started picturing tire tracks across my chest and found the idea amusing. I noticed, for the first time, that if you watch carefully, you can actually see the grass growing. It's like a bunch of little green eels, slithering out of the ground weaving their skinny little heads. In fact, once you think to look at the little fellows, they're all moving and dancing. I could hear the music they were dancing to. Van Gogh wasn't crazy, I realized. That's the way it all really looks.

"Is anything wrong?" Jane asked sweetly. Her face was glowing a lovely violet color.

"No, nothing," I said. "Just got to catch this…" My drink was floating upward from the table, and although it moved slowly, I found it difficult to grab. This is the way islands start, I thought. These little things are like seeds. You got your palm trees and your native girls and your flowers and they float away and land somewhere in the South Pacific, sprout roots and start growing. Pretty soon you've got Tahiti. Finally I caught it and pulled it down. Not this time, you little bugger.

"You haven't been sitting here in the sun too long, have you?" she asked. "You have to be careful in this climate."

"How do you do that?" Somehow she kept changing. One minute she was fully clothed, the next instant she was stark naked. It was a neat trick, but distracting. How did she expect me to carry on a conversation while she was doing that? Especially with my drink trying to escape, and the grass eels wiggling all around me.

Told you so, I told you so!

Shut up! Shut up!

"Finish your…" (Now her clothes were on) "drink and…" (Oops, naked again) "I'll take…" (clothed) "you in out…" (naked) "of the sun" (clothed).

Well, of course I hadn't been in the sun too long. I knew that. Still, I agreed and drank down my seed of an island. I did it for her. I thought her clothing trick might be considered a little strange even for Las Vegas. Might attract attention, cause her embarrassment. I didn't want that. She didn't know any better. She was just a naïve farm girl from Iowa. It was my duty to protect her. She was the one that needed to get inside.

I stood up and let her wrap one of her long tentacles around my waist three or four times and we floated a few inches above the ground into the hotel. It was pleasant, like ice-skating on a cushion of air. I did not remember doing this before, but promised myself I would do it more often. Much nicer than walking. I also liked that Jane had decided to maintain her naked state. Pressed against her warm body, I was pretty sure I was in love. Tentacles and all.

We managed to get into a hotel room without going through the lobby, or up an elevator, or down a hallway. We didn't even open a door. We were just in there.

"That's a good boy," Jane said, as she helped me stretch out on the bed. "Now, your wallet's in your jeans pocket isn't it? Of course it is. Let's just take them off, shall we? I saw all that nice money you have in there."

That was too complicated for me. Wallet? Pocket? Times like these make one appreciate the common sense approach of an Iowa farm girl. She knew all these big words and seemed completely in control. Using three or four of her hands, she undid my jeans and slid them off me.

"What's this?" She tapped the metal band around my leg. Oh yeah, that. I know what that is. There's a word for it. I thought as hard as I could.

"Butterfly?" I said.

"No," she laughed. "It's not a butterfly."

"Frisbee?"

"Is it something you keep money in?"

"Money. Toothpaste. Rat poison. The itsy bitsy spider da dum da dum da dum." I was sure I was getting close.

"Let's just look, shall we? Now where do you keep the key?" She checked my jeans pocket. No key. She felt my shirt pocket, found the change from the hundred and removed it for safe keeping. She unbuttoned my shirt. "You don't wear it around your neck, do you?" I wondered where I kept the key myself, and would have liked to help her look, but she was so darn quick. She'd think of someplace to look, and by the time I understood what she was talking about, she had already looked. I apparently did not keep it around my neck. I tried to remember, but could not. Anyway, the ceiling was doing something funny. It was sprouting more of those grass eels. Little green filaments were oozing out of it like hair, dancing from side to side. A wall-to-wall ceiling carpet of tiny snakes of grass.

"You don't keep it in your underwear, do you?"

A low sonorous gong sounded deep in my brain. Underwear. I knew I kept something in there. But what was it?

"Lisa?" I asked.

"No," she said. "Let's see here."

Quickly and expertly she slid my shorts down my legs and off my ankles. She resumed her search.

I discovered that Iowa girls are not only friendly, but playful as well. They can make a game out of anything, even searching for a lost key. The search became suddenly more interesting to me, and so did Jane.

"That feels good," I said. What a lovely woman! Nine breasts, and all of them perfect.

"You men are such sleazes," she said sweetly, continuing her search. "Slime bags and jerks." I loved the sound of her voice, although it was hard to concentrate on the words. Maybe she was speaking a different language. I could tell she liked me.

"Thanks," I said.

"Don't care a thing about women, really, do you? None of you do. We'd all be slaves if you had your way. Use us and then throw us away. Well, we don't all get used so easy. Some of us have wised up."

"Seven-Up?"

"This is the only way I can stand any of you. Helpless, stupid, barely conscious. Even then your true nature shows through."

"Ouch!"

"Only thing you're interested in is rape. Look at you. Can't even sit up and yet you're ready to rape me."

"Drapes?"

"You disgust me. All of you do. But that's enough of that." She stood up. "Where's the key to your money bracelet? Or do I have to cut it off?"

Another gong sounded somewhere across a foggy valley. It was early morning, the Buddhist monks were being summoned to prayer. There were little thatched roof huts, light was just beginning to ease away the darkness, flowers were thinking about opening. The gong sounded once more, deep and soft from the mountain temple.

Candles and incense were lit and the shiny black implements of worship were set neatly in a row upon the stone
altar. A tiny old man in a simple gray robe raised his calm
face to speak. "Listen, my son." he said. "This may be
important. Listen carefully."

"What?" I said.

"I said where's the key to your money bracelet, or
do I have to cut it off?"

"Listen carefully," the old monk said. "Think
slowly, slowly, one word at a time. It has to do with rat
poison. This may be important." I nodded. Suddenly it
came to me.

"I know!" I said. "L.V.'s got it. It's his thing! Let's
go find him. He'll give us the key. And he's got a swimming pool, too!"

"It's L.V.'s?"

"Yes! He put it on me. Let's go find him!" I tried
to sit up, but she pushed me back down.

"So, it's a collar. I've heard of these," she said
thoughtfully. "But I've never seen one. That changes
things a little, doesn't it?"

Something else entered my brain. It was a song.
What a joyous feeling to realize that you know a song! I
began to sing.

"Strangers in the night, exchanging glances... " I
was delighted to discover that I was a marvelous singer.
My voice was smooth and rich and perfectly on pitch.

"Shut up," Jane said. She opened her purse and
pulled out a roll of wide gray tape. "Put your feet together."
She paused for about an hour. "I said, put your feet together. No, stupid, like this." She helped me.

"Thanks," I said. She wrapped the tape around
them tightly. "I can't pull them apart now."

"That's the idea." She took my left hand and began wrapping tape around it until it was a fingerless gray

ball on the end of my arm. I thought it looked silly. Then
she did my right hand. I clapped the two gray stumps together. They made a neat thunking sound.

"Here, drink this," she said. "it will help you
sleep." She held the little plastic hotel glass to my lips
and I drank. "Good," she said. "Are we all comfy-cozy?
One more little thing… " She put a piece of the gray tape
across my mouth. "Because you're a singer," she said. I
beamed at the compliment, although I noticed that I
couldn't really sing or talk as well with the tape covering
my mouth. "Let's see, do we have everything?" She picked
up my jeans, felt to make sure the wallet was still in the
pocket, then put them into a white plastic trash sack. She
threw my underpants and shirt in it too. She put the roll of
tape back into her purse, looked around the room and
nodded. Then she sat down on the bed next to me. Her
hand moved slowly and tenderly on my leg, then up on
my chest. She touched my cheek and traced a line with
her finger down my body. It tickled, but in a nice way.

"I could almost like you," she said. "As long as
you were like this."

"Urghumm blmb," I said.

"Shh, it's OK, don't try to talk. You'll be asleep
soon." Her hand was on my leg again. "I hope you don't
hate me or anything. I mean, you know, it's nothing personal. It's just the way I make money. If it were up to you
men, women would never have any money. So we have
to use whatever we've got. Anything's fair. You taught
us that."

I did not see how she was making money at this.
We were just a couple of tourists playing games in Las
Vegas. I was sure I'd never played the duct-tape game
before, or the look for the key game, or the ice-skating-
on-air game. But money? How was money involved?
Shoot, if she needed money, I had several thousand dol-

lars back in my own room that she was welcome to. It wasn't going to do me any good. It was in the refrigerator. I told her about it:

"Frml:mm, gbll, rrmlumdi."

"Sure, honey. Really, you're kind of sweet. By tomorrow this will all be pretty hazy to you." She sounded sad. "And see, I haven't hurt you, have I? Not like some of the others. I just need a little time to move on. By the time you wake up and get loose, and figure out how to get some new pants... " She stopped and reached in her purse. "I almost forgot. " She took out a pair of scissors and cut the telephone line. "Room service would be cheating," she said. "Anyway, by that time I'll be a long way from here." Her hand moved gently over my skin. Her other hand still held the scissors. She giggled.

"This one guy," she said, her face bright with the memory. "He said he was going to call the cops. Pissed me off. You know what I did?"

"Urgllmmbb?"

She reached between my legs and grabbed me. Holding me firmly, in fact almost painfully tight, she leaned close to my face and smiled. She held the scissors in front of my eyes, opened them very wide and slowly closed them. The snap startled me.

"Yup," she said. "That's one bastard the girls won't have to worry about any more. You woulda' thought I cut off his goddamn head the way he thrashed around. Lucky I taped him good, or somebody would've heard him." She shook her head. "He probably survived. His kind always do."

The room was becoming foggy, Jane was a shadow and her voice was a dream. I was floating on a wine-colored sea with the sun setting on the horizon. The stars came out, one at a time, tiny blazing things. As I watched, they each put on a little white tuxedo and stepped down from their heavenly mezzanine to have cocktails on my chest. So glad you could come, I said. Pleased to meet you. Yes, and this is Jane. My pleasure. Have you met Sirius? Delighted. Jane smiled, an angel's smile and lowered her eyes shyly.

"The Bland Awful Free and Homer's Sausages," she said.

And a light began to flash.

Bingo! Bingo! Bingo!

Coins clattered from a machine, but there was no bucket to catch them and they spilled across a floor and rolled away.

Then she kissed my cheek. Her hair touched my forehead; I smelled her perfume. "I have to go now," she whispered. "Have a good dream." I loved her warmth against my skin. And though I tried to hold that warmth, I could already feel it fading, rolling away like lost coins. Despite the haze around me, I knew that if I did not go to sleep quickly, I would soon be too awake, and very lonely.

So, like a petal that has clung over-long to a rose, I simply released my grip and drifted lazily to the glassy surface of a warm dark pool.

"I've got it!" Olive said, bursting through the door. "Our problems are over.

"Where am I?" I answered.

"For the eighteenth time, you're back in our hotel suite, Las Vegas, remember? A couple hookers found you taped up like an old hockey player and hopping through the hallways naked. Trust me, it's just as well you don't remember. I don't know what happened to you, but you sure had a big grin on your face when they brought you here. They thought you were some big shot. Who else would act like that? But enough about that. We've got to come up with forty thou by tomorrow night. And I've got a plan."

"Taped up?" I tried to sit up, and something exploded within my skull. My head was a tiny jungle village suspected of harboring guerrillas. The United States Army was shelling it, bombing it, dropping napalm on it, exploding land mines beneath it, jamming its communications systems, targeting it with lasers and land-based missiles, surrounding it with lunatic marksmen, lighting it with flares, confusing it with buzz bombs and smoke bombs, burning down its houses with flame throwers, and shattering its windows with sonic cannons. I lay back down gently.

"Headache?" Olive asked. His voice was a marching band of a thousand accordions.

"Yeah."

"I'm not surprised. You got to learn to pace yourself. Anyway, here's our money." He dumped a bunch of plastic chips from a plastic bucket onto the bed. The sound was deafening, like all the garbage can lids in New York crashing against a marble floor. I covered my ears and cringed.

"Sorry," he said. He arranged the chips in little stacks.

"See, these are one dollar chips," he said. "And these are one hundred dollar chips. But if I paint the one dollar chips just right, you'd never notice the difference. At least a busy dealer might not. A new one. So I sit at a table, see, and I bet a few, then I trade my homemade hundred dollar chips for some twenties or fives. Then I go cash them in. The cashier gives me cash, because I'm turning in real house chips. Ten dollars becomes a thousand dollars."

"You'd have to do it forty times."

"Only if I lose every hand. If I start winning, I might double my money."

"What if they catch you?"

"Then tomorrow comes a little early. Anyway, I'll only do it once at every casino. Look for new dealers and hit 'em when they're busy. The chips will get replayed a dozen times before they discover them. Now go back to sleep. I've got to paint some chips."

I thought it was a hopeless scam. Then I caught myself. Hopeless scam? I couldn't imagine a scam more hopeless than the ones that seemed to be working. Insurance for example. And taxes. And television evangelists. If they wanted money to feed the poor, why didn't they just sell the Rolls-Royce and the villa in France? Religion in general confused me. If you get to Heaven by either faith or good deeds, why did each congregation need a million-dollar clubhouse? Couldn't they time-share or something? And lawyers who write laws that only lawyers can understand so that everyone else must hire a lawyer — was I the only person in the world who smelled a scam there?

Olive's plan seemed possible, after all.

Any sort of plan seemed an improvement to my life in general, and I relaxed for the first time in a week. I lay down on the bed, with the comforting drone of the air conditioner humming its mantra in the background. It sounded like summer sprinklers on green lawns, or a distant lawn mower. Its soothing buzz shut out all the smaller irritating sounds of Las Vegas.

I went back to sleep and had the most bizarre dream. In it, I was a life insurance salesman who lived in a tasteful suburban home with a perky wife and two daughters. We were getting ready to have a barbecue in the backyard and my wife was teasing me because a couple of dandelions had survived my recent chemical attack. I swore vengeance upon them while I fussed with charcoal that seemed slow to start. The two girls (I think they were twins), chased each other and their mother yelled at them to be careful. A golden retriever sat a few feet away from me, polite and endearing, smiling, trying to charm me out of a hamburger.

"I hope it doesn't rain," my wife said nervously, surveying a few clouds in the sky.

"Well, if it does, we'll just pretend we're camping, right girls?"

"Right daddy!" the twins shouted gleefully. "I hope it does rain," one of them declared bravely.

"You know honey," my wife said. "It would really be nice to have a second microwave. We could keep it in the family room and make popcorn in it when we're watching a movie on the VCR. Don't you think that would be nice?"

"We'll look at them tomorrow," I said. "Do you think we should have your new boss over sometime?"

"Probably," she said. "They have such a nice family. Besides, I think they play pinochle."

"Great!" I said. "Why don't you see how next Friday is for them. We don't have anything planned, do we?"

"Not unless you have a Rotary meeting."

"It's the week after."

"OK. I'll call them. Is the charcoal about ready?"

"I think we ought to wait a little longer."

"You're probably right. I hope it doesn't rain."

"We're going to need more ketchup. I'll see if there's another bottle. Girls, why don't you come inside now and wash your hands. Look at you! What a mess! Well, you're both going to have to take extra-long baths tonight."

"Me first, me first," they both shouted, then they giggled and followed her inside.

I thought about squirting more charcoal starter onto the little pile of briquettes, but I knew that was dangerous. The fire could follow that little stream of liquid right back up into the can and make it explode in your hand. I'd done it a few times, added starter to a smoldering fire, and been lucky, but that was when I was younger. Before I was a father. I couldn't take chances now. It wouldn't be fair to the girls.

I looked up into that blue, blue sky. The clouds were white and fluffy, not really threatening. Cheerful clouds. Still, it could rain. I ought to make sure there was plenty of windshield cleaner in each of the cars. I took a little pad of paper from my shirt pocket and made a note to myself. Check windshield cleaner. No sense in waiting until you were all the way out and driving through the city staring through grimy glass. That's how accidents happen. I decided to buy an extra gallon to have in the garage and made another note to myself.

I held one hand above the charcoal and felt it glowing warm. There's a little sense of satisfaction that comes from starting a fire, I thought. Oh, I could buy one of those electric charcoal starters, or buy the kind of briquettes that have wax or something in them so they're easy to start. My wife had even talked about converting to propane, but I didn't want to do that. I liked starting the barbecue this way, the old fashioned primitive way, with the smell of starter and the whoosh of the flames.

The coals were probably hot enough, but I decided to wait just a little longer, let them get white and perfect. My family admired my skill with charcoal. I'd wait just a little longer.

I looked at the pair of dandelions disturbing my otherwise perfect lawn. I did not need to make a note about them. "You're dead meat," I told them. The clouds skittered across the sky.

Secretly, I hoped it would rain.

When I awoke, I didn't know if it was day or night. Time is irrelevant in Vegas. Casinos never close, the lighting does not vary, the clanking coins don't rest, the lights keep flashing. Of course, if you go outside or look out a window you can tell. But such things are discouraged. Casinos don't have windows. You don't go to Vegas for fresh air or inspiring views. You come to be relieved of your money.

Weird dream, I thought, sitting up and shivering. Scary. Imagine a guy just drifting through his life like that, without taking control. Painting his life varying shades of off-white, never splashing purple or red in huge bold strokes, never sticking both hands into a fresh full paint can to sign his creation with hand prints, garish but uniquely his own. He must have made some choices very early that mattered.

And yet, in an off-beat sort of way, perhaps I had let that happen to me too. Maybe I was being too passive about this death thing. Maybe there was some way I could help Olive. I ought to take a little more control of my own destiny. It was, after all, my life. My death. My ankle that was collared. I decided to get involved.

I took a shower. It seemed a good first step. I put on clean clothes. Gingerly I removed several one hundred dollar bills from beneath the fuzzy gray sandwiches in my lunch pail. I developed a plan.

Olive knew what he was doing, that was sure. He'd been around. He'd worked in a casino. But his plan was risky. It only took one dealer spotting his bogus chips and he was out of business. If I could find him, maybe I could create a distraction just when he was trading them in. I could be a momentary flaw in the dealer's stony concentration. I could improve the odds, just a little. And isn't that what Vegas is all about really? The subtle shifting of odds?

I worried it might take me a long time to find him, but it did not. The third casino I walked through proved lucky for me. It also proved lucky for him. He was radiating optimism. A pretty young woman was beside him.

"Merle! What are you doing here?"

"I want to help."

"You can't help. You'll throw off my rhythm. Somebody might recognize you. Anyway, Linda here is helping me. She's bringing me luck. Oh, sorry. Linda, this is Merle. Merle, Linda."

I shook her hand. Something was familiar about her, but then every pretty woman seemed familiar to me. If I actually knew her, I'd remember it. Her hair was a huge condor's nest of blonde hair balanced on her head, her dress was tight and revealing, and she wore huge dark sunglasses.

"Have we met?"

"No, sah, mah name's Lindah." She spoke with a lazy southern drawl. "Ahm from Joe-Jah. Ahm afraid you've got me confused with anothah lady."

"Sorry."

She turned to watch Olive, but continued to speak softly to me. I could not see her face. "Unfortunately, y'all remind me of a man who once deceived me rathah cruelly. Why, if someone evah tries that again, I do believe aw'll cut their fingers off, one at a time, and hope they bleed to death. And ah'd be perfectly within my rights, don't you agree?"

"Well, that sounds a little harsh..." I said.

"Of course you would, sweetie," Olive interrupted. He circled his ear with his index finger. Bats in the belfry. "Of course you would. Now listen, Merle, get lost. Linda and I have some serious gambling to do. Don't we?" He had one arm around her waist and squeezed her harder than she would have preferred. She grimaced.

"When can we have a drink, dahling?" she said. He pulled out his wallet. It was fat with bills; I couldn't tell if they were real or not. He extracted a ten.

"Go get yourself something. I'm not ready to drink anything yet. Got to keep my head clear."

"Not even one teensy-weensie little drink?"

"Not yet. But you go ahead. I'll be right here."

She took the bill. "No, that's all raht. Ah can wait."

Olive took me aside a few feet, his arm around my shoulders, and whispered urgently in my ear.

"Change of plans," he said. "The chips have too much detail. Can't make 'em good enough. I'd get spotted in thirty seconds." He showed me his bucket, half full of hundred-dollar chips.

"They look pretty good to me," I said.

"Exactly! That's our new plan. There's only one safe bet in the world. Bet on greed. No dealer in town would accept one of these. But half the customers would."

"You're going to sell phony chips to tourists?" That did not seem right to me.

"Hell no! That would be a crime. This is much better. I'm going to let them steal them from me."

"I see."

But I didn't and Olive knew it. Impatiently he explained.

"I can tell a crook half a mile a way. I just sit down next to someone with a few hundred dollars in their bucket. Act drunk, make sure they see mine for a few seconds, then put my bucket down next to theirs. It looks like I've got thousands in here. First time I look away they'll grab my bucket and walk away fast leaving theirs behind so I don't notice right away."

"A few hundred dollars won't do it for us."

"Of course not. But I've got dozens of these ready to go. The bottom half is full of souvenir tokens, a penny a piece from the distributor. On top of that's a layer of my own special Mr. Oliver hundred-dollar chips. I've got about twenty bucks invested in each bucket."

"But there can't be that many thieves in Las Vegas."

He stared at me. "Merle, you got pure turnip juice flowing in your veins, don't you?"

"Excuse me?"

"Nothing. Go enjoy yourself. I've got work to do. I'm going to cleanse this casino of sinners."

Olive staggered toward some slot machines with the tightly packaged blonde attached to his elbow. He sat next to a young man in a college sweater. I saw the young man's eyes widen as he glanced into Olive's bucket. I also noticed a serious man in a dark suit watching them both from a discreet distance.

This was it. He was going to make his move, and I knew I had to help. We were cheating. What we were doing was wrong. We were stealing, sort of, taking advantage of the young man's weakness. But L.V. was going to kill us and that wasn't right either. Surely we had a right to do what we could to stay alive. Olive probably knew the risk he took with his little Keno scam. Maybe there was some sort of cosmic justice involved in that. But what had I done? I picked the wrong seat on the bus from Astoria to Portland and for that I was going to die. A universe that will kill you for sitting in the wrong spot surely would understand cheating a little to stay alive. It would probably even approve.

I sat at the closest blackjack table and threw down several hundred dollar bills.

"Shit," the dealer said, grimacing. "What in the hell's on that?" He looked at the pit boss. Within seconds the man in the dark suit came over to the table. The dealer handed him the bills, the man scowled and looked at me coldly.

"Braunshweiger," I said. "They were in my lunch pail."

The pit boss turned them in his hands a time or two, held them up to the light, and gave them back with a nod. The dealer pushed my bills into the slot on the table and slid a stack of chips toward me. His eyes were watering. I held my breath. This was the first time in my life I remembered doing something dishonest. It was oddly comforting to think that before I lost my memories I had probably done lots of dishonest things. I might be a wicked man, a mass murderer, a bank robber, an aluminum siding con-man. This was probably old hat to me. Still, it felt new and a little sickening.

But there wasn't time to worry about that now. I couldn't just pickup my chips and leave. Cards were being dealt, some of them to me, and everyone else knew what to do with them. It would seem suspicious if I sat at a table, got some chips, and then didn't have the foggiest notion of how to play the game. But I didn't. As I stared at the cards, I remembered how to play eights, and cribbage, and pinochle. But the blackjack synapses were tangled up in the back of the closet, useful only to a bored cat. I glanced toward Olive, but he was gone. So was the young man in the college sweater.

I was no longer innocent. I had helped Olive swindle the tourist. I was sure that anyone who happened to look at me would see warts sprouting from my face and horns pushing up through my hair. There was no way to go back. I had done something evil. I was wicked for life, without hope of redemption or forgiveness. The best I could hope for now was to fake my way through this card game and the rest of my life. At best, I would survive a little longer. At least now if the plan failed and L.V.'s goons came to get me, I could feel that justice had prevailed. I deserved to die. The pit boss watched me carefully.

No one spoke as the card game was played. Players put their chips on the table, the dealer dealt everyone cards, then went around the circle a second time. Some of the people scratched at the green table top with their cards and he'd throw them another card or two. Then the dealer would turn over their cards and take them and take their chips. Other people just waved their hand casually over the top of their cards as if blessing them, and he gave them more chips.

It's an adding thing, I thought, frantically trying to seem suave and self-assured. My cards add up to something, so do the dealer's. But do I want high scores or low? What do face cards count? I tried to watch the other players and imitated them while I struggled to retrieve this information. It can't be so difficult. But then, it doesn't matter. I just need to sit here for a minute and then leave. Don't worry about the silly card game.

When the dealer looked at me, I blessed my cards, and a moment later he gave me some more chips. I'll sit here for a minute, give Olive time to escape, then I'll go find him. The dealer looked at me. Oh yeah. I blessed my cards. It would be good if I had noticed which direction he'd gone. The dealer gave me more chips, then more cards. I blessed these new ones too. That girl, what was her name? Linda? Pretty woman, despite all that hair. Not as pretty as Jane, the farm girl I'd met briefly on the patio, but nice just the same. Maybe she had been lucky for Olive after all. More chips. More cards. More blessings. I wondered how you kept score in this game. Maybe I would find Jane again and then she and I and Olive and Linda could all go out to dinner together. That would be fun. I decided I'd probably sat there long enough. The pit boss was watching someone else.

"I have to go," I told the dealer.

"Cards have been dealt."

"You mean I can't leave yet?"

"Just as soon as this hand's done."

"Right. I knew that."

"Well?"

"Oh yeah." I blessed my cards. He turned them over, some people behind me gasped. He pushed more chips into my pile.

"Can I go now?"

"Yes. Please."

"Can I get some of my money back?"

"Just take your chips to the cashier."

"Thanks." I got a plastic bucket and scooped my chips into it. There were a lot of chips, but they were different colors and I didn't know which was which. They might all be peso chips.

I didn't know where to find a cashier. I wandered through a maze of clanking, flashing slot machines, long corridors of intense people feeding metal beasts coins from plastic buckets. Sometimes someone would win and not even remove the pile of coins from the metal basin, but just reach in there and take them out one at a time to feed back into the slot. Feed the slot, pull the handle. Feed the slot, pull the handle. Voracious animals, these machines, and their keepers seemed to fall willingly and easily into the numb rhythm of their care.

I walked into a gift store and picked up a magazine. It's title was all bold, capital letters run together. I pieced the words together. It said, "In the set, Imes." A cryptic message to some musician, an inside joke of some sort. It made no sense.

"You want to buy that?" the lady behind the counter snapped at me.

"Excuse me?"

"I said, you wanna buy a copy of *In These Times*? This ain't a library."

"Sorry." I put the magazine down and left the gift store.

Almost immediately I saw Mike, L.V.'s goon with the big gun. I panicked and turned around. Was our time up? Had Olive been caught in his little scam? I had to hide, but there was no place to hide.

"Change, sir?"

I nearly jumped out of my body. A gorgeous girl in a tight pink and very revealing outfit waited for my answer.

"I'd love to change," I said. "But I don't know how."

The girl smiled. "Would you like some change for the machines?"

"Right. What do you have?"

"I have anything you want, sir. Perhaps you'd like some dollars?"

"Yes, dollars. Can I trade you chips?" I held my little bucket out for her inspection. She peered into it, took out one chip, and gave me a roll of silver dollars. "Thanks. Can I play these in any machine?"

"The dollar slots are right over there, sir." I walked the direction she pointed. Let's see, this can't be too complicated, I thought. As long as my back was turned and I was playing some machine, maybe they wouldn't notice me. I put a coin into the slot, pulled the handle, and watched the little pictures go rolling past. One by one they stopped. No coins fell out the bottom. I put in another dollar and pulled the handle. The machine whirred optimistically, the little pictures spun around, stopping one by one. No coins fell out. I put in another dollar and pulled the handle.

"We've been looking for you, Mr. Merle." I knew the voice. Without turning around I could picture just where the gun was.

"I told you I didn't have anything to do with it." I was stalling. I think it was understandable. No coins fell. I put another dollar in, pulled the handle. It was pleasantly distracting to watch the bright colors spinning, flashing lights reflecting in the glass of the slot machine. The clanking and whirring of coins and machines and ice in glasses all blurred together into a dreamy haze around me. This was it. The end of the story. The Land of the Green and the Hole in the Face. Mike did not rush me. Instincts developed over a lifetime in Vegas told him to let me lose all my money first, then he could kill me. He stood behind me and spoke quietly.

"You know," he said, "in my business, no one ever has anything to do with anything. Everything's always a mistake."

I put in another dollar and pulled the handle and drifted along with the rolling images. No coins fell out.

"I don't get to make decisions," he said. "Otherwise my job would be tough. This way I'm just a tool. No responsibility. It's smart of L.V. to do it this way."

I inserted my last three dollars and pulled the handle. My roll of dollars had become sands in a cosmic hour glass, slipping into the machine. I watched the spinning colors. Mike would lead me out of here quietly. No need to cause a scene. If I protested, he would probably give me a shot of some fast-acting sedative. I could picture it clearly. We would drive outside of town, the car would stop. Mike would tell me that we were going to walk toward some distant landmark, a stone outcropping or something. He'd say that L.V. was there and wanted to give me one last chance to pay up. I would start walking, trying desperately to formulate a compelling argument, something that would sway L.V., make him see that he did not need to kill me. Before I walked eight steps, a bullet would shatter my skull. And that would be that.

The little rollers came to a stop, one by one. I closed my eyes.

Suddenly bells were clanging and whistles blowing and lights flashing. I leaped to my feet, terrified. Strong hands closed around my elbows.

"Well I'll be damned!" Mike said. People gathered round me shouting and pointing. "I'll be damned! You won the friggin' thing."

Sure enough. The machine I had been playing was a frenzy of flashing lights and sirens.

"How much did I win?" I asked, afraid to be hopeful. "In round numbers?"

"Sixty grand." His voice was filled with the awe that gamblers feel for remarkably good luck. The money meant nothing to him. "It's one of them special deals. I don't believe it." It only took a few seconds for him to become calm and businesslike. "OK, here's the deal," he whispered intently. "You assign your winnings to L.V. and you're off the hook. You walk out of here." He pulled a sheet of paper from his coat pocket.

"But Olive only owed forty." People slapped my back and tried to buy me drinks. I ignored them.

"Got to pay taxes, buddy. Look at it this way. You paid off forty G's with one silver dollar. And you get to live."

"And Olive?"

"He walks too. But you got to decide right now."

For just a moment I considered negotiating. How about forty-five thousand? Something like that. But luck can be capricious. You got to pull your weenie out of the campfire when it's done. You wait for the wind to shift, blow the smoke away from you, you might miss your chance. I did not want to contemplate making charcoal drawings with my weenie.

"Deal," I said, and signed the paper "Merle Haggard," but my hand was shaking and it was nearly illegible.

"Congratulations," he said, shaking my hand and nearly smiling. "Las Vegas loves a winner. We'll hire actors to pose as a couple from Omaha for the publicity photos. We'll handle everything."

There was some brief administrative work to be done with the casino manager. Mike made it very smooth. Then he removed the collar from my leg. I was surprised how much relief I felt.

"We ought to find Olive," I said.

"No problem." Mike produced a little device that looked like a hand calculator with a pair of antennae. "He's in this hotel somewhere." He aimed it upward. "In one of the rooms." I had been dragging my bucket of chips around, he looked at them.

"Look, we're even now. You don't owe us anything. Go cash in your chips and I'll meet you by the elevator."

I took the chips to the cashier and handed the bucket to the lady. She arranged them in stacks, counted the stacks, made a notation, got a young man to countersign, and then counted out my winnings.

"There you go, sir. Sixteen thousand dollars. Come back and visit us again soon. Thank you for playing mumble mumble casino."

"What?"

"I said thank you. Here's your money."

She was already helping the next customer. Sixteen thousand dollars? And alive beside? Surely I had found the Land of the Green. Which reminded me, I still had not completed my phone call. I stuffed the bills into my new wallet, removing the wad of stationery I had put in there. I still didn't know how I'd lost my old wallet. It didn't matter. But I had to make that call. Ironically, with all those bills, I only had two quarters and I felt I needed many more. I hoped I could find someone to make change for me.

Mike and his partner were waiting for me near the elevators. They didn't seem like such bad guys, after all. They talked about the upcoming football season as we rode up. When we reached the correct floor, Mike held the little tracking device in front of him and walked down the hall until it indicated which room Olive was in. It really was a neat device, I decided. Remarkably, Mike had a master key. He opened the door. This was exciting. After all his bad luck, Olive would not have to die. He wouldn't even have to go back to Oregon.

I stepped into the room, anxious to tell Olive the good news. Almost immediately I stopped. I have never seen such a strange sight.

Olive was laying stark naked on the bed, his feet bound together with gray duct tape and his wrists bound to the headboard. There was tape over his mouth and a massive blonde wig on the floor.

Jane, the girl from Iowa, was straddling him fully clothed and doing something to one of his hands. "That's one," she said to him. She didn't hear us come in. "Now, didn't I tell you I'd do that?" Olive was humming some song loudly and cheerfully through the tape. I didn't recognize it.

"What are you doing?" I asked. She whirled around, eyes wide with surprise. She had a pair of scissors in one hand and something small and pink and bloody in the other.

"You can't come in here!" she shrieked.

"Yes we can," Mike said, pulling his gun and pushing past me. Her face changed when she saw him. It wasn't fear, or recognition, or any emotion I understood. She stared at the gun, her eyes wide, her mouth open. Then she looked at his face. Then at the gun again. He froze in his tracks, staring at her.

"My name's Loretta," she said sweetly without any trace of an accent, putting the scissors down on the bedside table. She put the little pink thing neatly beside them and batted her eyelashes at him.

"I'm Mike," he said. They just stared at each other. Something was going on there that I couldn't grasp. The other man pushed past them both, surveyed the situation, and grabbed the phone.

"We need an ambulance for room 893," he said. "A man has had an accident. Looks like he's cut off his little finger."

I felt faint and leaned against the wall. Mike's partner quickly picked up the scissors and cut Olive free. Then he took the collar from his leg. He made a tourniquet around Olive's wrist with duct tape and threw the loose finger into the ice bucket. Then he wrapped a towel around the bloody hand, and finally, when he had done what he could, he removed the piece of tape from Olive's mouth.

"Just a spoonful of sugar helps the medicine go down," Olive sang loudly, but not very well. He was completely unaware of his problem.

"Give him his money back," the calm man said to the woman.

"Whatever you want," she said. "It's mostly newspaper anyway. Pissed me off. It's in the sack."

He pulled Olive's clothes from the plastic trash sack and threw them on the floor. Then he cleaned the scissors with another towel. He threw the collar and all the bits of duct tape into the sack and picked it up.

"We got to get out of here," he said.

"Spoonful of sugar, spoonful of sugar... Brown sugar, just like a dum dum dum."

Mike and Loretta (or Jane, or Linda, or whoever she was) were still staring at each other.

"Look, we got to get out of here now," the other man said.

"I always liked the name Loretta," Mike said.

"Why, thank you," she said, looking shy and girlish.

"Listen, I'm going up to Montana this weekend, do some fly fishing. You come with me."

"We gotta get out of here!"

"I'll pick you up in front of this hotel, eight o'clock Friday morning."

Then he turned and walked out. She blushed.

"What a sweet man," she cooed. "Imagine meeting someone like that in Las Vegas! A real outdoors man, and a gentleman too. Why I do believe I'm in love!" She picked up her purse daintily and pranced out of the room.

"Spoonful of sugar makes the mayonnaise go bad..."

The other guy shook his head. He stared at the door Loretta had just gone through, then at the ice bucket, then at Olive, naked and singing on the bed. He shook his head again and looked at me. "Sometimes I wish I was a bus driver. Come on, he'll be fine. When he comes to, he'll think it was a small price to pay. I'll take you to the airport."

I just nodded. Las Vegas is nice, I thought. Lots of interesting people. But I was pretty sure it wasn't my home.

The Land of Debris

"This ain't Nawlins, I guaron-tee that, bud. Whoo-ee! None o' that fancy dancy whoo-dall and fall-derall down thisa' way, no sir. This here's the gritty true of the thing, what I'm sayin', the gritty true. You eatin' some o' that jen-you-wine Cajun cookin' now, bud, not like that Nawlins shit. Crayfish so fresh one'll bite jer nose you don't git 'im chunked down quick like. Whoo-ee! Not like that Nawlins shit. More coffee?"

"Sure. Where did you say I was?" I pushed my cup toward him. The man behind the counter had shrimp-pink skin, a sweaty forehead that stretched to the top of his head, and a belly the size of three watermelons. A dilapidated stationwagon of a man.

"You's between heaven and a pretty woman, son. Heaven and a pretty woman. Bo's Place, edge of the swamp, best of the best for God's true. And you just off the bus in each and every sense of the word."

"I'm looking for the Band on TV and the Homely Parade."

"Well, now, sure you are son, as you said before. And sure as Jesus' mama never slow danced with strangers, you's found what you been lookin' for. I guar-on-damn-tee. Now ain't that the most righteous coffee to ever slippy-slide down your throat?" He filled my cup with thick brown fluid; I finished eating my craw dads, rice, and green weeds.

"It's fine coffee. Are you Bo?" I hadn't seen anyone else since I'd come in an hour ago. The place was a wooden shack on a mud road somewhere in Louisiana, with six tables and a Formica counter. It looked like it was about to sink into the wet ground. It looked like it ought to sink into the ground. The air was muggy as a locker room. An electric fan in the corner pushed the greasy smell around. But the food was good. Especially for something that looked like big cooked bugs.

"Born Bo, been Bo, be buried Bo, I warrant." He laughed and whooped and did a little dance step. The old wooden floor creaked and shook beneath his weight. Then he leaned on the counter, his fast-talking silliness gone for the moment. "Now, what's the deal, son? You didn't dangle-foot in here 'cause your travel agent recommended it. You been sashayin' and buck dancing like a swamp-bug on a hot grill. Why'd ya' need to see old Bo?"

I took a deep breath. Sometimes you just have to trust somebody. Even if you shouldn't. Even if it's a stupid risk. Right now, my need to trust somebody outweighed the risk of being stupid. Anyway, Bo seemed pretty reliable.

"I was on an airplane flying out of Las Vegas," I said. Bo grimaced, but said nothing. "And I was sitting next to this woman of color. A... substantial woman. She called herself Magnolia."

Bo's eyes lit up. "Ah Magnolia! You talked to Magnolia? Lord, it's been what, two, three years? What a woman! Fat as a lard truck and twice as greasy. But whoo-ee! Can that woman dance! Takes her a little bit to git all them wheels and pistons turnin' and a'cranking, like a big old train on a cold mornin', but once you get her a'shakin' and a rollin' and she'll wear out a dozen good men, one night, Lord a'mercy! Never saw a woman move like ol' Magnolia, all that good black skin just a wigglin' and a jigglin'. Tell me, how'd she look, bud? She look all right?"

"She looked fine. Real healthy. Said to tell you watch out, she'd come down some dark night and skin your fat... that is, she said she'd be disappointed if she ever hears you're with another woman."

"Whoo! Lord a'mercy! I can hear her now. But she don't need worry. The woman flat spoiled me for the rest of her gender. Them pretty little girls come flirtin' with ol' Bo, I cain't even see 'em. Tells 'em don't even waste yer juice. Happens all the time."

"Right," I said. "Anyway, she said she could tell something was bothering me, and so I told her, and she said I should come see you. Told me what bus to take from New Orleans and everything. Said for a hundred bucks, Bo was my best shot. Said to say she sent me."

Bo looked serious.

"Well, if Magnolia sent you, I'll do what I can. You got a hundred bucks?"

I pulled a new bill from my shirt pocket. I kept the rest in my wallet. Mike's associate had advised me against flashing a lot of money around outside Las Vegas. Said it just makes poor people feel bad. Makes the bad folks want to steal from you, and the rich folks want to advise it away from you, or invest it away from you. Best to let 'em know you can pay your beer tab and that's it. Just before he put me on the airplane, he told me that the one thing he understood about people, after all his years of working with L.V., was that poor people will cheerfully give you their money. Rich people will give you advice.

Bo nodded and slid the bill back toward me. "Only if I can help," he said. "Now, what's the form of tribulation you afflicted with, bud? Voodoo? That's usually it, ain't it. A curse? Some dark-woman spell? Now, come on, boy, you got to give me somethin' to chew on here."

"Well, the truth is, I don't know," I said. "I was in Oklahoma, and I realized that I didn't know who I was. Didn't know my own name, or how I got there, or anything about my past. I just knew this telephone number, but every time I call it, I get a bad connection and a recording that says it's not in service."

"You drink much of that real cheap red wine, son?"

I shrugged. "Don't know. Maybe that's it. Anyway, it's starting to bother me. I thought I was going to die in Las Vegas and that really got my attention. It could be my life is going on somewhere without me. Maybe I'm missing dentist appointments. Maybe I'm missing paychecks or vacations. I might have a lawn that's desperate to be mowed. Or a boat that needs to be painted. Or mail piling up in a mailbox. Maybe somebody loves me and thinks I ran away and they're giving up on me and falling in love with someone else. Maybe they'll take away my seat on the Armed Services Committee. See what I mean? There might be something out there that's important to me that's just slipping away because I can't remember what it is."

"Hmm," he said thoughtfully. "You could be right, sure as you say. That's the way it usually goes, bud. Things slips away when you forget they's important to you. Mean trick, I warrant you that. Helluva goddamn mean trick."

"So Magnolia said that there's a lot of things you can try in a case like that. And something's going to work. But she said I looked like a guy who would read books to find an answer, or go to somebody's office, or take a quiz in a magazine. White stuff, she called it. She said that wasn't bad or anything. Nothing wrong with white stuff. It's just not the only stuff. And she said I was one of those guys who might never try the stuff that was a little harder to find, just 'cause I wouldn't know about it, and she said you were the guy I ought to go to. I don't know what she's talking about, really. But that's my story."

"So you been kickin' around a bit, tryin' this'n that and it ain't cooked your chicken for you?"

"I've done some traveling," I said. "And I met some folks. But I don't know that I've tried to do much of anything. You know, really tried. Now I want to."

"Mmm, yes, sure as you say. Didn't try,'cause you didn't know what to try."

"I guess so."

"But you remember some things?"

"Yeah. Funny stuff. I know the capitals of all the states. I remember different actors, a few musicians, some songs, things like that. I know whole Star Trek episodes by heart, for example. It's weird to know Captain Pike's life on Talus Four better than I know my own." I paused. I didn't know how to put this. "So what exactly do you... do?"

He whooped and laughed and stamped the floor. Then he was calm again.

"I just knows folks, son, that's all. I just knows folks. This little spot's kinda' unusual. We right on the edge of the bayou, we got Cajuns comin' and goin' all the time. This is about the last spot the buses and trucks get to. I got a little store round back, sell that sugar and kerosene and coffee in the big cans. Yes sir. But we also close to a little village of black folks, folks from Haiti and Jamaica mixed in with folks lived here since their great granddaddies was slaves. They don't like to live too close to the road, but they come in like the Cajuns. We all friends'round Bo's Place, I guar-on-tee."

He poured himself a cup of thick black coffee and topped off mine.

"They's even a little band of them old-timey Indians always movin' around, movin' and movin', yes sir. They don't talk much, but they leave you alone. It's a big swamp, son. You can flat-bottom for a week and never see sign one of a human. But they out there. Escaped convicts that won't never get caught. Crazy folks that'd get locked up in a city. They just don't know any better, see, but they do fine out in the wet country. No crazier than a big old mama gator, I warrant. And they all know ol' Bo, yes sir. They all know ol' Bo. Well, one of them swamp people might have what you need. And you won't find it in any magazine quiz. You come to the right place, all right."

I hoped it was not one of the crazy people or escaped convicts that had my answer. I hoped it was a nice Cajun family, and they'd say, shoot, you just got to drink some red wine and dance to accordion music and your memories will return. Or a pretty girl from Jamaica with skin the color of coffee with cream, who could sing some soft magical song, something from an old Belafonte album, and make my spell disappear. Or even a big black woman like Magnolia, who could perform some voodoo ritual. A few pins in a doll, burn a little incense, clap your hands three times, and presto. This is your life.

"So how do I start?"

"That's the simple thing. I've decided I can help you. You give me a hundred bucks. Kinda like a good faith deposit, ya know?"

I nodded, not at all surprised, and gave it to him. He stuffed in his shirt.

"Good boy, and that's the gritty truth, yes sir. You onto it now. You be ol' Bo's guest until we get you figgered. Sounds like a woman to me, off the bat, or voodoo. It's usually one or t'other, you know. But now you my guest. Startin' right there."

He pointed at my plate, empty except for a few bits of crustacean tail and some antennae and things that looked like insect eyes.

"The meal?"

"Yes sir. On the house. "

"Well, thank you," I said.

"Not at all. You tote your stuff on back through this clearing here, see that little pathway? You bet. Back that-a-way. I got me a little house back there, and a guest house to boot. Ain't fancy, but it's free. Tonight we go flat-bottomin'."

I got up to go. There was something else Bo wanted to say, and he cleared his throat.

"You say Magnolia looked pretty good, did ya?" His voice was quiet.

"She looked real strong to me."

"Ain't that God's truth! Ain't nobody messes with that woman." He looked down at the floor. "And she said she might come down and see ol' Bo?" I swear the man was blushing.

"I think you can count on it."

"Lord a'mercy!" he said softly and shook his head. "Would that be somethin'!"

The "guest house" was a creaking carcass of a shed that was being slowly sucked into the muddy ground. Standing inside, you could look in any direction and see light through the planks. Bo had nailed screening to the inside of the walls and ceiling, probably to keep out the bugs. My guess was that the bugs that lived around here could karate-kick their way through both the rotten wood and rusty screen if they thought there was a meal inside. At least there was a cot and a kerosene lamp, and a tree outside the crooked door covered with huge white blossoms the size of my head that smelled like the perfume section of a big department store.

I lay down to test the cot. The air was hot and sweet and still and full of moisture. An army of birds chirped and whistled outside. Insects made low, lazy, buzzing sounds. A drop of sweat fell from my nose to my lips and I licked the salt away. The cot was hard beneath me, but not unpleasant. Light through the planks and from the single window made blurred designs on the wooden floor.

I must have dozed off, because the next thing I knew Bo was outside knocking on the door and it was dark.

"Up and at 'em, Slick," he said. "Rise and shine. Sleep too long out here and the moss'll grow between your toes. Come on, come on. That's a way."

I stumbled out the door. The moon was full and red through the humidity. The air felt just as hot as it had in the daytime and the birds and insects as noisy. The moonlight softened everything into dreamy patches of mellow light and black velvet shadows. A bat swooped past, low and fast and silent.

"Where are we going?"

"I have some errands to tend to, bud. And you comin' along for the ride. You can meet some folks, let them see you. These folks a little shy sometimes. Can't tell what a guy from the city might be about, ya know? Ain't nothin' gonna happen tonight. We just gonna run some errands." He pulled a bottle of whiskey from his back pocket and took a swig. "Insect repellent," he explained, wiping the mouth of the bottle with a corner of his shirt. "You better have some too."

"No thanks," I said. He insisted.

"You be nothin' but clean white bones time we get back you don't protect yourself, son. Here take a bit."

The stuff burned my throat and nose and made my eyes water.

"Made it myself," he said. "I just use this fellow's bottles." He pointed to the white-haired gentleman pictured on the label. "They don't understand insect repellent up there in Kentucky. Come on."

We walked down the path toward a creek where his boat was tied. Fireflies turned on, flew in gentle zigzags for a moment, then casually turned off amid the bushes and weeds as he started the motor. The boat was comfortably wide, an oversized rowboat with a flat bottom. A half-dozen cardboard boxes were stacked toward the rear. The engine was noisy, drowning the sound of bugs and birds and the occasional eerie hoot or howl. Still, the swamp seemed very mysterious, a deep and secret place, a place for vampires and silent sliding snakes and slow moving phosphorescent ghosts and huge shadowy fishes and insane murderers who hide behind trees to stalk unsuspecting newcomers. We rocked from side to side as he eased the craft through the water. I reached over the side and let my fingers trail through the warm water.

"Know what we call that?" Bo pointed to my hand. I shook my head. He lit a cigarette and blew the smoke into the night. The water felt good moving through my fingers. "Trollin' for gators."

I pulled my hand out of the water and dried it quickly on my jeans. Bo chuckled. He steered easily through channels that connected to lakes, that narrowed to passageways between hills, then spread to marsh meadows before constricting again in a twisting maze of waterways — a liquid roadway that existed on no map. Sometimes we'd head straight for a thicket drooping with Spanish moss and vines. He'd slow down and we'd go right through, ducking our heads as he somehow found a passage beneath the leafy canopy.

"Watch this," he said, slowing the boat, letting it drift in a broad expanse of water. He aimed a flashlight onto the water. It reflected a dozen of pairs of fire-red eyes floating on the surface.

"Gators," he said simply. "Best meat in the world." We moved on. The swamp was not merely spooky in a vague psychological way, real prehistoric violent danger lurked just beneath the water's surface and slithered through the vegetation. Hungry things and poisonous things and evil things watched us, waiting for a mistake.

He eased the nose of the boat onto a sandy bank and turned off the motor. "Come on now, son," he said. He handed me a box to carry, took one himself, and we walked down a path in the moonlight. A cluster of ramshackle homes emerged from the darkness ahead of us, their windows yellow with lantern light. I could hear someone playing blues on a cheap guitar, and, much farther away, the sound of drums. The two were not related. They were like radios tuned to different stations surrounded by the night sounds that enveloped us as soon as the boat motor no longer kept them at bay.

"Hey, Bo," a deep male voice startled me.

"Hey, Mr. Whitney," Bo spoke toward the shadows on a porch.

"You gone kinda' uptown ain't you? Hirin' help to do the heavy work." The voice was slow and relaxed. A lazy musical bass.

"Lord a'mercy, I try," Bo said. "I do try. Sooner'r later they all want paid, though. Ain't figured past that one yet."

The shadows laughed, low and easy.

"Reckon thats'a stuff I ordered?"

"Reckon so. Where d'ya want it?"

"I s'pose you could set it about anywheres. Right where you standin' might not be bad."

We set the boxes down.

"This fella here was sent by Magnolia," Bo said. "That so?"

"Yes sir," Bo said. I decided I'd talk if somebody asked me a question. I still couldn't make out a person on that dark porch. "He might be needin' a session."

"Hmm." The man made it sound like a long word, with many syllables, rising and falling, a whole sentence comprised of a single low humming sound.

"He'll be with me a spell, like as not. We'll come visit. Magnolia herself might be stoppin' in."

"Hmm." The shadow on the porch made a whole new sentence of the hummed sound. This time there was surprise and pleasure. "That would be somethin'."

"Whoo-ee! I hope to shout. Bet your daddy's suspenders. Lord a'mercy! Anyway, he's all right." There was a long pause. "Yeah, he's all right."

"What kinda' session you figger we'd be havin?"

"You're the expert, Mr. Whitney. He lost his memory. That's all I know. You know me, I just cook and sell life's little necessities."

"Lost his memories? Ha! Nobody loses their memories. They get took, that's what. The problem I see is findin' out who it was took 'em. Or what it was. I guess I could ponder on it a bit. 'Specially you says Magnolia might be down herself."

"It's what she told him. Yes sir."

"Hmm."

"Anyway, I got errands to run. You don't let them skeeters eat you dead, hear, Mr. Whitney?"

"I got me some fine new insect 'pellent."

Bo laughed. "We be seein' you."

"Hmm. "

We went back to the boat, eased it off the bank, and headed deeper into the swamp. The motor sounded a little muffled, a natural part of the soft, hot blackness. I had no idea how Bo could tell where we were or where we were going. After a while he slowed the boat and pulled up next to a huge tree that was growing right out of the water. "Ain't no way this fellow'll show hisself tonight. Not with a stranger along. We just leave his stuff here.

185

He'll pay me bye and bye." He set a small box in a low crook of branches, then turned the boat back to the center of the channel.

The swamp changed as we traveled farther. The waterway deepened, becoming more like a river and less like a marsh. The land became more hilly, with a few areas that were not thickly congested with vegetation. In daylight they might have been meadows or fields. A wooden dock materialized ahead of us. Bo skillfully parked the boat beside it.

"Grab me up them boxes, son." Bo stood on the dock and I handed them to him. We walked up a hill of thick wet grass that was alive with fireflies, their cool white flares advertising enduring insect lust. Beyond the hill stood a dozen houses. I could hear someone strumming soft slow chords on a banjo, not frenetic bluegrass or ragtime. Just a chord, then silence, then another chord. Someone else was playing an accordion with them, equally soft and easy, a one note melody. Children yelled at each other in the distance. A mother's voice threatened them, a wooden screen door slammed. Dogs started barking as we approached a house.

"That you, Bo?" A woman's silhouette appeared against the half-opened door, a yard light came on.

"Hell no," Bo said. "It's old Scratch come lookin' for souls to take on home and roast. Who you think it is?"

The woman laughed. She sounded young. "Well, I figger if there's a buck to be made, it's either Bo or old Scratch. But them dogs don't bark so much if it's only the Devil."

"I got me a helper tonight. Dogs don't know 'im."

"That so?"

"Yes, ma'am. Friend of Magnolia's." We stood on her porch, each of us holding a box. The light from inside lit my face and reflected off Bo's forehead as she inspected me quickly, but her face was still shadowed. She opened the door wider and stepped aside.

"Well, don't stand outside all night," she said. "Bring that stuff on in." She turned and yelled into the darkness. "Hush, you dogs, or I'll sell you to a city boy." She put a hand gently on my shoulder as I walked through the doorway and spoke softly. "No offense. It's just a sayin'."

We walked through a small, neat living room to a kitchen lit by a single electric light. What a wonderful luxury, electricity. My eyes had become so accustomed to the darkness that it seemed very bright. We put the boxes on the big wood table.

"How about some berry wine?" the woman asked pleasantly, following us into the kitchen. She was in her early thirties, dressed simply in jeans and a dark blue blouse. She wore her long brown hair in a ponytail. She was pretty and clean and her eyes were alive. She seemed out of place in the swamp. "Or are you too full of your own vile home brew?"

"Lord a'mercy, a small glass would be just fine, Marci."

She smiled, nodded, and poured us each a glass of crimson liquid. It was sweet and strong with just a little carbonation. I thanked her.

"Here's your money, Bo. I do appreciate your totin' these out here for me." She turned to me. "They ain't no bookstores quite this far out. Nor shoppin' malls, either."

"I sure didn't see any," I said.

She opened a box. "Did you get that sheet music?" There was a little excitement in her voice.

"You bet I did, honey. Marci's a fine piano player, Merle. Just got herself a new piano. That's gonna make this swamp a little easier to take, ain't it?

She smiled. "Gonna make it heaven," she said.

"Is little Jeff about?" Bo asked.

She nodded. "Just like always. He's out back workin' away." There was pride and a little sadness in her voice. "But he ain't so little any more."

"Grab up your wine, son. They's somebody you got to meet."

We walked out the kitchen door, a flimsy frame of wood with screening stretched tight over it. A spring slammed it behind us. I couldn't see a thing in the darkness. As if reading my mind, a light came on over the door and lit a pathway. There was a shed behind the house. Light shone beneath the door.

"Yes, sir," Bo said quietly, "This fellow is somethin' else." He opened the door. Inside was a teenage boy with shaggy dark hair sitting on a stool, carving on a block of wood. He was probably about the same age as Earnest.

"Hey, Jeff," Bo said.

"Hey yourself, Mr. Bo." The boy's face lit up, but his voice was slow and awkward. He did not look away from his carving, but he kept smiling shyly.

"You got no time for licorice?"

The boy said nothing, but he tapped on his chisel a little faster and his grin got a little bigger.

"Well, shoo-ee, that's a sad case, when a boy got no time for life's finer pleasures. Don't you agree, bud?"

"It's hard for me to imagine," I said. Bo had a little paper sack full of candy. He set it on the floor next to Jeff.

"I want to show my friend here some o' your work, Jeff. Would you mind if I did that?"

Jeff just tapped a little faster, grinned, and looked away.

"Come on back here," Bo said. I followed him past piles of junk to a shelf against the back wall full of wooden sculptures. "Ol' Jeff, he don't talk much," Bo whispered. "And he ain't never learned to read or do much of anything. He just ain't got that kind of mind. But Lord a'mercy, can the boy cut on wood!"

It was true. There were dozens of shiny-smooth wooden animals leaping and dancing and swooping, living things that seemed only momentarily still. A hawk perused a rabbit. A cougar leaped from a branch. A dog scratched his ear.

"These are really good," I said in amazement.

"I hope to shout," Bo said. "Marci lived in the city for a time before she had the boy. Went to regular school and all. Could o' done just fine. But when they saw that Jeff was slow, her old man split, and she knew it wouldn't work. They wanted to put Jeff in some institution. She couldn't afford that, and it weren't right anyway. Came back up here where he'd fit in a little better. Swamp don't care much if you're like everybody else. And the folks stick together. Then they found out how he can cut wood."

"Do they sell these?"

Bo chuckled. "I should say! Jeff's got hisself a little industry goin'. I haul his stuff to the city every now and again. Them folks thinks it's gold. He don't know, o'course. Don't care. His mama saves up every dime. Says someday there might be somethin' he wants real bad, and then he can get it with his own money." He paused. "'Course, that won't happen. He won't ever want nothin' real bad. He's got everything in the world right now." He paused again. "He bought that piano for her. Only time I saw him get kinda firm. Told her she was going to get it, and if it was his money and he could buy what he wanted, that's what wanted. Sounded like her daddy or somethin' just for that little bit. We had to pontoon the thing in special."

We walked back to the front of the shed and watched Jeff chip away at his wood, slowly releasing an antelope from within it. I could almost see a gleam in the animal's eyes as it was finally able to stretch its long legs and leap free. From the happy look on Jeff's face, he could see it too. Piano music drifted through the muggy night. There was a little black drop of licorice juice on the corner of Jeff's mouth.

I lived in the swamp with Bo for two weeks, sharing my cot with various flying and crawling critters. I adapted to the humidity, the heat, spicy rice with stir-fried arthropods, and Bo's speech patterns. I made no progress toward regaining my memories. Because of some sort of misunderstanding about the monthly bill, Bo's telephone wasn't working so I couldn't try the number. But now I had something else to distract me. We were headed toward what Bo would describe only as a "big meeting."

"That's our spot," Bo said softly. The boat's engine puttered slowly as we coasted toward a hill rising from the dark water. Twilight suffused the swamp with a golden glow. The hillside before us was remarkable only for its lack of trees. The knee-high grass looked like something snakes would enjoy.

"Toss me that tie-down," Bo said, stepping out of the boat and into the warm water. I gave him the rope, he pulled the boat onto the muddy shore and tied it to a massive log next to several other boats.

Just beyond the hill, two dozen people were busy setting up camp. They erected several large tents around a campfire, strung kerosene lanterns from poles, and boiled coffee on camping stoves. The smell of food cooking assaulted me: meats and spices, oregano and pepper and cayenne. Insects and birds chattered; they never slept.

An indescribable assortment of people arrived by boat and on foot as the twilight faded and the kerosene lanterns lit the area in flickering yellow. Thin, hard, quick-eyed men in worn clothing drifted from shadow to light and back again. Closer to the fire, smiling black men in T-shirts and jeans joked. Their wives, in bright cotton dresses, gossiped and clucked at the packs of noisy, happy children that raced through the camp. Freckle-faced men wore straw hats and short-sleeved shirts; some maintained a handy pack of cigarettes under their sleeves. Heavy women laughed loudly while they attacked their cooking projects like field generals. Dark-eyed Indians hung back at the edge of the light. Other figures, even more shadowy, lurked in practiced stillness in the darkest spots. Everyone was welcome. Every shade of skin was represented and irrelevant. Old men teased young girls. The girls feigned embarrassment and pretended to ignore eager young men who strutted for their benefit. Excitement filled the air. This was not a routine get-together.

Magnolia had come. Huge and regal and pitch black, she was the queen of this court and her presence was the center of every circle. She wore a simple green dress, a tent for her bulk, and stood like a continent while people swirled around her, her eyes half closed, a dreamy, confident smile on her face. The woman radiated something. If she had been young and pretty, I would have called it sex. But she was neither young nor pretty. Still, people were drawn to her. They wanted to touch her and listen to her low voice and make her laugh. She was a mountain of a woman, full of power and life. Maybe it was sex, after all.

Magnolia had summarized her life for me on the plane. She grew up in the bayou, but had gone to college in New Hampshire. The cadences of the Deep South faded in and out of her speech. For just an instant she'd sound like a Yankee professor, then like an escapee from Gone With the Wind.

"All right, boy," she said to me. Her voice was deeper than mine. "We got food to eat and liquor to drink. We ain't got all night to get you set to rights. Why don't you explain your problem to Magnolia one more time. Don't leave out nothing."

She sat on a tree stump next to the fire, I sat on an aluminum folding chair.

"I don't remember who I am," I began. She held up a hand and I stopped.

"I don't think that's precisely what you mean, Sunshine. I think you know who you are. What you forgot is who you used to be."

It seemed a semantic fine point, but I agreed.

"First thing you ought to think on is this: you got it better than most folks. Most folks remember who they used to be, but they got no idea who they are right now. Go on."

"Yes, ma'am. Anyway, all I remember is this phone number, but it's not working any more. It's the only clue I've got."

"I see. Well, now, it could be a clue all right. But then again, it might not be. That's the hard part of detective work. Sorting out which things are clues."

"It's all I've got."

"You always got more than you think you got. Tell me what you tried so far."

I told her about Oklahoma, and New Mexico, and Oregon, and Las Vegas.

"And I haven't remembered much except some TV shows and a couple songs."

"And you sure you want your old life back?"

"Of course I do! Who wouldn't?"

Magnolia stared into the fire. "I had a good friend once. Darlin' woman, pretty as spring. Married a guy who took to drinkin'. A nasty drunk, beat her up all the time.

But she couldn't leave him. Just couldn't do it. Couldn't leave him, couldn't stop him. If I'd been around, I'd a killed him myself. But she was too damn sweet. They found her body in a little meadow, pretty little wildflowers all around her, still holding his shotgun." She paused. "Shotgun's a helluva way to do yourself."

"I'm sorry."

"It was a long time ago. Point is, I wish she'd lost her memories, forgot who she was and where she lived. Every day of my life I wish that."

"And you think I've got something terrible in my past?"

"Not up to me to know. I'd just be guessin'. It's up to you. You ain't bad off just the way you are."

"But it's my life. I want it back."

Magnolia shrugged. "You sure? How hard you tried?"

"I think about it all the time. I try to call this phone number and…"

"You been to a doctor?"

"What?"

"A doctor. First thing anybody'd suspect is you got hit in the head."

"I don't have a bump…"

She laughed, the way a mountain range would laugh. "If you really wanted them memories back, first thing you would'a done is found a doctor. But I don't believe you got conked in the head."

"Then what did happen?"

"You just shut down part of your brain. Maybe for a little bit, like an experiment. Maybe forever. Part of you still remembers everything. You just got that part turned off."

"Why would I do that?"

"Death or love, Sunshine. Death or love. Someone close to you dies, part of you closes up like a flower. Lose too many flowers, you might as well go dormant for the winter. Come spring, you heal up a bit and start sproutin' memories like dandelions on a new lawn.

"Love's different. Love's the meanest bastard Nazi ever played doctor on his prisoners. But lord, can he waltz! He puts on that fine, crisp uniform, with his medals gleaming and his hair slicked back, and holds out his hand. I swear, your sores'll still be oozing, but you'll limp out onto the dance floor. You don't let yourself think about tomorrow morning, and that clanging bell, and the cold white room. Sometime the only smart thing to do about love is forget it. You might'a just took things a bit far."

"Love or death, eh?"

"That's right, Sunshine. That's where I'd put my money."

"So what do I do?"

"Rituals. Only way to deal with spirit matters is rituals. Always has been. But you got a special problem. You don't remember yours. You might've been raised in some church, taught yourself to believe in its dance book. If you'd been raised to voodoo, we'd be set." She looked at me for a moment then shook her head. "Kind of unlikely. Business folk got rituals, farmers got 'em, everybody's that's got any spirit left in 'em at has their own brand. But you, you got to make up your own."

"I don't know how."

"Ain't no rule book, Sunshine. But deep inside, you know. That's the problem with civilization. Folks think someone else got to make up their rituals for 'em. Every now and again, someone finds somethin' works for them. Everybody else just copies his rituals for a few hundred years. Might work for 'em, might not. Sooner or later, you got to make up your own. Them's the clues you need to look for. Something'll ring a bell in you. You try it and see if it works. Can't be feeling silly, can't worry how you look. Thinking about it won't do you no good. You got to do something. Almost anything. Now, tell me again what you remember."

"I remember some science facts, some things about business…"

"That's good. Maybe you made money as a scientist, or a businessman. But your job might not be the part of you you're looking for."

"I remember some songs…"

"I like that. Music. Lots of folks use music. We can jump-start that engine."

I felt impatient. "But what do I do?"

"You got to go inside yourself, look in a real deep mirror. Everybody's got a whole raft of folks inside 'em. There's a big old monster you crank up when you get mad. Everybody's got one. You got a little kid that feels sorry for hisself. Your mama's in there somewhere, and maybe your papa, if you knew him. You got Jesus, and the Devil, and a bunch of animals, and maybe an angel or two." She winked at me. "Your case, I bet you got a pretty girl or two in there most of the time. Shoot, Sunshine, all that noise and confusion inside a person, sometimes you just got to shut 'em all up." She stretched and looked over toward the food.

"Now, you go fill up a plate, no need to do this hungry. Just don't let Bo pour any of his wicked home brew down your gullet. When it gets a little darker, we'll get you started. Just remember, you didn't live your life in one night, no reason you have to get it all back in one night either. Easy does it."

A United Nations smorgasbord was spread out on card tables and makeshift benches. Crabs and shrimp and chicken lounged in thick spicy sauces. White rice and corn steamed in the darkness. Beef sizzled, coffee pots perked cheerfully over Coleman stoves, carrots and potatoes baked together in the campfire. Green leafy vegetables were punctuated with slices of bright red peppers. A pot of gumbo sat beside a colorful bowl of fresh sliced fruit in a sweet liquor. Marci poured me a glass of her dark wine, while Jeff stood shyly behind her. Bo toasted every woman there, and several that weren't there. He toasted his favorite football team, Robert E. Lee, every bowl of food, most of the planets, and several Norse gods.

Finally, everyone was full; the youngest children were sleeping. My head buzzed with Marci's pleasant wine. Magnolia approached me.

"You set yourself down on that little mound, Sunshine, we'll get this show on the road."

I did as I was told. I was nervous but felt I had no choice. The grass was damp beneath me, the air was still very warm. She nodded in the direction of an old black man who hobbled toward us and sat on the ground a few feet away. Two young boys brought him a hollowed-out tree stump with alligator hide stretched tight across it. He spit into his hands, rubbed them together, and struck it with his palm.

Whump! The drum made a very low sound. He nodded his head in time to some internal metronome.

Whump! People looked in our direction.

Whump! Magnolia nodded. Yes, just like that, she seemed to say. Another man came and sat beside him, a fiery Cajun with red hair. He held a copper kettle upside down between his crossed legs. He listened to the old man for a few minutes, nodding his head, stretching his fingers, and nibbling bits of shrimp that clung to the inside of the kettle. Then, using only his index fingers, he started to tap on the kettle, just a few beats, in-between the old man's steady bass. One by one others joined them,

forming a circle around me. Each one had a handmade
drum of some sort: drums made of old metal barrels; of
boxwood covered with leather; mayonnaise jars with metal
lids, partly filled with water. Deep drums beat a slow
steady pace, others tapped higher and more urgent, conga
drum sounds and bongos and frantic little rappings in layers of syncopation. Each drummer found his own pattern,
immersed himself in it and repeated it over and over again
until it was part of the larger rhythm, and he was part of
it. Then someone would change their beat, just a little
and that single subtle shift changed the entire sound. I
could feel the intensity of this activity, the attempt to keep
track of the incredibly complex interplay of sounds as it
evolved, while each player maintained his own distinct
pattern.

I relaxed into the sound, releasing conscious control. It was not a mental activity. My brain couldn't keep
track of the rhythms. This was deeper and more primitive
than thought. Not something you make yourself do. You
had to let yourself do it. Magnolia sat beside me and set a
copper pot on the ground. She lit a twisted rope made of
twigs and leaves, then blew it out. Bittersweet smoke rose
from it as she put it in the little incense pot and blew on it.
Then she sprinkled other leaves on top and the scent
changed just a little.

"I'm a healer, son," she said, taking my hand and
holding it between her own huge hands. You need
healin'?"

"I don't think so," I said. "I'm not sick. I just can't
remember who I am."

She nodded gravely, like a doctor.

"Happens all the time." She stared at me. "You
got kind eyes, son. You ain't a criminal." It was as if she
could read my deepest fear. I did not want to learn I was
someone I despised. She leaned her head back and

laughed. "Leastways, you don't have a criminal's mean soul. Altogether possible you broke some laws. If so, you ain't alone in this crowd. Anything like that ring bells in yer head?"

I remembered the gas station attendant in Oklahoma who thought I might be an escaped convict. I blushed. She smiled, her white teeth bright piano keys against her face.

"Don't matter to me, son. Your eyes, that's what matters. You don't scare ol' Magnolia." I could not imagine a truckload of terrorists scaring her.

"Thanks."

"Like I say, it happens all the time. More than you'd think. And what kind of folks d'ya suppose it happens most to?"

People who've done something terrible, I thought. I shook my head and said nothing.

"Healers, son. Healin' takes a lot out of a body. But if it's in yer blood, if you got the gift, you jest can't say no, someone needs healin'. Only way to get a vacation is to forget who you are for a spell. Then, when you strong again, it all comes back to you."

She laughed again.

"There's one old coot I know, fine man, but crazy as a loon. Thinks it happened to Jesus Christ hisself. Believes every word of the Bible right up to where Jesus ascends to Heaven. He thinks The Man just lost his memory for a while, like healers do, and they added all that fancy stuff just to make the story better. Thinks Jesus probably got a job building houses or sanding floors. Thinks he's still out there, healin' hisself, waitin' till it all comes back to him."

She smiled and shook her head.

"'Course, some days the old coot thinks it's him. Believes he's Jesus Christ, living in a two-room hole above a topless joint in The Quarter, moppin' floors to pay the rent. So I guess you never can tell."

"I don't think I'm Jesus."

"That's a start, son. That's a fine start. But hell, don't rule it out." Her eyes twinkled with firelight.

"I'm pretty sure."

She shrugged. "Fine by me. But the answer ain't out here." She gestured broadly toward everything in the world. "Answer's inside your own head. All we can do is help you relax a bit, tell you it's OK to remember, whenever you ready. Might come back a bit at a time, might wash in sudden, like a flood. Might never come back, none of it. Would that be the worst thing in the world?

Maybe not, I thought. But it is what I spent a hundred bucks for.

"Forgettin' you a healer ain't the worst thing," she said, answering her own question. "Way worse, all those folks that never know they got the gift."

"How can they not know?"

"Because they never try to use it, son. They never even try. So they never know. Saddest thing in the world."

"So what do we do?"

"You just sit there and look around inside yourself. And I'll sit right here and protect you. I won't let nothin' bad happen to you, son. You believe that?"

I nodded. No one was going to mess with me while Magnolia was holding my hand.

Beyond the drummers, people gathered to watch. I felt conspicuous sitting in the center, but gradually the feeling dissipated. Faces glowed with wine and laughter and firelight. No one watched me especially. Eyes closed, or half-closed and unfocused, they nodded in time and swayed. A young woman rotated her shoulders sensuously as the beat began to saturate her body. In another situation she would have kept my attention all evening. But I was busy being a Mayan priest, trying to invent a ceremony that did not require bloodletting.

I closed my eyes. "Don't fall asleep, Sunshine," Magnolia whispered. "Just look inside yourself. Look for clues." She released my hand and began kneading my shoulders with her powerful hands. "You tight as a banjo string, Sunshine. You got to tune that string lower and lower. Take some deep breaths and push all that crap out'a your insides. Don't need to worry about it. You safe here. Ol' Magnolia ain't gonna let them demons touch you here. You safe, Sunshine."

Her fingers pushed at the knotted ropes in my shoulders and I felt them softening. She was right. Surrounded by escaped convicts and renegade Indians and wild-eyed Cajun musicians and the descendants of runaway slaves and illegal Cuban refugees and men too crazy to survive in the city, I felt safe.

I nodded my head to the complicated beat of the makeshift orchestra and let my mind drift. The noisy music pushed aside all my internal chattering and confusion. I reached out, not like a dying man for a buoy or a hungry man for food, but gently, as one would reach to touch the smooth marble of a fine sculpture. Or perhaps as someone would reach out to touch a sculpture in a museum he had been admiring just before all the lights went out. I simply relaxed while the music wove a lovely and complex cloud around me.

The swirling clouds coalesced into a woman's face. A beautiful woman with perfect skin and laughing eyes. Her face showed both amusement and exasperation as she watched me. I was patting my pockets and walking around quickly, looking for something.

My feelings were jumbled. The part of me that was inside the vision seemed confused, harried, and embarrassed. Some other version of myself stood offstage, watching the scene, no longer a part of it. As audience, I ignored the character that played me and focused every ounce of my attention on the woman. The swamp disappeared, confusion faded, and warm peaceful joy engulfed, nestled, and rocked me like an infant. I watched her push an errant strand of hair from her forehead and thought I would burst from happiness. She put one hand on her cocked hip and shook her head in exasperation. I wanted to sing a boisterous Greek folk song and dance around her on my knees. But the vision continued.

The woman said, "If you'd just leave your keys the same place every time, then you'd always know where they were." She must have told me that a thousand times.

But I couldn't find them.

Finally she said, "That's OK. I've got time. I'll drop the twins off on my way to work." Then she kissed me quickly on the cheek and ran out the door, leaving a wake of spicy perfume in the air. I inhaled slowly and for a long time, savoring the scent, then held my breath as if I could save it within me.

Then, somehow, I was in a car, driving down a tree-lined street. Birds sang and the sun was bright but traffic moved slowly. It crept a few feet, then stopped, then moved again. Irritated, I honked and shouted at the car ahead of me.

A few moments later I saw the problem. There had been an accident. A car had run a stop light and plowed into another car smashing it to junk. The pavement was wet beneath the two cars. Glass and metal glistened everywhere. As I crept through the intersection, a policeman motioned me to keep moving. Lights flashed and sirens wailed in the distance. There was something very familiar about the car. I tried to figure out what it was, but the sun must have gone behind a cloud because everything suddenly became dark and unfocused. I couldn't see a thing.

I stopped the car without bothering to pull over, as if I was hypnotized. and had been ordered to do so. It never occurred to me to close the car door behind me as I walked away. I ignored the honking horns and angry shouts as I moved between moving vehicles back toward the accident.

People stood on perfect, clean sidewalks staring at the wreckage. Ambulance lights flashed with supernatural brilliance. I pushed my way through the crowd toward the street. I must have looked like some sort of monster because each person I nudged aside reacted identically. They paled, their eyes opened wide, and they stepped back to let me through. Women put their hands to their lips, as if to stifle a scream.

Just as I reached the front of the crowd, something happened that confused me. The lights on the ambulance stopped flashing and it drove slowly away. There was no siren. I breathed a sigh of relief. No siren meant no one had been injured.

Before I could turn and walk back to my life, I saw the vehicle beyond the ambulance. A white van with neat black lettering spelling out the single word "coroner." It made no sense. I'd already decided that no one had been injured. Someone had made a terrible mistake. It was all too confusing; I felt faint and there was no reason to stay there. Reality had been cracked open like an egg and drained of all substance, leaving only a fragile shell rocking on the basement floor of the universe. I retreated, pushing my way back through the crowd. When I reached the open sidewalk, I began to run as fast as I could, ignoring traffic, stumbling on uneven pavement, crossing streets to screeching tires, honking horns, and cursing drivers. I ran for five or six blocks, seeing nothing until I came to a familiar bar, an oasis of reality in a desert of surreal images.

"Straight tequila," I said to the bartender, panting like a terrier. I threw a twenty in his direction. "As much as that'll buy."

He poured, I drank, and he poured as if we were two prize fighters exchanging jabs until the hazy blur that soon surrounded me seemed much more real and concrete than the fantasy world outside. This was better.

But walking was a problem I realized as I stumbled toward the men's room, crashing from wall to wall in the narrow hallway. I leaned and rested for a moment, letting the swirling world settle to predictability before proceeding.

A pay phone hung like a saint's statue from the wall. Of course. Everything became clear and beautiful. The Mormon Tabernacle Choir erupted in glorious song and rainbows shot from stained glass windows. I pushed a quarter into the lovely instrument and held my breath. A woman's voice spoke to me and sunshine and gravity returned.

"This is Lana DeVries and the Tones of Toledo Music Store. Please leave a message and I'll get back to you as soon as I can..."

I returned to the bar, my steps steadier. "I need some quarters," I said and gave him a ten.

"Ten dollars' worth?" He sounded surprised.

"Yes. It's all I have on me."

He shrugged and gave me the change.

With heavy pockets I went back to the pay phone and called the number over and over again.

"...I'll get back to you as soon as I can..."

"...Music Store..."

"…back to you…"

Finally I had only two quarters left. Reluctantly I decide to save them. As long as I had them, I had not yet heard that voice for the last time.

An owl called out from deep in the swamp, a banjo joined the drumming, and Magnolia's hand squeezed my shoulder.

"Easy, Sunshine. What did you see?"

"A bar, and some quarters, and I think there was a pay phone. It's all so hazy…"

My cheeks were wet.

"That's fine, then, don't you worry about it. Gonna take a little time, that's all. I'm right here, ain't goin' no place. You just do what you gotta do, and we ain't gonna worry 'bout none of the rest of it. That's it."

I closed my eyes again. But now everything was different. If I had been in a museum before, touching statues gently in the dark, the museum had changed. Now it felt like a prison and each statue and painting became an obstacle in my path. I crashed into things, cursed, stumbled, and struck at everything I touched. I ripped tapestries from doorways and kicked them aside. Pottery and glass shattered around me. If only I had a baseball bat, I thought, I could escape this tangled maze of delicate and useless crap.

Then I was moving quickly and effortlessly through a black tunnel, perhaps a subway…no, I was in a huge cave of some sort, lit infrequently by primitive torches, and riding on something, maybe a horse. As I approached the lighter area near a torch I could see it was no horse. I rode something that looked like a dinosaur and we were barreling along much too fast. I tried to scream, but the rush of air into my open mouth silenced me. I clutched the massive leathery scales beneath me and hung on for my life. We shot like a locomotive through the blackness. A light in the distance rushed toward us.

We burst out of the side of a mountain like a cannonball. The beast kept galloping along, down the hillside, through a meadow, along the bottom of a canyon, and out onto a prairie. I could see a four-lane interstate highway ahead. Civilization! Human beings! Safety! When we reached the pavement, my reptilian vehicle changed its course and started racing down the white line. We began to overtake cars.

"Slow down!" I shouted, but the creature was oblivious. I could imagine the drivers ahead, cruising along, windows rolled up against the outside world, humming absentmindedly to their favorite CD. I could picture them glancing casually into their rearview mirrors, secure in the belief that their radar detectors would protect them. No highway patrol back there, they'd think. A few cars, nothing remarkable except perhaps that one dinosaur barreling down on me at two hundred miles an hour. They'd look away, then they'd jerk their heads back up to stare into the rearview mirror once more in terror and disbelief.

"Slow down!" I shouted again, but it was no use. We were gaining quickly on a big green station wagon.

Its brake lights came on, the car swerved to the right, bounced over the shoulder, landed in a field of green wheat, and just kept going. The monster ignored it. A red sports car screeched to a stop; we sailed right over it. A Mercedes ahead of us did not react at all. We passed it on the left, smoothly, as if it were standing still. I twisted back and for an instant saw its driver, a tiny white-haired woman sitting forward, holding herself up with the steering wheel, squinting through her glasses straight ahead. She never saw us. Two other cars spun off the road in panic.

There was an exit ramp ahead. Billboards advertised gas stations and motels. The reptile didn't bother with the exit ramp. It just slowed to a clumsy trot and plowed through the fences. As we passed through a gas station, the beast's massive body knocked down all the gas pumps and took out a corner of the building.

It crushed cars in the parking lot like aluminum cans beneath its feet. Customers screamed as they ran out of the restaurant. The beast reared back in terror at the sound, then leaped out of the parking lot, onto the highway, and raced back toward the mountain. In seconds we reached the foothills.

Suddenly it stopped, cocking its head to one side, sniffing the air. It crouched low to the ground and inched its way up the hill. When it had slithered near enough, it raised its knobby head and peered over. I raised up a little on its back so I could see too.

Beyond the crest of the hill a road construction crew worked frantically. There had been an accident. A boulder the size of one of the Mount Rushmore heads had fallen on a pickup truck, crushing its bed to the ground. The cab had escaped the full weight of the mammoth stone and protruded from beneath it. The driver was still alive, but trapped inside.

The boulder was just too big. Their huge bulldozers were helpless against it. They cut at the truck metal with torches, but the man was pinned tightly against the frame and they had to stop frequently to let the metal cool. At this rate, they'd cook him before they got him free. Someone said he was losing a lot of blood. I had an idea.

"Could you move that boulder?" I whispered to the beast. It pretended that it couldn't understand me.

"Listen to me, you hippopotamus!" I grabbed a fleshy lump that looked vaguely like an ear and twisted it as hard as I could. The creature winced in pain and whined like a puppy. "You're going to lift that boulder off that truck or I'll beat you back to the Pleistocene. Comprende?"

The beast nodded sheepishly. I released its ear, climbed down, and ran toward the men.

"Hey!" I shouted. "Can I help?"

"Who are you?" They looked at me suspiciously.

"Listen. I've got a piece of equipment that might be able to lift that boulder."

"There's no piece of equipment in the state that could lift that boulder."

"This isn't from around here. "

"If you think you can help, stop talking and get it in here. This man's dying."

"Have your men move away." I clapped my hands together once, authoritatively. The beast lumbered into the light. "Easy now, gentle," I whispered. "This isn't a game."

"What in the hell?" The men gasped.

"They must be shooting a movie around here," one said. "What do you suppose it cost to build that thing?"

"All right now," I said to the monster. "Be careful. The idea is to help them, not kill them." It nodded, concentrating. This was a new concept. Much easier to sashay and swashbuckle over things and let someone else clean up the mess. It was confused.

"Just lift the rock off the truck and set it down over there."

It crouched on its haunches, grasped the rock with its front claws, and easily lifted the boulder.

"See if you can open a hole in the roof of the cab."

With one claw it ripped the metal.

"OK you guys," I shouted. "Come and get him out of there." Men ran to the truck. Their amazement at the beast was tempered by the urgency of the situation. We sat back and watched. In a few minutes the foreman came over to me.

The foreman turned to me. "Exactly what is this thing, anyway?"

"No idea. We just met."

"Is it dangerous?"

I thought about that for a moment. I would not want it in the bathtub with me. "It's not malicious. It just doesn't know any better."

"Hmm."

"Can I buy it from you?" the foreman asked quietly.

"Why would you want it?"

"We build mountain roads. A lot of clearing boulders away, digging, hauling. Boy, with one of those around we'd be ten times as efficient."

I stared at the beast with an odd fondness. It certainly might be useful to a construction crew, and I didn't really have a place to keep it. "It's yours," I said. But the beast turned and began loping back toward its cave and disappeared into the evening.

"And where do you want to go?" the foreman asked.

"Excuse me?" He looked somehow younger now, and his work clothes had become a neat uniform.

"We have several flights leaving the airport in the next hour. What's your destination?" He held out a paper with dozens of numbers and cities listed.

"There," I pointed at random to a city I'd never visited.

"Of course. Will you be charging that today?" I set my wallet on the counter and handed him a credit card. "This will just take a moment."

We shook hands and I walked up the hill. From the top, I heard drums, and a low wailing song. Down below there was a circle of men beating on a variety of home-made instruments with lanterns strung on poles beside them for light. The wailing sound was a huge black woman singing deep and slow. Someone sat in the center of the circle. That's supposed to be me, I thought. The rest was foggy. I walked toward them.

No one noticed as I moved through the crowd like a phantom and joined the fellow sitting in the middle of the circle. Almost immediately the music changed, becoming louder and more intense. The black woman rolled to her feet and shook in time to it. Her formless moaning changed to a melody, a blues song, loud and sharp. An accordion joined in. I heard a washtub bass, then a guitar playing fast chords. A wooden flute played quick trills and a banjo chunked in time. The people in the crowd began to dance, and I could not resist. I stood up and joined them.

It felt good to move around awkwardly to the music. I could almost make out the words to the song: "The Sand of the Sea and the Homeward Refrain…"

Bo danced over to join Magnolia. His skin was flushed, and he held a mason jar of home brew in one hand. His face exploded in a smile as he reached for her hand. She glowed like a lighthouse and rolled like the ocean as they danced away from the crowd to an open area of trampled grass. Bo was a huge little boy, all elbows, knees, and joyful exuberance, whooping and twisting with the music. Magnolia danced like a planet would dance, rotating and orbiting, confident in her own gravity. Everyone else moved back and out of their way. It didn't take memories or brains to recognize two people who were supposed to be together. Or to understand that when you get that much love, and that much mass, up to speed, all you can do is shake your head in wonder and stand clear.

"Drink some coffee."

I opened my eyes. The drums were silent, the sky was beginning to lighten. People slept in clusters around the dying fire.

"What time is it?"

"You got an appointment?" Magnolia laughed, a rolling bass drum of a laugh.

"I guess not."

"Well, then you got time for a cup of coffee." I sipped at the black liquid. "You remember your dreams?"

"Some of them. A little bit. I was looking for a key. Seems like it was just starting, then it was over."

"People's lives are like that, Sunshine, once you get old enough. A quick snap in the bushes behind you. A book you read once."

"And at the end of the book?"

"When a book ends, the good parts get folded up and carried around in somebody's pocket. The rest gets sold at a garage sale for a nickel. I got a bus to catch. You comin'?"

"I ought to say good bye to Bo."

"Good bye's don't do anybody no good. Come on, son. Time you got on with your life."

She started Bo's boat and drove it skillfully back to his store, a contented smile on her face.

"You'll miss Bo, won't you?" I asked.

"Bo's somethin' else, ain't he? But we'd drive each other crazy if we spent too much time together. We don't have one of them every day things. This is the only way it'll work." She turned off the motor. "But hell, yes, I'll miss him."

With a little embarrassment I thought about the hundred bucks I'd paid Bo. Cheap for a two-week vacation. But I had to say something.

"I still don't have my life back."

She nodded and smiled. "Seems to me you got a pretty good life. A person's memories, that's part of him all right, but it ain't who he is. When they write your life story, they'll edit out all them hours of staring out a window. The way you made your living, probably not too important. Hell, son, you know who you are already, and you got a world of choices. Best part, you got no regrets."

I didn't say anything. She thought for a minute.

"A person's what they fear and what they love."

I wasn't sure that was worth a hundred bucks either. But a guy who spent sixty-five thousand dollars for the key to an ankle bracelet might not be the world's best shopper.

I really wasn't afraid of anything, especially, except my own condition. Fear must be a thing one learns, and easy to forget. If I had once been fearful, amnesia was an improvement.

But did I love anything? I thought for a moment. I loved the sun on my face. I loved fried chicken. I loved looking at pretty girls. I loved music, and working hard, and driving down the road. It was a very pleasant list, and everywhere I turned I thought of additions to it. Was that who I was? A list?

I felt unsatisfied. A person is more than the things they love. They are also the people they love. And that's what I'd lost. If I'd ever had any. Somehow, I couldn't make myself say that.

"What if I had hobbies?"

"Buy some cigarettes, learn to smoke. Number one hobby in the country."

A local bus was waiting at Bo's store. We rode in silence to the nearest town. At the depot, buses headed in every direction. I picked a destination at random and bought a ticket. Magnolia hugged me and left on a different bus.

I headed north. The bus ride was sleepy and monotonous, and I lost track of time. We passed swamps and forests and farms. When next I woke, the trees had become more sparse, the fields vast oceans of corn and wheat. The signs said "Kansas." The bus stopped at a small town. I got off and entered a small cafe.

Middle-aged men sat in small groups. A single waitress fussed over them, filling their coffee cups, joking and teasing with each one. I sat at the counter and ordered a hamburger basket. The radio was unobtrusive in the background. This morning's doughnuts and cooking French fries perfumed the air. Fat flies buzzed their daily business. I sipped coffee and waited for my meal.

A tall blond man came in and sat one stool away. He wore jeans and canvas sneakers that had once been white, with holes worn through the sides. He looked vaguely familiar but I said nothing. I had learned that lesson, at least. Trying to be inconspicuous, I observed him.

His features were Scandinavian, he was lanky but with the beginnings of a pot belly. His hair was a mop of fine yellow straw stuck to his head in a random, wind-blown fashion that covered his ears and collar. He wore a light blue long-sleeved shirt rolled to his elbows and not completely tucked in. His short blond beard needed a barber's touch. His eyes were clear and very blue. For a fellow who appeared so disorganized and unkempt, he seemed cheerful and confident. Not sloppy like a bum, exactly, more like someone who just doesn't notice, or care, what they look like. Someone who forgets to look in the mirror before they leave the house.

"So how are you today?" the waitress asked as she gave him a glass of water.

He smiled like she was an old friend. Or like a man who is comfortable with women and simply expects them to like him too.

"Well, on a scale of one to ten..." he paused for effect, "I know I'm on the scale."

God, get this guy away from me, I thought. The waitress giggled and took his order. I couldn't believe she was buying that crap. "And would you like some coffee?"

"It's not a question of like," he said. "It's a question of need." He reached down the counter for a newspaper someone had abandoned.

"What a world," he said in my general direction as he began reading out loud. "Pigs break into secret stash of beer in Kenya, get drunk, and chase the villagers around the town." He shook his head, smiling. "You couldn't make up something like that. Or get this one: 'Lightning kills twenty cows in India'. One bolt. What do you suppose, they were all playing golf together or something?" I didn't answer. "And this is no tabloid. This is a respectable big city newspaper. Oh, I love this one: 'New government study indicates that people who exercise a lot tend to be thinner.' How much money do you suppose they spent on that study? A couple hundred thousand?" He put down the paper for a moment. "You live around here?"

"No," I said. The man had slopped coffee onto his saucer and it dripped from the bottom of his cup onto his shirt when he drank. He hadn't noticed, being more intent on all the bizarre events that had occurred around the world since yesterday morning. As he read, he twisted and ripped his paper napkin relentlessly, building a little pile of debris around him on the counter.

"Me either. Kind of a pretty little town, though, isn't it?"

"I just got here."

"You been down to Winfield?"

"No."

"Biggest bluegrass festival in the country, plus the factory where they make all the colored crayons. Shame to go through Kansas and not hit Winfield."

"Is that where you're going?" I asked.

"Just came from there. Heading for Lawrence. Business. And you?"

"I was on a bus heading north and just decided to get off here. No reason."

"Well, there's probably a reason. You just don't know it yet."

"Could be. What do you do?"

"If you mean, 'what do I do,' like, am I a plumber, well, I do lots of things. I painted a house yesterday in exchange for a neat old guitar. So, I guess I'm a house painter. Last night I made twenty bucks playing the guitar at a bar in Wichita. So I guess I'm a guitarist. Wrote a song once, 'Sometimes I'm Bambi, sometimes I'm Blitzen, but right now I feel like venison.'" He made an exaggerated shrugging gesture. "I do a lot of things. I don't know who I am. Probably not a song writer. How about you?"

I thought for a second. "I'm a businessman." That was broad enough to cover it. I'd made money playing pool, and gambling, and working for a rock star. You make money without a job, you're a businessman. I left it at that. This guy liked to play little word games. A waste of time.

The door opened and a young man burst through. He was a big guy with a wholesome boyish face, probably late twenties, with marvelously neat hair. A Kansas farm boy, I guessed, who stayed in town to raise his family. He carried three cigar boxes under one arm. He stopped just inside the door and waved his other arm around wildly. His mouth opened. All conversation stopped. The waitress whispered, "That's the editor of the local newspaper." Then she spoke out loud. "OK, Joe, don't keep us in suspense. We can tell what happened. Was it a boy or a girl?"

His face lit up like Disneyland at night, but he was so excited the words couldn't find their way to his mouth. Finally they erupted out of him.

"It's a baby!" he shouted. "A perfect baby!" The cafe burst into loud applause and laughter. The man at the counter and I joined in. It was not possible to resist.

"Easy, Joe," the waitress laughed. "Was it a boy or a girl?"

But Joe just nodded his head vigorously, like a six-foot woodpecker on a mountain pine, and began distributing cigars to everyone. I was afraid he'd knock over a table in his exuberance.,

"Here, take two. Hell, take six. I was right there! I saw it. I can't believe it." He handed me a fat cigar, kissed the waitress on the cheek, loud and wet, then scrambled back out the door.

The blond man slipped his cigar into a shirt pocket. "Now that's a man who never really believed in magic until today," he said quietly.

The man offered me a ride to Lawrence. He was working on some complicated deal that made no sense to me and sounded pretty improbable. We got into his old blue Dodge van. "Now, don't get worried or anything," he said as we rolled down the interstate, miles from the nearest town. "I had a flat tire this morning and I'm not sure how long my patch will hold. It's kind of an experiment. I found the hole and injected some house paint into it with a syringe. They're about the handiest tools in the world, syringes. Anyway, I just wondered how that would work." He grinned at the highway stretching before us. "Seems to be holding pretty good. I sure hope it keeps on holding, because I don't have a spare." This did not seem like the prudent approach to the problem. I wished he would have mentioned it to me before I climbed into his rattling, clanking old vehicle. But it was too late now. "If I ever write my life story," he said, "I ought to call it something like 'No Brakes, No Spare.'" He laughed, turned toward me, and arched one eyebrow. "Just kidding," he said. "The brakes aren't all that bad." He patted the dashboard the way Heliotrope patted Michelle. "Don't worry about Big Blue."

I looked around the van. Boxes contained all the implements of living. Cans of food rolled loose on the floor. A pile of clothes spilled from an old pillow case. At the back was a makeshift bed, a mattress sitting on a piece of plywood above the wheel wells. A guitar lay partly concealed beneath a blanket on the mattress. I glanced out the back window and froze.

We were being followed by a white van.

Quickly I turned to stare out the front window.

"You OK?" he asked. I couldn't answer. He looked at me for a long moment, then casually glanced in the rearview mirror. "Friends of yours?"

"I'm not sure."

He nodded, completely unconcerned.

"We could try to outrun them if you want," he said quietly. "Might be a good test for my tire patch. Big Blue ain't scared of nothing."

I thought for a moment.

"I'm not either," I said with as much conviction as I could muster. "No, I don't want to outrun them. I want to catch the bastards."

He looked at me for a moment. "You know, the windmill never loses."

"I don't care."

The blond man smiled and nodded. "No prob," he said. "Let's call their bluff."

He slowed down and vehicles began to pass us. The white van slowed and stayed behind us, too far away to see inside it.

"Kind of pesky, aren't they?" he said cheerfully.

"Pull over," I said.

Without a word or turn signal he turned onto the shoulder and slowed nearly to a stop. The white van slowed but did not follow us onto the shoulder. When it finally passed us and began to accelerate, he turned to me and arched one eyebrow. "Well?" he said. I nodded. He threw the stick into first gear, patted the dashboard, and spoke to his vehicle. "Go get 'em, honey."

The squeal of the van's tires surprised me as our acceleration pushed me back against the seat. He worked the gears smoothly and we began to pass cars. The white van was a quarter of a mile ahead and driving just at the speed limit.

"They won't stop on the interstate," he said. "Might as well settle in and see where they go."

I nodded and we drove an inconspicuous distance behind our prey. I kept my eyes fixed on the white rectangle ahead of us. The blond man seemed to have forgotten about it completely.

"You know what the neatest thing in the world is?" he asked. My mind drifted to all the possibilities: love, money, friends, a dependable car.

"The surface to volume ratio," he said confidently. "You cut something in half. You haven't changed its volume at all, but now it has more surface. Cut it again, and the surface increases again, but the volume doesn't. The

˅ smaller the thing, the more surface it has compared to its volume."

"Yes, that does sound neat." I wasn't sure it qualified as the neatest thing in the world. We maintained a steady speed.

"It's the key to everything. Cell division, house painting, heating buildings — everything. I bet it controls the concentration of chemicals in a cell, for example. Tells it when it's time to divide. I bet when they finally figure out cancer, they'll discover it's controlled by a flaw in the cell membrane that screws up the concentration of a cell division instigator. Screws up the natural effect of the surface to volume ratio.

"That's why fireworks are possible, you know. Iron filings, magnesium filings, all that stuff that won't burn in a big chunk. You cut it into tiny enough pieces, it gets hot enough, and there's enough surface exposed to oxygen, and bingo. A billion sparks and a happy Fourth of July."

"Like cutting a diamond?" I asked cautiously.

"Exactly! Every tiny chip they remove increases the surface for light to reflect off of. It doesn't really change the stone much, but it sure looks different."

Life is kind of like that, I thought.

"Why don't they teach that to kids in school?" he continued. "How can they miss such a cool concept? It's a damn shame. And then there's plasmids and fibrils in cells..."

He talked quite a bit, but he steered the conversation toward facts. He seemed a lot more shy talking about himself. The only thing I learned about him as a person was that he had been so nearsighted as a child that people thought he was retarded. Sports had been impossible. Friendships were few, because he couldn't recognize the other children unless they were practically sitting on his lap. No waving to someone across a playground, no flirting with a girl two desks away. So, he spent his childhood reading. His first major epiphany was getting glasses in high school and realizing how different all the girls looked. Since then, nothing had seemed impossible to him, and nothing bothered him too much. If you manage to get through school without being able to see blackboards, or softballs, or girls, things like flat tires and poverty and chasing a hitchhiker's enemies were just interesting challenges. Little chips to remove from your diamond.

"I'm a little jealous of you, though," he said.

"Excuse me?"

He smiled at the highway. "When I was a kid, I read a lot about Indians. At one point, I wanted to be an Indian when I grew up. But with the blond hair and blue eyes, it wasn't a real practical career choice."

"Probably not."

I waited for him to explain why he was jealous of me, but he didn't.

The white van took an exit on the outskirts of Lawrence. Without a word, we followed. It pulled into the parking lot of a tiny motel and parked. We parked on the other side of the building.

My friend smiled and started to open his door. "Shall we?" he said, as if asking his prom date for a dance.

"I've got to do this alone," I said.

He stopped opening his door and frowned. "Are you sure?" I nodded and got out. He watched for just a minute, then shrugged.

"Suit yourself," he said. "Give 'em hell." He flashed a thumbs-up sign and drove away.

My heart was beating fast as I walked across the parking lot. My legs resisted every step, but I forced them to propel me. Each step toward the white apparition seemed to take several minutes.

The side door of the van was open and a man in blue coveralls was leaning into it. Inside, shelves were built into the walls. The shelves were filled with tools and wires and pipes. I stopped a few feet behind the man. This is it, I thought, summoning my courage. The man didn't seem to notice me behind him. I cleared my throat. He didn't react. He was struggling to move something across the floor of the van.

"Excuse me," I said rather loudly. "Can I help you?" I meant it as a threat, the way a policeman would say it to someone who was walking around a restricted area. I hoped my voice sounded menacing.

The man jumped, obviously startled, and turned around. He must have been eighty years old, very thin with snow white hair and a kind face. A vegetarian Santa Claus. He smiled and confused me completely.

"Why, yes you can, son. Thank you very much. This old tool box just gets heavier every year. If you could just grab that end there..."

I stared at him, he waited, his smile undimmed. "There's a handle on the end there," he said, pointing. He pulled at the other end of the metal box, moving it slightly. I awoke from my daze and moved quickly to help him.

"Let's see, they say there's a leak in number seven. If you could just help me get this over to that door there..."

We carried the tool box to the door, him using both hands and moving slowly. I could have easily carried it alone in one hand. "Thanks a lot," he said. "Now if I can just get that new day guy to let me in, we'll have it fixed good as new in no time."

He walked stiffly toward the office. I let the palm of one hand settle on his van for a moment. It contained no devils, only an old man's tools and memories and job. A train mourned in the distance, cars flew past on the interstate, the air smelled of fertile soil and motel disinfectant. Behind the motel, men in a field threw bales of hay onto a pickup truck.

I would not want to spend a lifetime here, I thought. But it would be just fine for tonight. I walked toward the office and rented a room.

My room had a television and neat little bars of soap and clean sheets. I had an overwhelming desire to take a shower.

The hot water cleaned the swamp mud and bus smell from my skin. It occurred to me that my life before Oklahoma might have consisted of the same kind of thing as my life since then: a series of random adventures, some people I'd grown fond of but had abandoned in my quest for the next bus out of town. Perhaps I'd loved no one. If I had, I might not have realized it at the time.

I stared at my face in the foggy mirror. My eyes were very dark, my hair black and a little shaggy, my skin darkly tanned. Yes, it could be an Indian's face. I'd never considered that possibility. There were probably other possibilities I had missed as well. Examining the face closely, this stranger's face, I saw lines around my eyes and across my forehead. I looked older than I'd realized but it didn't bother me. I liked the face in the mirror. It did not look evil or dangerous. I made it smile, and deep lines spread from the corners of its eyes and mouth. Whatever past had shaped it, that face had smiled enough to engrave marks on its skin. I smiled again. "Pleased to meet you," I said.

Perhaps I would never regain my past and was marooned forever in the present. If I wanted friends or lovers, I would have to grow them out of the fields of strangers around me. Whatever poems I had written, or diseases I had cured, or money I had accumulated, no longer belonged to me. I was a leaf that had released its hold on the tree. This was my moment of motion, of individual flight, my solitary dance through the air, separate from my billion twins. No longer green and faceless on the tree, not yet crushed and decomposing on the forest floor.

I watched television until I became sleepy. The shows seemed brand new to me, each commercial imaginative, every news report remarkable.

The next morning, I walked to the college campus.

It was Saturday morning and I was the only person in the student lounge. I sat on a hard plastic chair near the pool tables, pinball machines, and coffee machines. The smoking section. I had just bought a pipe and wanted to try it out. I followed the pipe-store owner's instructions: just a little tobacco in the bowl, tamp it down, apply a wooden match. Suck. Cough. Suck.

It went out. I tamped it tighter and applied another match. Suck. Cough. Suck. Blow out the smoke. I surrounded myself with the rich aroma. But it doesn't taste at all like that in your mouth. It tastes like burning weeds. And smoking anything is dumb. I knew that. Still, smart people smoke pipes. Writers and professors and nuclear physicists smoke pipes. People with memories. Perhaps they love the paradox of its fragrance: It only smells beautiful to someone who's not smoking. They choose to smoke. For some of them, that choice matters. It kills them.

I had a thick wad of cash in my pocket and decisions to make. Without rent or car payments or responsibilities, the money could last me a long time. Maybe even until I regained my past. I could sleep outside. Go south during the cold months. I could work at odd jobs for food, maybe earn a little extra for bus fares and new socks. Make it last. Or, I could spend it on something. Invest it. Start a business. I determined that I would decide what I was going to do. I would not just hang around waiting for the jokester universe to push me into something. I inhaled a bit more smoky death and thought of possibilities.

Maybe I should start a little photography business, I thought, with no idea where the thought came from. Take pictures of people and products. Pamper them. Make them look better than they are. Or maybe not.

Any life would be fine, really, I thought. Any series of simple repetitions, strung together like patterns in a cloth. Lives seemed to be like that: Huge paintings made up of tiny, similar dots of color that only makes sense from a distance.

The pipe went out. It surprised me how tough it is to keep that little fire burning. It's not like operating a cigarette, that, once lit, is an automatic device. No. You have to keep puffing and tamping and stirring the tobacco or it simply expires. It's the price you pay for that lovely aroma. I put the troublesome implement down.

A young couple came in and sat a few tables away. They didn't seem to notice me. I couldn't tell if they were deep in conversation or practicing lines from a play. She described their experiences together. He disagreed and described them completely differently. It astonished me. Had these two people lived the same relationship? It sounded like they had each fabricated partners and convinced themselves that the other was the person of their imagination. And neither had realized it. Their memories were intact, but useless. It had to be a play.

"There is no room for us," the girl said firmly.

"It's a big world."

"No," the girl said. They both stared into their Styrofoam cups as if they were very deep wells.

I carried my coffee outside into brilliant sun light. A fountain bubbled and danced in a pool of water. Leaves bobbed amid the reflections of fluffy white clouds and a perfect blue sky. The leaves were brown. Somehow, improbably, it was autumn.

The couple inside were obviously in love, but they weren't happy. Another paradox to consider.

Three young men walked past carrying books and teasing each other.

"You still cruising around in that bondo-buggy? You'll be lucky if it gets you to the junkyard."

"Hey, man, that's not my car, that's my life."

"You got that right. You spend more time fixing that wreck than you spend on all your classes put together. You're gonna wake up some day and you'll be putting car parts into boxes, shipping them off, and thinking about retiring."

"My choice, man. My choice."

They laughed and kicked at the dried leaves, then sauntered off and disappeared into the dappled autumn.

I need a plan, I thought. I have a life to invent.

"Step one," I said to the leaves, reaching into my pocket and withdrawing the two quarters I had hoarded for my entire life. I rubbed them together for a moment. The sun was warm on my skin, but the air was crisp. I shivered and stared at the mysterious coins in my hand, worn bright and clean. Reflected sunlight flashed from them and they looked like jewels. I repeated the phone number one last time.

Then I threw them into the pool.